Richard Garnett

The Age of Dryden

Richard Garnett

The Age of Dryden

ISBN/EAN: 9783337423834

Printed in Europe, USA, Canada, Australia, Japan

Cover: Foto ©Andreas Hilbeck / pixelio.de

More available books at **www.hansebooks.com**

THE

AGE OF DRYDEN

BY

R. GARNETT, LL.D.

LONDON

GEORGE BELL AND SONS

1895

PREFACE.

THE plan of a general history of English literature in a series of introductory manuals, each dealing with a well-defined period and individually complete, as set forth in the preface to Mr. Dennis's *Age of Pope*, is advanced a stage further by the present volume.

The period described,.from its chief literary figure, as *The Age of Dryden,* and which might with equal propriety have been entitled *The Age of the Restoration,* extends from 1660 to 1700. Some very important writers, such as Milton and Clarendon, the composition or publication of whose principal works falls within this epoch, have been passed over as belonging in style and spirit to the preceding age; and in a few instances this procedure has been reversed. In the main, however, the last forty years of the seventeenth century constitute the period of literary activity represented, and will be found to be demarcated with unusual precision from both the preceding and the ensuing era.

The writer of a literary history embracing works on a great variety of topics will soon discover that he is expected to impart more information than he possesses. If in any measure endowed with the grace of modesty, he will frequently feel compelled to acknowledge with Mr. Edward Gibbon Wakefield, when, after having overcome every other difficulty in the foundation of his colony, he came to provide it with a bishop: 'I fear I do not very well understand this part of the subject myself.' Trusty guides, however, fortunately are not wanting. The author's warmest acknowledgments are due for the assistance he has derived from personal communication with Professor Hales, and from the writings of Macaulay, Matthew Arnold, Mr. Gosse, Professor Saintsbury, Mr. Churton Collins, and Dr. Fowler. He is indebted for the Index to Mr. J. P. Anderson, of the Reading Room of the British Museum.

R. G.

October, 1895.

CONTENTS.

THE AGE OF DRYDEN.

INTRODUCTION.

THE accession of Charles II. as king *de facto*, which in the political history of England marks a Restoration, in her literary history marks a Revolution. Not that the transition from one mode of writing and thinking to another was instantaneous, or enjoined by legislative or academical decree. It had long been slowly progressing, and its unequivocal triumph would probably have come to pass sooner but for the obstruction to the intellectual life of the nation occasioned by twenty years of civil commotion. The magnitude of this impediment appears from the fact that all the writings of even so great a scholar and poet as Milton, produced during this interval, were of a polemical nature. When at last society found sufficient stability to allow its members to write for fame, emolument, or the extension of knowledge, it quickly became manifest how wide a gulf yawned between the men of that day and the men of twenty years ago. The new influence, indeed, had long been at work. A comparison, for example, of the last of the old dramatists, Massinger and Shirley, with their predecessors, evinces how much even in their day the stage was losing in poetry, in imagination, and in the charm of musical metre; how rapidly its personages were degenerating from vital indi-

B

vidualities into conventional types; how much, on the other hand, always excepting Shakespeare's pieces from the comparison, it was gaining in logic and construction. An examination of other forms of literature would reveal a similar clarifying process, a steady discouragement of the quaint affectation which was the bane of Elizabethan literature, combined, unfortunately, with increasing sterility of fancy, and growing insensibility to the noble harmonies of which English prose is capable. An Elizabethan poet, indeed, Samuel Daniel, had in some of his works almost anticipated the style of the eighteenth century; in general, however, writers during the period of the Civil War seem to our apprehension more or less encrusted with the mellow patina of antiquity, conspicuously absent from nearly everyone who wrote under Charles II. Hence the accession of this monarch, in whose person the new taste might be said to be enthroned, is justly regarded as the commencement of the new era. Charles's personal influence on letters was not insignificant. ' The king,' says a contemporary, Burnet, ' had little or no literature, but true and good sense, and had got a right notion of style, for he was in France at a time when they were much set on reforming their language. It soon appeared that he had a true taste. So this helped to raise the value of these men [Tillotson and others], when the king approved the style their discourses generally ran in, which was clear, plain, and short.' Burnet, therefore, had no doubt that correct principles of taste had been established in England in Charles II.'s time, and partly by the king's instrumentality—a dictum equivalent to the condemnation of all preceding English literature as barbarous. Such was also the opinion of one of the masters of English style in the succeeding century, David Hume.

Charles II. was not a man who could under any circumstances have sympathized greatly with the poetry of Spenser, or the prose of Raleigh or Hooker. The native bent of his mind was, moreover, strengthened by contingencies, among which Burnet justly gives a foremost place to his residence in France. It must be added that this influence coincided with a movement which, if for the time disadvantageous to English literature, was, nevertheless, essential if it was to cease to be merely insular. Until the time of Charles I. this literature, in so far as it owed anything to external patterns of modern date, had been chiefly dependent upon Italy. This might have long continued but for the decay of Italian letters consequent upon the triumph of foreign oppression and spiritual despotism throughout the peninsula. France stepped into the vacant place, and developed a literature qualified to impress other nations no less by its defects than by its virtues, by its want of elevation as well as by its sprightliness and lucidity. Ere long French ideas of style had pervaded Europe, and approximation to French modes was the inevitable qualification for the great mission of human enlightenment which was to devolve upon Britain in the succeeding century. Up to this time the literature of England had resembled that of Spain, original and racy of the soil, grander and more noble than the less dignified literature whose statutes it was to keep and whose laws it was to observe for a season, but on this very account comparatively out of touch with the common needs of men. Had British writers continued to indite the prose of Hooker and Milton, their ideas would have found no entrance into the Continent; and grievous as was the declension from the poetry and music of these great writers to the *sermo pedestris* of their successors, this was more than counterbalanced by the acquisition of lucidity, logic, and cogency. The loss was but temporary, the gain was everlasting; for the nineteenth century has found it possible to restore much of the solemn pomp and musical and pictorial charm of Elizabethan English, without parting with the clearness and coherence which are indispensable for a literature that would deeply affect the world. In becoming for a moment French, English literature first became European—happy that the new influence did not, as elsewhere, penetrate too far, and that when all of good that the foreigner could proffer had been assimilated, speech and style regained their nationality. They did not, however, thus revert to their old channel. 'The Restoration,' says Matthew Arnold with justice, 'marks the real moment of birth of our modern English prose.' This prose, indeed, has since been vastly enriched by recurrence to antique models, but gains from this source have always been felt to partake of the nature of importation. The vital point of Restoration practice is accepted by all who do not deliberately aim at the composition of poems in prose. 'It is,' says Arnold, 'by its organism—an organism opposed to length and involvement, and enabling us to be clear, plain, and short—that English style after the Restoration breaks with the style of the times preceding it, finds the true law of prose, and becomes modern; becomes, in spite of superficial differences, the style of our own day.'

This age of metamorphosis, therefore, is one of the most important in the history of English literature, and if the men of the Restoration could have beheld themselves in their relation, not only to their predecessors, but also to their successors, their complacency would not have been unjustifiable. Their inability to apprehend their true relation to either was a failing by no means peculiar to them, but it has exposed them to a double measure of the ridicule of posterity, who roar with laughter over Pepys's dictum that *A Midsummer Night's Dream* 'seems but a mean thing' after Sir Samuel Tuke's *Adventures of Five Hours*, and are hardly more merciful to Dryden's conversion of *Paradise Lost* into an opera. It must be owned that the conception of poetry as something awful, spiritual, and divine, became for a time extinct. Shelley's Defence of Poetry, could such a work have existed, would have seemed even more absurd to that age than Mr. Pepys's critical deliverances do to ours. The excuse is that the particular work assigned to the period was incompatible with a very high standard of poetry. This work, as we have seen, was the regeneration of English prose by the elimination of those elements which unfitted it for clear precise reasoning and practical business, and the making English a tongue in which Bunyan and Cobbett might be classics equally with Bacon and Sir Thomas Browne. Such an achievement implies a prosaic age. If the latter part of the seventeenth century could have produced Miltons, these would have continued to write as Milton did: it was therefore fortunate for the language in the long run that supreme genius should have for the time died out, and have been replaced by a vigorous, terrestrial, unideal genius that, having no oracle, required no tripod. For a time, no doubt, the contrast must have seemed very dismal to any who yet retained a perception of the richness and glory of the Elizabethan epoch. But we, if we compare, not to say the letters of Cromwell, but those of Charles I., with the despatches of Wellington, cannot but be sensible of an enormous advance, not merely in the effectiveness of speech, but in its dignity and simplicity, and of a great enrichment of the language by the newly acquired power to deal with common things, For this the men of the Restoration are to be thanked: and it must be added that their work could not have been done if they had not thoroughly believed in it; and that this belief necessitated, except in such superior minds as Dryden's, contempt for their predecessors and a genuine preference of their sorry foreign models to Shakespeare. The revolution which they effected in matters of taste may be compared to the contemporary revolution in politics. The Restoration government was a sad decline from the enthusiastic visions of Milton and Vane, or even from the wise and sturdy sway of Cromwell. Nevertheless the English nation accepted and maintained it as the best arrangement which the circumstances of the time admitted. So the new style in 'literature was universally accepted because the old style was for a time effete; because tasks had been imposed and needs had arisen to which it was unable to respond; because, in short, a prosaic age craved a prosaic literature. We look, therefore, on the Restoration period as anything but an ideal epoch, but at the same time as a most momentous one; as one to which we are indebted for much of our present command over the resources of our language; and to which Britain owes very much of her present power over the world. Acquaintance with its leading representatives also proves that, if less picturesque figures than their predecessors, they were not inferior in mental power. And, although the age is justly regarded as in the main an age of prose; yet, as poets respond most readily to the influences of their time, and are usually in the van of intellectual revolutions, so the leading figure in the literary history even of this epoch of prose is a poet—Dryden, doubtless the most prosaic of all our great poets, but inferior to none in intellectual force; and one whose poverty and pliability made him the mirror of the less worthy tendencies of his time on the one hand, while his higher aspirations and the force of his genius rendered him no less the representative of its better qualities on the other. With Dryden, therefore, we commence our survey.

CHAPTER I.

JOHN DRYDEN AS A POET.

JOHN DRYDEN was born August 9, 1631, at Aldwinkle All Saints, between Thrapston and Oundle, in Northampton-shire. He was the grandson of Sir Erasmus Dryden, baronet, of Canons Ashby, in the same county; and his father possessed a small landed property, which he trans-mitted to the poet. Dryden maintained a connection with his native county all his life, but it was never close; of the rest of the world, outside London and Cambridge, he only occasionally saw anything. Few of our great writers have been so thoroughly identified with the metropolis, of which he became an inhabitant at an early age by his entry at Westminster School, the precise date of which is unknown. Locke and South were among his schoolfellows. He must have distinguished himself, having been elected to Cam-bridge in 1650. Before leaving Westminster he had made his first appearance as an author by the publication of a copy of verses on the death from small-pox of his school-fellow Lord Hastings, an unintentional *reductio ad absurdum* of the reigning fashion of extravagant conceits in the style of Marino and Gongora. This composition, otherwise worthless, foreshadows in a manner the whole of Dryden's career. He was not one of the writers who themselves form the taste by which they are ultimately judged, but rather one of those who achieve fame by doing best what all desire to be done; the representatives of their age, not its reformers. Little is known of his career at Cambridge except that he was on one occasion 'discommoned and gated' for some irregularity, that he took his degree in 1654, and, though obtaining no fellowship, continued to reside until about 1657, when he removed to London, with what precise plans or expectations is uncertain.[1] The general knowledge displayed in his critical writings (he scarcely ever, says Johnson, appears to want book-learning but when he mentions books) justifies the conclusion that his time had been employed in study: how greatly his mind had matured was attested by his verses on the death of Cromwell (1658), which, if disfigured by some conceits, exhibit a more sustained elevation than any contemporary except Milton or Marvell could have attained. They were rivalled by his congratulatory verses on the Restoration (1660), which naturally exposed him to the reproach of inconsistency, but, as Johnson remarks, 'If he changed, he changed with the nation.' There can, indeed, be no doubt that the establishment of a settled government was approved by the good sense as well as by the loyalty of the country, and although circumstances were to make Dryden the most formidable of political controversialists upon paper, his temperament was not that of a polemic, and, save when he had committed himself too far to retreat, he was always ready to acquiesce in what commended itself to the general sentiment of his countrymen. The Restoration was also a joyful event to men of letters, if for no other reason than that it re-opened the stage,

---

[1] He was an ungrateful son of his *alma mater*, having pointedly declared his preference for Oxford. Perhaps this disloyalty may be connected with the appearance at Cambridge of a pamphlet against him, in the form of a mock defence against "the censure of the Rota," in the same year (1673).

which, while as yet the periodical press was not, afforded the best market and the readiest opportunity for literary talent. Dryden is said to have had a play ready soon after the Restoration, and it is difficult to understand, except from a certain inertness in his constitution, ever most readily responsive to the spur of necessity, why he should have so long delayed his appearance as a dramatist. The determining motive may ultimately have been his marriage (not, apparently, a very fortunate one) to Lady Elizabeth Howard, eldest daughter of the Earl of Berkshire, in December, 1663; for in that year he produced his first play, *The Wild Gallant*, and from that time we find him, for many years, sedulously at work to earn money by a description of literary activity notoriously uncongenial to him. Only one of his numerous plays, he tells us, was written to please himself. The long list includes, *The Indian Emperor* (1665), in which, instead of reforming the weak blank verse of his day, which would have been a most important service, he fell in with the prevalent fashion of rhymed tragedy; *Tyrannic Love* (1669), and *The Conquest of Granada* (1672), in which he carries rhymed bombast as far as it would go, but at the same time displays surprising energy and vigour; *Aurengzebe* (1675), also a rhyming play, but a great improvement; *All for Love* (1678), and *Don Sebastian* (1690), examples of a purer taste; and *The Spanish Friar* (1683), and *Amphitryon* (1690), his best comedies. These pieces, the chief landmarks of his dramatic career, will be subsequently considered.

Returning to the incidents of Dryden's life, we find little to chronicle for several years except the births of three children, his elevation to the laureateship in 1670, and various literary controversies of no interest at this day except as they served to call forth the admirable

critical prefaces by which he did more for English prose
style than his poetry was at that time effecting for English
verse. It is remarkable how late his genius flowered, and
how long he was in discovering his proper path. He might
never have found it at all but for the accidental coincidence
of the political controversies of his time with his official
position as poet laureate. This seemed to impose on
Dryden the duty of coming to the assistance of the Court,
and his recognition of the obligation produced (1681)
Absalom and Achitophel, which at once gave him the distinction of the greatest satirist our literature ·had yet
produced; the most consummate artist in the heroic
couplet, and the most cogent reasoner in rhyme. *The
Medal*, occasioned by a medal struck by the City in honour
of the failure of the indictment of Shaftesbury, was suggested as the subject of a poem by Charles II. The fact
has been doubted, and does not rest upon very strong
external authority, but is confirmed by a letter from
Dryden to the Treasurer, Hyde, now in the British Museum,
shown by internal evidence to have been written after the
publication of *Absalom and Achitophel*, and consequently
after the striking of the medal on occasion of Shaftesbury's
acquittal. In this, after speaking of his expense in the
education of his children, complaining of the irregular
receipt of his pension, and remarking that even a quarter
in advance 'is but the Jesuits' powder to my disease, the
fit will return a fortnight hence,' he adds, 'I am going to
write somewhat by his Majesty's command, and cannot
stir into the country for my health and studies till I secure
my family from want.' This can hardly have been anything but *The Medal*.[1] The appeal, after some delay,

---

[1] Malone thinks that it was the translation of *The History of the
League*, but Dryden can have hardly deemed country retirement
necessary for a work of this nature.

brought Dryden an addition to his pension and a sinecure office in the Customs.

This was the most active period of Dryden's life as a poet. A personal altercation occasioned by an attack on *The Medal* by Thomas Shadwell produced *MacFlecknoe*, the bitterest of his satires, and in the same year of 1682 appeared the second part of *Absalom and Achitophel*, chiefly by Nahum Tate, but containing upwards of two hundred lines from Dryden's own pen, dealing with his literary antagonists in a style of sovereign mastery. Almost simultaneously appeared *Religio Laici*, 'a serious argument in verse on the credibility of the Christian religion and the merits of the Anglican form of doctrine and church government.' Dryden's mastery over metrical ratiocination made the subject attractive; but the Church of England had hardly done rejoicing in her champion when she was scandalized by his exodus to the Church of Rome. It is not likely that he was altogether insincere; but it can hardly be doubted that the death of a monarch of taste and parts, who valued him for his genius, and the accession of a successor who valued men only for their theology, and gently hinted the fact by docking his salary of a hundred pounds, had more to do with his resolution than he quite acknowledged to himself. The position of the Protestant laureate of a Popish sovereign called upon to bid Protestants rejoice over the birth of a Popish Prince of Wales, generally in that age believed to have been smuggled into the palace in a warming-pan, would assuredly have presented difficulties even to those who found none in extolling George II.'s patronage of the arts. Dryden was too deeply committed to expect anything from the other side. The apology for his conversion was given to the world in his *Hind and Panther* (1687), a poem displaying even augmented power of reasoning in rhyme, and which might have ranked with

his best but for the absurdity of the machinery. Soon
afterwards the unsoundness of the foundation on which he
had built his fortunes was demonstrated by the Revolution, which deprived him of the laureateship and swept
away all official sources of income. But for his change
of religion he might have taken the oaths to the new
government without censure, but he had broken down the
bridges behind him, and seemed for a moment to have
left himself no alternative between want and infamy. A
third nevertheless remained, hard labour for the book-
sellers. To his great honour, Dryden grappled with the
situation with all the sturdy tenacity of his lymphatic
temperament, and in the same spirit which Scott afterwards displayed under similar circumstances. He may
probably have reformed his system of living, which can
hardly have been other than extravagant; certain it is
that if he could not keep entirely out of debt, he at least
kept out of disgrace, and that the years which followed
his apparent ruin, if not the most brilliant part of his
life, were the most honourable and honoured. It should
be added that he appears to have been largely assisted by
the generosity of friends, especially Dorset.

The work which Dryden now found to do, for which he
possessed extraordinary qualifications, and for which there
was a genuine demand in the age, was that of translation
from the Latin classics. The derivative character of Latin
literature was not then recognized, and Roman authors
received the veneration due of right only to the greatest
of the Greeks. No one doubted that they gave unsurpassable models of style in their respective branches, and
not many among Dryden's contemporaries questioned that
he had given a definite and durable form to English
poetry. In 1667, a few days before the publication of
Paradise Lost, Pepys had overheard men saying that there

would never be such another English poet as Cowley, and
Dryden now stood in Cowley's place. It seemed then a
highly desirable thing to bring these two classics together,
and Dryden was perfectly competent to do whatever was
expected of him. He would hardly have succeeded so well
with the Greek writers, even had his knowledge of the
language been more extensive; but he was well qualified
to reproduce the more distinctive qualities of Roman
poetry, its dignity, sometimes rising into majesty, its
manly sense, its vehemence, pregnancy, and terseness. By
1693 he had rendered all Persius, much of Juvenal (the
remainder was supplied by his sons), considerable portions
of Ovid, the first book of Homer, and something from
Theocritus, Horace, and Lucretius. In this year he commenced a more ambitious work, a complete version of
Virgil. Of the merits of these works we shall speak here-
after; it is sufficient to observe here that they for a long
time prescribed the laws of metrical translation in English.
It is pleasant to notice how many of them were executed
at the country seats of friends, where the old man, dis-
charged from the strife of faction and the noise and glare
of theatres, relieved his intellectual toil by the simple
amusements of a country life. Virgil was published in
1697, and remained, in the judgment of the age, at the
head of all English translations until Pope's *Homer* came
to dethrone it. It was immediately succeeded by a greater
work still, his *Fables* from Chaucer and Boccaccio. Though
the representative of the literary taste of his time, Dryden
was by no means the representative of its prejudices. He
saw much more in Chaucer than his contemporaries were
capable of seeing, and, rightly judging that the antiquated
style of the old poet (who, however, appeared to him much
more uncouth than he really was) would effectually keep
him out of readers' hands, he determined to modernize and

adapt some of his stories, to which narrative poems founded on Boccaccio were afterwards added. The undertaking precisely suited the genius of Dryden, which lay more in expressing and adorning what he found ready to hand than in original invention, and his *Fables*, published in 1699, are deservedly placed at the head of his works. It is of course impossible that they should exhibit the same intellectual strength as his argumentative and satirical poems, but this is more than compensated by their superior attractiveness, the additional scope offered for the display of art, and their comparative freedom from everything that can repel. The same volume contained his greatest lyrical effort, the universally known *Alexander's Feast.* He received forty pounds for it; the Virgil is said to have brought him twelve hundred; for the *Fables* he got only three hundred. From a private letter of about this date it appears that there was some idea of his receiving assistance from the government, which he seems not unwilling to accept, provided that it proves to require no sacrifice of principle. It is not likely that he would have been allowed to die in want; and indeed, early in 1700, a dramatic performance was got up for his benefit. He died shortly afterwards (May 1st, 1700) in narrow pecuniary circumstances, but in the enjoyment of a more unquestioned literary supremacy among his contemporaries than any Englishman had held before him. The cause of his death was the mortification of a toe inflamed by gout. He was buried in Westminster Abbey. The funeral, for the splendour of which Farquhar vouches in a contemporary letter, is said to have been accompanied by tumultuary scenes, but the absence of any reference to these in a malevolent contemporary libel, ascribed to Thomas Brown, is sufficient evidence that they did not occur.

There are few English writers of eminence whom it is so

difficult to realize satisfactorily to the mind's eye as Dryden. Personal enough in one respect, his writings are singularly impersonal in another; he never paints, and seldom reveals himself, and the aid which letters or reminiscences might have afforded is almost entirely wanting. No one noted his conversation; his enemies' attacks and his friends' panegyrics are equally devoid of those traits of character which might have invested a shadowy outline with life and substance. The nearest approach to a portrait is Congreve's, which leaves most of the character in the shade, and even this is somewhat suspicious, for Congreve was Dryden's debtor for noble praise, and the vindication of Dryden's repute had been imposed upon him by the poet himself. The qualities, however, which he commends are such as seem entirely reconcilable with the lymphatic temperament which, partly on his own authority ('my conversation,' he says, 'is slow and dull, my humour saturnine and reserved'), we have seen reason to attribute to Dryden. We are told of his humanity and compassion, of his readiness to forgive injuries, of a friendship that exceeded his professions, of his diffidence in general society and horror of intrusiveness, of his patience in accepting corrections of his own errors, of which he must be allowed to have given a remarkable instance in his submission to Jeremy Collier. All these traits give the impression of one who, though by no means pedantic, was only a wit when he had the pen in his hand, and entirely correspond with his apparent aversion to intellectual labour, except under the pressure of want or the stimulus of Court favour. When at length he did warm to his work, we know from himself that thoughts crowded so rapidly upon him that his only difficulty was to decide what to reject. Such a man may well have appeared a negative character to his contemporaries, and the events of his life were not of a nature to force his virtues or his failings into notice. We can only say that there is no proof of his having been a bad husband; that there is clear evidence of his having been a good father; and that, although he took the wrong side in the political and religious controversies of his day, this is no reason why he may not, according to his light, have been a good citizen. His references to illustrious predecessors like Shakespeare and Milton, and promising young men like Congreve, indicate a real generosity of character. The moral defects of his writings, coarse licentiousness, unmeasured invective, and equally unmeasured adulation, belong to the age rather than to the man. On the whole, we may say that he was one whom we should probably have esteemed if we could have known him; but in whom, apart from his writings, we should not have discovered the first literary figure of his generation.

Dryden's early poems, the *Heroic Stanzas* on the death of Cromwell, the *Astraea Redux* on the Restoration, the panegyric of Clarendon, and the verses on the Coronation, are greatly marred for modern readers by extravagant conceits, but are sobriety itself compared to the exploits of contemporary poets, especially the Pindaric. In a more important particular, Dryden, as Scott remarks, has observed a singular and happy delicacy. The topic of the Civil War is but slightly dwelt on; and, although Cromwell is extolled, his eulogist abstains from any reflections against those through whom he cut his way to greatness. Isolated couplets in the other poems occasionally display that perfection of condensed and pointed expression which Dryden habitually attained in his later poems:

> 'Spain to your gift alone her Indies owes;
> For what the powerful takes not, he bestows:
> And France, that did an exile's presence fear,
> May justly apprehend you still too near.'—*Astraea Redux.*

These early attempts, however, were completely thrown into the shade by the *Annus Mirabilis, a poem on the* memorable events of 1666, written at Charlton, near Malmesbury, the seat of Lord Berkeley, where Dryden and his family had resorted in 1665 to escape the plague, and published in February, 1667. The author was then thirty-five, and, judged in the light of his subsequent celebrity, had as yet achieved surprisingly little either in quantity or quality. Youth is generally the most affluent season of poetical activity; and those poets whose claim to inspiration is the most unimpeachable—Spenser, Milton, Wordsworth, Shelley—have irradiated their early writings with flashes of genius which their maturer skill hardly enabled them to eclipse. This cannot be said of Dryden, who of our great poets, unless Pope be an exception, probably owed least to inspiration and most to pains and practice. Even Pope at this age had produced *The Rape of the Lock, The Temple of Fame, Eloisa to Abelard,* and his translation of the Iliad, enough to have given him a high place among English poets. The *Annus Mirabilis* was the first production of Dryden that could have insured him remembrance with posterity, and even this is sadly disfigured with conceits. After all, the poet finds only two marvels of his wonderful year worthy of record—the Dutch war, which had been going on for two years, and which produced a much greater wonder in the year ensuing, when the Dutch sailed up to Gravesend and burned the English fleet; and the Great Fire of London. The treatment of the former is very tedious and dragging; there are many striking lines, but more conceits like the following, descriptive of the English attack upon the Dutch East Indiamen:

> ‘Amidst whole heaps of spices lights a ball,
>   And now their odours armed against them fly;

> Some preciously by shattered porcelain fall,
>   And some by aromatic splinters die.'

The second part, treating of the Fire of London, is infinitely better. Dryden exhibits one of the most certain marks of a good writer, he rises with his subject. Yet there is no lack of absurdities. The Deity extinguishes the conflagration precisely in the manner in which Dryden would have put out his own candle :

> 'An hollow crystal pyramid he takes,
>   In firmamental waters dipt above ;
> Of it a broad extinguisher he makes,
>   And hoods the flames that to their quarry drove.'

Nothing in Dryden is more amazing than his inequality. This stanza is succeeded by the following :

> 'The vanquished fires withdraw from every place,
>   Or, full with feeding, sink into a sleep ;
> Each household genius shows again his face,
>   And from the hearths the little Lares creep.'

Other quatrains are still better, as, for instance, this on the burning of St. Paul's :

> 'The daring flames peeped in, and saw from far
>   The awful beauties of the sacred quire ;
> But since it was profaned by civil war,
>   Heaven thought it fit to have it purged by fire.'

A thought so striking, that the reader does not pause to reflect that the celestial sentence would have been equally applicable to every cathedral in the country. Perhaps the following stanzas compose the passage of most sustained excellence. In them, as in the apostrophe to the Royal Society, in an earlier part of the poem, Dryden appears truly the *vates sacer*, and his poetry becomes prophecy :

' Methinks already from this chymic flame
   I see a city of more precious mould ;
Rich as the town which gives the Indies name,
   With silver paved, and all divine with gold.

' Already labouring with a mighty fate
   She shakes the rubbish from her mounting brow,
And seems to have renewed her charter's date,
   Which heaven will to the death of Time allow.

' More great than human now, and more august,
   Now deified she from her fires doth rise ;
Her widening streets on new foundations trust,
   And opening into larger parts she flies.

' Before, she like some shepherdess did show,
   Who sat to bathe her by a river's side ;
Not answering to her fame, but rude and low,
   Nor taught the beauteous arts of modern pride.

' Now like a Maiden Queen she will behold
   From her high turrets hourly suitors come ;
The East with incense and the West with gold
   Will stand like suppliants to receive her doom.

' The silver Thames, her own domestic flood,
   Shall bear her vessels like a sweeping train ;
And often wind, as of his mistress proud,
   With longing eyes to meet her face again.

' The wealthy Tagus, and the wealthier Rhine,
   The glory of their towns no more shall boast ;
And Seine, that would with Belgian rivers join,
   Shall find her lustre stained and traffic lost.

' The venturous merchant, who designed more far,
   And touches on our hospitable shore,
Charmed with the splendour of this northern star,
   Shall here unlade him, and depart no more.'

For several years after *Annus Mirabilis*, Dryden produced but little poetry apart from his dramas. Fashion,

Court encouragement, and the necessity of providing for his family, had bound him to what was then the most conspicuous and lucrative form of authorship. In one point of view he committed a great error in addicting himself to the drama. He was not naturally qualified to excel in it, and could only obtain even a temporary success by condescending to the prevalent faults of the contemporary stage, its bombast and its indecency. The latter transgression was eventually so handsomely confessed by himself that but little need be said of it. Bombast is natural to two classes of writers, the ardent and the phlegmatic, and those whose emotions require the most working up are frequently the worst offenders. Such was Dryden's case, and his natural proclivity was much enhanced by his adoption of the new fashion of writing in rhyme, beloved at Court, but affording every temptation and every facility for straining after effect in the place of Nature. Mr. Saintsbury justly reminds us that Dryden was not forsaking the blank verse of Shakespeare and Fletcher, the secret of which had long been lost; nevertheless, although, as we shall see when we come to his critical writings, he pleaded very ingeniously for rhyme in 1665, his adoption of it was condemned by his maturer judgment and practice. It was, however, fortunate in the long run; his rhyming plays, of which we shall speak in another place, would not have been great successes in any metre, while practice in their composition, and the necessity of expressing the multitude of diverse sentiments required by bustling scenes and crowds of characters, gradually gave him that command of the heroic couplet which bestows such strength and brilliancy on his later writings. His 'fourteen years of dramatic practice,' as Mr. Saintsbury justly says, 'acted as a filtering reservoir for his poetical powers, so that the stream, which, when it ran into them, was the turbid and rubbish-laden current of *Annus Mirabilis*, flowed out as impetuous, as strong, but clear and without base admixture, in the splendid verse of *Absalom and Achitophel*.'[1]

This great poem, published in November, 1681, at the height of the contest over the Exclusion Bill and its consequences, remains to this day the finest example of political satire in English literature. The theme was skilfully selected. James II. had not yet convinced the most sceptical of the justice and wisdom of the Exclusion Bill, and its advocates laboured under the serious disadvantage of having no strong claimant for the succession if they prevailed in setting the Duke of York aside. James's son-in-law, the Prince of Orange, would not, it is safe to say, ever have been accepted by the nation as king if James's folly and tyranny had not, years afterwards, given him the opportunity of presenting himself in the character of Deliverer; and, failing him, there was no one but the popular but unfortunately illegitimate Monmouth. The character of Absalom seemed exactly made for this handsome and foolish prince. The resemblance of his royal father to David, except in matters akin to the affair of Bathsheba, was not quite so obvious. Dryden might almost have been suspected of satirizing his master when he wrote:

'When nature prompted, and no law denied
Promiscuous use of concubine and bride;
Then Israel's monarch after heaven's own heart
His vigorous warmth did variously impart
To wives and slaves; and, wide as his command,
Scattered his Maker's image through the land.
Of all the numerous progeny was none
So beautiful, so brave as Absolon.'

[1] It is perhaps worth remarking that, although not yet a Roman Catholic, Dryden in this name employs the orthography, not of the authorized English version, but of the Vulgate.

The management of Absalom was a difficult matter.
With all his transgressions, the rebel Monmouth was still
beloved by his father, and Dryden could not have ventured
to treat him as his prototype is treated by Scripture. He
has extricated himself from the dilemma with abundant
dexterity, but at some expense to his poem. The catastrophe
required by poetical justice does not come to pass, and the
conclusion is tame. All such defects, however, are forgotten
in the splendour of the execution. The versification is the
finest in its style that English literature had yet seen, the
perfection of heroic verse. The sense is weighty and
massive, as befits such an organ of expression, and, whatever may be thought of Dryden's flatteries of individuals,
there is no reason to doubt the sincerity with which he
here expresses his political convictions. He unquestion-
ably belonged to that class of mankind who cannot discern
principles apart from persons, and his contempt for
abstractions is pointedly expressed in one of his ringing
couplets :

> ' Thought they might ruin him they could create,
> Or melt him to that golden calf—a state.'

This is not a very high manifestation of the intellect in its
application to political questions, but it bespeaks the class
of persons who provide ballast for the vessel of the state
in tempestuous times; and, on the whole, *Absalom and
Achitophel* is a poem which the patriot as well as the
admirer of genius may read with complacency. The royal
side of the question could not be better put than in these
lines placed in the mouth of David :

> ' Thus long have I, by native mercy sway'd,
> My wrongs dissembled, my revenge delay'd ;
> So willing to forgive the offending age,
> So much the father did the king assuage.

But now so far my clemency they slight,
The offenders question my forgiving right.
That one was made for many, they contend ;
But 'tis to rule ; for that's a monarch's end.
They call my tenderness of blood, my fear ;
Though manly tempers can the longest bear.
Yet since they will divert my native course,
'Tis time to shew I am not good by force.
Those heap'd affronts, that haughty subjects bring,
Are burdens for a camel, not a king.
Kings are the public pillars of the state,
Born to sustain and prop the nation's weight :
If my young Sampson will pretend a call
To shake the column, let him share the fall.
But oh, that he yet would repent and live !
How easy 'tis for parents to forgive !
With how few tears a pardon might be won
From nature pleading for a darling son !
Poor, pitied youth, by my paternal care
Raised up to all the height his frame could bear !
Had God ordain'd his fate for empire born,
He would have given his soul another turn :
Gull'd with a patriot's name, whose modern sense
Is one that would by law supplant his prince ;
The people's brave, the politician's tool ;
Never was patriot yet, but was a fool.
Whence comes it, that religion and the laws
Should more be Absolom's than David's cause ?
His old instructor, ere he lost his place,
Was never thought endued with so much grace.
Good heavens, how faction can a patriot paint !
My rebel ever proves my people's saint.
Would they impose an heir upon the throne ?
Let Sanhedrims be taught to give their own.
A king's at least a part of government ;
And mine as requisite as their consent.
Without my leave a future king to choose,
Infers a right the present to depose.
True, they petition me to approve their choice ;
But Esau's hands suit ill with Jacob's voice.

> My pious subjects for my safety pray ;
> Which to secure, they take my power away.
> From plots and treasons heaven preserve my years,
> And save me most from my petitioners ! '

It will be observed that ' the right the present to depose,' is mentioned by Dryden as something manifestly prepos- terous, and the derivation of it as a logical corollary from the Exclusion Bill is assumed to be a sufficient *reductio ad absurdum* of the latter. In the view of the majority of the nation, this was sound doctrine until the Revolution, which reduced Dryden's poem from the rank of a powerful political manifesto to that of a brilliant exercise of fancy and dialectic. As such, it will never cease to please and to impress. The finest passages are, no doubt, those descriptive of character, whether carefully studied portraits or strokes against particular foibles imputed to the poet's adversaries, such as this mock apology for the parsimonious kitchen of the Whig sheriff, Slingsby Bethel :

> ' Such frugal virtue malice may accuse,
> But sure 'twas necessary to the Jews :
> For towns, once burnt, such magistrates require,
> As dare not tempt God's providence by fire.'

The elaborate and glowing characters of Achitophel (Shaftesbury) and Zimri (Buckingham) it is needless to transcribe, as they are universally known. It may be remarked that the character of the turbulent and adven- turous Shaftesbury does not match very well with that of the Ulyssean Achitophel of Scripture, but Dryden has wisely drawn from what he had before his eyes.

The Medal, which we have seen reason for attributing to the suggestion of Charles II. himself, appeared in March, 1682. It is a bitter invective against Shaftesbury, its theme the medal which his partisans had very naturally

struck upon the occasion of his acquittal in the preceding
autumn. It is entirely in a serious vein, and wants the
grace and urbanity of some parts of *Absalom and Achitophel*, but is no way inferior as a piece of strong, vehement satire. Shaftesbury's conduct as a minister, before
his breach with the Court, is thus described:

> ' Behold him now exalted into trust ;
> His counsel's oft convenient, seldom just :
> Even in the most sincere advice he gave
> He had a grudging still to be a knave.
> The frauds he learned in his fanatic years
> Made him uneasy in his lawful gears ;
> At best, as little honest as he could,
> And, like white witches, mischievously good.'

The second part of *Absalom and Achitophel* appeared in
November, 1682. It was mainly the work of Nahum Tate,
who imitated his master's versification with success, but
has numerous touches from the pen of Dryden, who in-
serted a long passage of unparalleled satire against his adversaries, especially Settle and Shadwell:

> ' Who by my means to all succeeding times
> Shall live in spite of their own doggrel rhymes.'

The character of Shadwell (Og) is well known, but it is
impossible to avoid quoting a portion of it:

> ' The midwife laid her hand on his thick skull,
> With this prophetic blessing—" Be thou dull ;
> Drink, swear and roar ; forbear no lewd delight
> Fit for thy bulk ; do any thing but write.
> Thou art of lasting make, like thoughtless men,
> A strong nativity—but for the pen ;
> Eat opium, mingle arsenic in thy drink,
> Still thou mayst live, avoiding pen and ink."
> I see, I see, 'tis counsel given in vain,
> For treason, botch'd in rhyme, will be thy bane ;

Rhyme is the rock on which thou art to wreck,
'Tis fatal to thy fame and to thy neck.
Why should thy metre good King David blast?
A psalm of his will surely be thy last.
Darest thou presume in verse to meet thy foes,
Thou, whom the penny pamphlet foil'd in prose?
Doeg, whom God for mankind's mirth has made,
O'ertops thy talent in thy very trade;
Doeg, to thee, thy paintings are so coarse,
A poet is, though he's the poet's horse.
A double noose thou on thy neck dost pull,
For writing treason, and for writing dull.
To die for faction is a common evil,
But to be hang'd for nonsense is the devil.
Hadst thou the glories of thy king exprest,
Thy praises had been satire at the best;
But thou in clumsy verse, unlickt, unpointed,
Hast shamefully defiled the Lord's anointed.
I will not rake the dunghill of thy crimes,
For who would read thy life that reads thy rhymes?
But of King David's foes, be this the doom,
May all be like the young man Absolom;
And, for my foes, may this their blessing be,
To talk like Doeg, and to write like thee!'

Only a month before the appearance of this annihilating attack, Dryden had devoted an entire poem to Shadwell, who had justly provoked him by a scandalous libel. The title of *MacFlecknoe* is derived from an Irish priest and, with the exception of some good lines pointed out by Southey and Lamb, a bad poet, already satirized by Marvell. It is a vigorous attack, but not equal to the passage in *Absalom and Achitophel*, and chiefly memorable inasmuch as the machinery evidently suggested that of Pope's *Dunciad*.

Dryden's next poetical efforts, the dramatic excepted, were of quite another kind. Simultaneously with the second part of *Absalom and Achitophel* appeared *Religio*

Laici, an argument for the faith of the Church of England as a *juste milieu* between Popery and Deism. In one respect this takes the highest place among the works of Dryden, for it is the most perfect example he has given of that reasoning in rhyme of which he was so great a master. There is not and could not be any originality in the reasonings themselves, but Pope's famous couplet was never so finely illustrated, except by Pope himself:

> ' True wit is nature to advantage drest ;
> What oft was thought, but ne'er so well exprest.'

At the same time the poetry hardly rises to the height which the theme might have justified. There is little to captivate or astonish, but perpetual admiration attends upon the masterly conduct of the argument, and the ease with which dry and difficult propositions melt and glide in harmonious verse. The execution is singularly equable ; but perhaps hardly maintains the elevation of the fine exordium :

> ' Dim as the borrow'd beams of moon and stars
> To lonely, weary, wandering travellers,
> Is reason to the soul : and as, on high,
> Those rolling fires discover but the sky,
> Not light us here ; so reason's glimmering ray
> Was lent, not to assure our doubtful way,
> But guide us upwards to a better day.
> And as those nightly tapers disappear,
> When day's bright lord ascends our hemisphere ;
> So pale grows reason at religion's sight,
> So dies, and so dissolves in supernatural light.
> Some few, whose lamp shone brighter, have been led
> From cause to cause, to nature's sacred head,
> And found that one First Principle must be :
> But what, or who, that universal He ;
> Whether some soul, encompassing this ball,
> Unmade, unmoved ; yet making, moving all ;

Or various atoms' interfering dance
Leap'd into form, the noble work of chance ;
Or this great All was from eternity.—
Not even the Stagyrite himself could see,
And Epicurus guess'd as well as he.
As blindly groped they for a future state,
As rashly judged of providence and fate ;
But least of all could their endeavours find
What most concern'd the good of human kind ;
For happiness was never to be found,
But vanish'd from them like enchanted ground.
One thought content the good to be enjoy'd ;
This very little accident destroy'd :
The wiser madmen did for virtue toil,
A thorny, or, at best, a barren soil :
In pleasure some their glutton souls would steep ;
But found their line too short, the well too deep,
And leaky vessels which no bliss could keep.
Thus anxious thoughts in endless circles roll,
Without a centre where to fix the soul :
In this wild maze their vain endeavours end :—
How can the less the greater comprehend ?
Or finite reason reach infinity ?
For what could fathom God were more than he.'

Dryden's next important poem brought obloquy upon
him in his own day, and must be perused with mingled
feelings in this. Between 1682 and 1687, the date of the
publication of _The Hind and the Panther_, the laureate
of the Church of England had, as we have seen, become a
Roman Catholic, and most reasonably desired to justify
this step to the world. The Court also expected his pen
to be drawn in their service, and hence the double purpose
which runs through the poem, of vindicating his personal
change of conviction and of justifying the political
measures to which James had had recourse for establishing
the supremacy of his church. All this was perfectly
natural ; the extraordinary thing is that so great a master

of ridicule should have been blind to the ludicrous character of the machinery which he devised to carry out his
purpose. The comparison of the true church to the milk-
white hind, and of the corrupt church to the beautiful but
spotted panther, might have been employed with propriety
as an ornament or illustration of the poem, but the endeavour to make it the groundwork of the entire piece is pregnant with absurdity. Animals may very well be introduced
as actors in a fiction upon condition that they behave like
animals ; and their faculties may even be expanded to suit
the author's purpose so long as their exercise is confined
to visible and concrete things ; but the notion of a pair of
quadrupeds discussing the sacraments, tradition, and the
infallibility of the Pope, is only fit for burlesque, and con-
stitutes, indeed, a running burlesque upon the poem.
Dryden probably took up the idea without sufficient consideration, and when he had made some progress in his
work he may well have been too enamoured with the beautiful but preposterous exordium to surrender it to common
sense. Perverse and fantastic as is the plan of his poem,
none of his works is richer in beauties of detail. 'In none,'
says Macaulay, 'can be found passages more pathetic and
magnificent, greater ductility and energy of language, or a
more pleasing and various music.' The power of reasoning
in rhyme is little inferior to that displayed in *Religio Laici*,
and the narrative character of the piece allows of a diversified variety excluded by the simply didactic character of its
predecessor. The invective against Calvinists and Socinians,
typified by the wolf and the fox, is an average, and not beyond an average, example of Dryden's matchless force.
Near the end, it will be perceived, he suddenly bethinks
himself that, as the apologist of James's ostensible policy,
it is his business to recommend not persecution but toleration, and he caps his objurgation with a passage conceived

in a widely different spirit, a severe though unintentional
reflection upon the practice of his own church :

> ‘ O happy pair, how well you have increased !
> What ills in church and state have you redress’d !
> With teeth, untried, and rudiments of claws,
> Your first essay was on your native laws ;
> Those having torn with ease, and trampled down, ⎫
> Your fangs you fasten’d on the mitred crown,   ⎬
> And freed from God and monarchy your town.   ⎭
> What though your native kennel still be small,
> Bounded betwixt a puddle and a wall ;
> Yet your victorious colonies are sent
> Where the north ocean girds the continent.
> Quicken’d with fire below, your monsters breed
> In fenny Holland, and in fruitful Tweed ;
> And, like the first, the last affects to be
> Drawn to the dregs of a democracy.
> As, where in fields the fairy rounds are seen,
> A rank sour herbage rises on the green ;
> So, springing where those midnight elves advance,
> Rebellion prints the footsteps of the dance.
> Such are their doctrines, such contempt they show ⎫
> To heaven above, and to their prince below,   ⎬
> As none but traitors and blasphemers know.   ⎭
> God, like the tyrant of the skies, is placed,
> And kings, like slaves, beneath the crowd debased.
> So fulsome is their food, that flocks refuse
> To bite, and only dogs for physic use.
> As, where the lightning runs along the ground,
> No husbandry can heal the blasting wound ;
> Nor bladed grass, nor bearded corn succeeds,
> But scales of scurf and putrefaction breeds ;
> Such wars, such waste, such fiery tracks of dearth
> Their zeal has left, and such a teemless earth.
> But, as the poisons of the deadliest kind
> Are to their own unhappy coasts confined ;
> As only Indian shades of sight deprive,
> And magic plants will but in Colchos thrive
> So presbytery and pestilential zeal
> Can only flourish in a commonweal.

From Celtic woods is chased the wolfish crew ;
But ah ! some pity e'en to brutes is due ;
Their native walks, methinks, they might enjoy,
Curb'd of their native malice to destroy.
Of all the tyrannies on human kind,
The worst is that which persecutes the mind.
Let us but weigh at what offence we strike ;
'Tis but because we cannot think alike.
In punishing of this, we overthrow
The laws of nations and of nature too.
Beasts are the subjects of tyrannic sway,
Where still the stronger on the weaker prey ;
Man only of a softer mould is made,
Not for his fellows' ruin, but their aid ;
Created kind, beneficent and free,
The noble image of the Deity.'

Dryden produced yet one more poem in the interest of the
Court, his *Britannia Rediviva*, an official panegyric on the
birth of the Prince of Wales, June, 1688. Literature has
perhaps no more signal instance of adulation wasted and
prediction falsified. Many lines are spirited, but others
betray Dryden's fatal insensibility to the ridiculous in his
own person :

' When humbly on the royal babe we gaze,
The manly lines of a majestic face
Give awful joy.'

The raptures of the Byzantine courtiers over the imperial
infant Protus were nothing to this. Dryden did not want
eloquence or dignity to celebrate the hero if he could have
found him ; it was his and our misfortune that when the
hero did at last come to the throne the poet had disqualified
himself from extolling him. The landing in Torbay and the
triumphal march to London ; the victory at the Boyne and
the defence of Londonderry were transactions as worthy of
epical treatment as any history records ; but the only man

in England who could have treated them epically deemed them rather matter for elegy; and to have indulged in elegy he must have fled to France. Public events and political and religious controversy were no longer for him : stripped of his means and position he betook himself to translation and playwriting as the readiest means of repairing his shattered fortunes, and it was not until the mellow sunset of his life that he turned to the compositions which, of all he ever wrote, have given the most delight and the least offence, his *Fables.* These, published at the beginning of 1700, include five adaptations from Chaucer, and three stories told after Boccaccio, as well as *Alexander's Feast,* and a few other pieces. It would not be too much to say that this book achieved two things, either of which would have immortalized a poet : it fixed the standard of narrative poetry, (except of the metrical romance or ballad class, and also that of heroic versification. The latter, indeed, was thought for a time to have been transcended by Pope, but modern ears have tired of the balanced see-saw of the Popian couplet, and crave the ease and variety of Dryden, restored to literature in Leigh Hunt's *Story of Rimini,* and afterwards imitated by Keats in *Lamia.* The freedom which so great a master allows himself in rhyming should be a lesson to modern purists : final sounds so slightly akin as *guard* and *prepared, placed* and *last,* are of continual occurrence. In matters still more important than versification Dryden is in general equally admirable. He subjected himself to a severe test in competing with Chaucer—severer than he knew, for Chaucer was not yet, even by Dryden, valued at his full worth. In some respects Dryden certainly suffers greatly by the comparison. He is pre-eminently an intellectual poet, to whom the tree of knowledge had been the tree of life; there is perhaps scarcely a thought in his writings that charms by absolute simplicity and pure nature. Wherever, therefore, Chaucer is transparently simple and unaffected, we find him altered for the worse in Dryden. The very important part, however, of *The Knight's Tale* which is concerned with courts, camps, and chivalry is even better in Dryden than in his model. He might have defined his sphere in the words of Ariosto, a poet who has many points of contact with him :

> ' Le donne, i cavalier, l'arme, gli amori,
> Le cortesie, l'audaci imprese io canto.'

If this is true of portions of *Palamon and Arcite*, it is still truer of *The Flower and the Leaf* (then believed to be a genuine work of Chaucer's), throughout a most brilliant picture of natural beauty and courtly glitter, painted in language of chastened splendour. The other pieces modelled after Chaucer are of inferior interest, yet all excellent in their way. Two of the three tales from Boccaccio are acknowledged masterpieces, *Cymon and Iphigenia* and *Theodore and Honoria*. The interest of the first chiefly consists in the narrative itself, and that of the second in the way of telling it. The story, indeed, though striking, is fantastic and hardly pleasing, but Dryden's treatment of it is perhaps the most perfect specimen in our language of *l'art de conter*.

An example of Dryden's descriptive power may be given in a passage from *The Flower and the Leaf* :

> ' Thus while I sat intent to see and hear,
> And drew perfumes of more than vital air,
> All suddenly I heard the approaching sound
> Of vocal music, on the enchanted ground :
> An host of saints it seem'd, so full the choir ;
> As if the bless'd above did all conspire
> To join their voices, and neglect the lyre.

D

At length there issued from the grove behind
A fair assembly of the female kind :
A train less fair, as ancient fathers tell,
Seduced the sons of heaven to rebel.
I pass their forms, and every charming grace ;
Less than an angel would their worth debase :
But their attire, like liveries of a kind,
All rich and rare, is fresh within my mind.
In velvet white as snow the troop was gown'd,
The seams with sparkling emeralds set around :
Their hoods and sleeves the same ; and purpled o'er
With diamonds, pearls, and all the shining store
Of eastern pomp ; their long-descending train
With rubies edged, and sapphires, swept the plain.
High on their heads, with jewels richly set,
Each lady wore a radiant coronet.
Beneath the circles, all the choir was graced
With chaplets green on their fair foreheads placed ;
Of laurel some, of woodbine many more,
And wreath of Agnus castus others bore :
These last, who with those virgin crowns were dress'd,
Appear'd in higher honour than the rest.
They danced around ; but in the midst was seen
A lady of a more majestic mien ;
By stature, and by beauty, mark'd their sovereign queen.
    She in the midst began with sober grace ;
Her servants' eyes were fix'd upon her face,
And as she moved or turn'd, her motions view'd,
Her measures kept, and step by step pursued.
Methought she trod the ground with greater grace,
With more of godhead shining in her face ;
And as in beauty she surpass'd the choir,
So, nobler than the rest was her attire.
A crown of ruddy gold inclosed her brow,
Plain without pomp, and rich without a show :
A branch of Agnus castus in her hand
She bore aloft (her sceptre of command ;)
Admired, adored by all the circling crowd,
For wheresoe'er she turn'd her face, they bow'd.
And as she danced, a roundelay she sung,

In honour of the laurel, ever young.
She raised her voice on high, and sung so clear,
The fawns came scudding from the groves to hear,
And all the bending forest lent an ear.
At every close she made, the attending throng
Replied, and bore the burden of the song :
So just, so small, yet in so sweet a note,
It seem'd the music melted in the throat.'

One remarkable feature of the principal poets of the
seventeenth and eighteenth centuries is the infrequency of
the casual visitations of the Muse.   They seem to have
hardly ever experienced an unsought lyrical inspiration, or
to have sung merely for singing's sake.   Hence Dryden is
permitted to appear only twice in the *Golden Treasury*.
His songs, to be treated of more fully when we consider the
lyrical poetry of the period, though often instinct with true
lyrical spirit, seem to have been deliberately composed for
insertion in his plays, and the same is the case with almost
the whole of what he would have called his occasional
poetry.   His two chief odes, *Alexander's Feast* and the
memorial verses to Anne Killigrew, were indubitably commissions; and it is probable that few of the epistles, elegies,
dedications, and prologues which form so considerable a
portion of his poetical works were composed without some
similar inducement.   As a whole, this collection is creditable to his powers of intellect, quickness of wit, and command of nervous masculine diction.   It is frequently the
work of a master, though conceived in the spirit of a jour-
neyman.   The adulation of the patron or the defunct is
generally fulsome enough; yet some compliments are so
graceful that it is difficult not to believe them sincere, as
when he apostrophizes the Duchess of Ormond :

'O daughter of the Rose, whose cheeks unite
The differing titles of the Red and White !

> Who heaven's alternate beauty well display,
> The blush of morning and the milky way.'

Or the conclusion of his epistle to Kneller:

> 'More cannot be by mortal art exprest,
> But venerable age shall add the rest.
> For Time shall with his ready pencil stand,
> Retouch your figures with his ripening hand,
> Mellow your colours, and imbrown the teint,
> Add every grace which Time alone can grant;
> To future ages shall your fame convey,
> And give more beauties than he takes away.'

Or these from the epistle to his kinsman, John Driden, more likely than any of the others to have been the unbought manifestation of genuine regard:

> 'O true descendant of a patriot line!
> Who while thou shar'st their lustre lendest thine!
> Vouchsafe this picture of thy soul to see,
> 'Tis so far good as it resembles thee.
> The beauties to the original I owe,
> Which when I miss my own defects I show;
> Nor think the kindred Muses thy disgrace;
> A poet is not born in every race;
> Two of a house few ages can afford,
> One to perform, another to record.
> Praiseworthy actions are by thee embraced,
> And 'tis my praise to make thy praises last.'

The last couplet, excellent in sense, is an example of Dryden's one metrical defect. He is not sufficiently careful to vary his vowel-sounds.

Dryden's translations alone would give him a conspicuous place in English literature. The most important, his complete version of Virgil, has been improved upon in many ways, and yet after all it remains true, that 'Pitt is quoted, and Dryden read.' Had he never translated Virgil, his renderings or imitations of Juvenal, Horace, and others, would suffice to entitle him to no inconsiderable rank among those who have enriched their native literature from foreign stores. His principle of translation was correct, and accords with that of the greatest of English critics. Coleridge assured Words- worth that there were only two legitimate systems of metrical translation, strict literality, or compensation carried to its fullest extent. Dryden most probably had not sufficient Latin to be literal; but in any case his genius would have disdained such trammels, not to men- tion the more prosaic, but not less potent consideration, that what is written for bread must usually be written in haste—a fact which weighed with Dryden when he discon- tinued rhyme in his tragedies. Thus thrown back on the system of compensation, he has richly repaid his authors for the beauties of which he has bereaved them, by the beauties which he has bestowed—or which, as he maintains, were actually latent in them—and has expressed many of their thoughts with even enhanced energy. He has, in fact, made them write very much as they would have written if they had been English poets of the seven- teenth century, and his work is less translation than trans- fusion. They necessarily appear much metamorphosed from the originals, but the fault is less that of Dryden than of his age. Could he have attempted the same task in our day with equal resources of genius, and on the same principles of workmanship, he would have succeeded much better, for he would have enjoyed more comprehension of the spirit of his originals than was possible in the seventeenth century. The scholarship of that age had not vivified the information which it had amassed; the idea- lized, but still vital conceptions of the Renaissance had given place to inanimate conventionality; the people of

Greece and Rome appeared to the moderns like people in books; and such warm, affectionate contact between the souls of the present and the past as afterwards inspired Shelley's versions from Homer and Euripides was in that age impossible.

So great and versatile were Dryden's powers that, after all that has been said, his performances as a lyric poet, as a dramatist, and as a critic remain to be spoken of, and his rank in each has to be recognized as that of the foremost writer of his country in his own day. These will be treated in their appropriate places. The present is, perhaps, the most appropriate for a few words on his position as a poet. It is most difficult to determine whether he and his successor, Pope, should be placed at the bottom of the first class, or at the head of the second class of great English poets. If the very highest gifts of all—originality, creative imagination, unstudied music, unconscious inspiration, lofty ideal, the power to interpret nature, are essential conditions of rank in the first class, then assuredly Dryden and Pope must be contented with the second. If not positively excluded by the very nature of the case—if deficiency in the very highest qualities can be compensated by consummate excellence in all the rest—if intellect will supply the place of inspiration, and art that of nature—then they stand so high above the average of the second rank that it seems injurious not to place them in the first. The principle of exclusion, logically carried out, might involve the elevation above them of other writers whom we instinctively feel to be their inferiors; too absolute an insistence, on the other hand, upon the claims of intellectual power and perfect execution as qualifications for supreme poetical rank, must result in preferring Pope to Dryden. Inferior to his successor in both these respects, Dryden may

still justly be preferred to him on the ground of his more
ample endowment with that divine insanity without which,
as Plato truly says, no one can be a poet. But this consideration cannot be invoked in his favour against Pope
without admitting his inferiority to poets of the very first
order; and it may be seriously questioned whether any
poet can belong to the first order who is so exclusively a
town poet as Dryden and Pope, and has so little knowledge
of nature. The resemblances and contrasts between him
and Pope have been frequently discussed; there are two
other poets with whom comparison is less hackneyed and not
unprofitable. In fecundity, in versatility, in energy, in the
frequent application of his poetry to public affairs, in his
influence on contemporary literature, position as head of a
school, and incontestable superiority to all the poets
around him, no less, unfortunately, in bombast and incom-
prehensible breaches of good taste, he strongly reminds us
of Victor Hugo. Hugo, undoubtedly, was a much greater
lyrical poet than Dryden, and was enkindled by spontaneous inspirations which never visited Dryden; yet the
two are essentially of the same genus; the differences
between them are rather characteristic of their eras than of
themselves; and while Hugo's imagination would have
pined in the seventeenth century, Dryden's intellect and
Dryden's modesty would have been highly serviceable to
Hugo in the nineteenth. Another poet, whose talent
and career offer many analogies to Dryden's, is one
whom Dryden himself disparages upon metrical grounds.
Claudian, like Dryden, is a remarkable instance of a poet
owing a large portion of his fame to his dexterous treatment of occasional subjects. As Dryden drew material for
his most powerful writings from the political and religious
controversies of his day, so Claudian found his themes in
the exploits of Stilicho and the misdeeds of Rufinus. Both

have made uninteresting subjects attractive by admirable treatment; both are greatly indebted to art and little to nature; both in their latter days [1] sought relief from politics in more ideal compositions, Dryden in his *Fables*, Claudian in his *Rape of Proserpine*, a poem imbued with the characteristic qualities of Dryden.

Among the greatest services which Dryden rendered to our language and literature are to be reckoned his improvements in heroic versification, of which he has left an unsurpassed model.

> 'Waller was smooth, but Dryden taught to join
> The varying verse, the full majestic line,
> The long-resounding march, and energy divine.'

His changes, nevertheless, were not always improvements. He is too uniform, though not absolutely uniform, in confining the sense to the couplet; and, in adding dignity to Chaucer's verse, he has lost something of its sweetness. Leigh Hunt well observes: 'Though Dryden's versification is noble, beautiful, and so complete of its kind that to an ear uninstructed in the metre of the old poet all comparison between the two in this respect seems out of the question and even ludicrous, yet the measure in which Dryden wrote not only originated, but attained to a considerable degree of its beauty in Chaucer; and the old poet's immeasurable superiority in sentiment and imagination, not only to Dryden, but to all, up to a very late period, who have written in the same form of verse, left him in possession of beauties, even in versification, which it remains for

---

[1] In his dedication to the second book of *De Raptu Proserpinae*, Claudian says:

> 'Tu mea plectra moves,
> Antraque Musarum longo torpentia somno
> Excutis et placito ducis ab ore sonos.'

some future poet to amalgamate with Dryden's in a manner worthy of both, and so carry England's noble heroic rhyme to its pitch of perfection.'   It need not be said that Pope's magnificent eulogy solely respects Dryden as a rhyming poet.   His blank verse, though in general good enough for the stage, and better than that of most of his contemporaries, is utterly destitute of the sweetness and variety of the Elizabethans.

Dryden's works were edited with exemplary zeal and fidelity by Sir Walter Scott. The standard modern edition is Mr. Saintsbury's; the one most convenient for general use, Mr. Christie's.

CHAPTER II.

THE contemporary of Dryden who approached him most
nearly in satiric force, and, generally speaking,
in the borderland between poetry and prose,
was John Oldham (1653-1683). Not much
is known of his life. The son of a Nonconformist minister,
he nevertheless obtained a university education, but after
leaving college was glad to accept the position of usher in
Archbishop Whitgift's free school at Croydon. Coming to
town he filled the post of tutor in various families, and by
his *Satires upon the Jesuits* (1681) gained the acquaintance
of Dryden and other men of letters and the patronage of
the Earl of Kingston, who seemed likely to provide for
him, but at whose seat in Nottinghamshire he died of the
smallpox, December, 1683.

Oldham (1653-1683).

Oldham's poems consist partly of odes, formal and elaborate compositions, and partly of the satires which in his
age in some measure supplied the place of the modern
journal and review. A secret and unconscious harmony
pervades all branches of the contemporary art of every
epoch; and in the stately and somewhat stilted lyrics of
Oldham and his compeers we discern the counterpart of the
elaborate frontispieces with temples and triumphal arches,
chariots and cornucopias, tritons and nereids, which the
engravers of the age prefixed to its literature. The en-

graving is hardly art, and the verse is hardly poetry ; we are
nevertheless conscious of a vigour and a substance which
command respect. The work is compact and solid at any
rate, and displays much of the force of the Giants, if little
of the inspiration of the Gods. Oldham would fain be
extravagant in praise of wine ; but there is not the least
trace of genuine Bacchic frenzy in his laboured dithyramb.
The epicedion on his friend Mouvent is a serious composition indeed, forty-two mortal stanzas, with, nevertheless,
sufficient good things to justify the praise bestowed on it
by Pope. The ode to Ben Jonson is remarkable as expressing the feelings of the men of the Restoration towards the
poet who they really thought had reformed the stage, and
delivered it from the reprehensible licentiousness of Shakespeare. Like Oldham's other lyrical compositions, it
abounds with most dissonant lines, but has also some noble
ones, as these, for example :

‘ Let meaner spirits stoop to low precarious fame,
    Content on gross and coarse applause to live
    And what the dull and senseless rabble give ;
    Thou didst it still with noble scorn contemn,
    Nor wouldst that wretched alms receive,
The poor subsistence of some bankrupt, sordid name :
    Thine was no empty vapour, raised beneath,
        And formed of common breath,
    The false and foolish fire, that's whisked about
By popular air, and glares awhile, and then goes out ;
But 'twas a solid, whole, and perfect globe of light,
    That shone all over, was all over bright,
And dared all sullying clouds, and feared no darkening night.'

Oldham's principal celebrity, however, is derived from
his satires. He had the knack of stinging invective, and
has been not unjustly compared to Churchill. His *Satires
on the Jesuits* exactly suited the time of the Popish Plot,
at present they repel by their one-sidedness. All satire,

except that inspired by fancy, is apt to become repulsive
by its natural tendency to dwell upon the meanest and
lowest aspects of human nature ; and this is pre-eminently
the case with Oldham, who is always ridiculing or de-
nouncing, always drawing his illustrations from the base
and offensive, and seldom diversifies his low matter with
an ennobling thought.   Yet he evinces so much manly
sense, and his style is so nervous, that it is impossible not
to admire his vigour, and wish him a more inviting subject.
His metre and rhyme frequently stand in need of Dryden's
generous apology :

> ' O early ripe ! to thy abundant store
> What could advancing age have added more ?
> It might, what Nature never gives the young,
> Have taught the smoothness of thy native tongue.
> But satire needs not these, and wit will shine
> Through the harsh cadence of a rugged line.'

All this notwithstanding, Oldham had the root of the
matter in him, and has described, as only a poet could, the
ambition, the toil, and the triumph of a poet :

> ' 'Tis endless, Sir, to tell the many ways
> Wherein my poor deluded self I please :
> How, when the fancy lab'ring for a birth,
> With unfelt throes, brings its rude issue forth :
> How, after, when imperfect, shapeless thought
> Is, by the judgment, into fashion wrought :
> When at first search, I traverse o'er my mind,
> None, but a dark and empty void I find :
> Some little hints, at length, like sparks break thence,
> And glimm'ring thoughts, just dawning into sense :
> Confus'd, awhile, the mixt ideas lie
> With nought of mark to be discover'd by ;
> Like colours undistinguish'd in the night,
> Till the dusk images mov'd to the light,
> Teach the discerning faculty to choose,
> Which it had best adopt, and which refuse.

Here rougher strokes, touch'd with a careless dash,
Resemble the first setting of a face :
There finish'd draughts in form more full appear,
And in their justness ask no further care,
Meanwhile, with inward joy, I proud am grown,
To see the work successfully go on ;
And prize myself in a creating-power,
That could make something, what was nought before.
   Sometimes a stiff unwieldy thought I meet,
Which to my laws, will scarce be made submit :
But when, after expense of pains and time,
'Tis manag'd well, and taught to yoke in rhime,
In triumph, more than joyful warriors would,
Had they some stout and hardy foe subdu'd :
And idly think, less goes to their command,
That makes arm'd troops in well-placed order stand,
Than to the conduct of my words, when they
March in due ranks, are set in just array.
   Sometimes on wings of thought I seem on high, ⎫
As men in sleep, tho' motionless they lie,   ⎬
Hedg'd by a dream, believe they mount and fly : ⎭
So witches some inchanted wand bestride,   ⎫
And think they thro' the airy regions ride,   ⎬
Where fancy is both trav'ller, way and guide : ⎭
Then straight I grow a strange exalted thing,
And equal in conceit at least a king :
As the poor drunkard, when wine stums his brains,
Anointed with that liquor, thinks he reigns ;
Bewitch'd by these delusions, 'tis I write,
(The tricks some pleasant devil plays in spite)
And when I'm in the freakish trance, which I,
Fond silly wretch, mistake for ecstacy,
I find all former resolutions vain,
And thus recant them, and make new again.
   " What was't I rashly vow'd ? shall ever I
Quit my beloved mistress, Poetry ?
Thou sweet beguiler of my lonely hours,
Which thus glide unperceiv'd, with silent course :
Thou gentle spell, which undisturb'd dost keep
My breast, and charm intruding care asleep :

They say thou'rt poor, and un-endow'd, what tho'?
For thee, I this vain, worthless world forego :
Let wealth and honour be for fortune's slaves,
The alms of fools, and prize of crafty knaves :
To me thou art, whate'er th'ambitious crave,
And all that greedy misers want or have.
In youth or age, in travel or at home ;
Here, or in town, at London, or at Rome ;
Rich, or a beggar, free, or in the Fleet,
What'er my fate is, 'tis my fate to write." '

Oldham's talent, depending upon masculine sense and vigour of expression rather than upon the more ethereal graces of poetry, was of the kind to expand and mellow by age and practice. Had he lived longer he would undoubtedly have left a name conspicuous in English literature. As it is, he can only be regarded as a bright satellite revolving at a respectful distance around the all-illumining orb of Dryden. Before passing to Marvell and Butler, the only two really original poets after Dryden besides the veterans Cowley and Waller, who belong to the preceding period, it will be convenient to despatch a group of minor bards, whose inclusion in the standard collections of poetry, involving memoirs by a master of biography, has given them more celebrity than they in most instances deserve.

John Wilmot, Earl of Rochester (1647-1680), is principally known to posterity by his vices and his repentance. The latter has helped to preserve the memory of the former, which have also left abiding traces in a number of poems not included in his works, and some of which, it may be hoped, are wrongly attributed to him. For a number of years Rochester obtained notoriety as, after Buckingham, the most dissolute character of a dissolute age; but at the same time a critic and a wit, potent to make or mar the fortunes of men of letters. 'Sure,' says Mr. Saintsbury,

Lord Rochester
(1647-1680).

' to play some monkey trick or other on those who were unfortunate enough to be his intimates.' Many a literary
cabal was instigated by him, many a libel and lampoon
flowed from his pen, among others, *The Session of the Poets*,
correctly characterized by Johnson as ' merciless insolence.'
Worn out by a life of excess, he died at thirty-three, and
his penitence, largely due to the arguments and exhortations of Burnet, afforded the latter material for a narrative
which Johnson, entirely opposed as he was to the author's
political and ecclesiastical principles, declares that ' the
critic ought to read for its elegance, the philosopher for
its arguments, and the saint for its piety.'

Rochester's acknowledged poems fall into two divisions
of unequal merit. The lyrical and amatory are in general
very insipid. The more serious pieces, especially when expressing the discomfort of a sated votary of pleasure,
frequently want neither force nor weight. Four particularly fine lines, quoted without indication of authorship
in Goethe's *Wahrheit und Dichtung*, have frequently occasioned speculation as to their origin. They come from
Rochester's *Satyr against Mankind*, and read :

> ' Then Old Age and Experience, hand in hand,
> Lead him to Death, and make him understand,
> After a search so painful and so long,
> That all his life he has been in the wrong.'

Goldsmith's ' best-natured man, with the worst-natured
muse,' is purloined from Rochester, who is also the pro-
pounder of the paradox, ' All men would be cowards if they
durst.' Some of his songs are not devoid of merit. After
all, however, nothing of his is so well known as the antici-
patory epitaph on Charles II., ascribed sometimes to
him, sometimes to Buckingham, and very likely due to
neither :

> ' Here lies our mutton-eating king,
>   Whose word no man relies on ;
> Who never said a foolish thing,
>   And never did a wise one.'

Wentworth Dillon, Earl of Roscommon (1633?-1684), was a very different character, both as a man and as a poet. He is accused of no fault but a love of gaming, and the purity of his Muse merited the well-known eulogium :

> ' In all Charles's days
> Roscommon only boasts unsullied bays.'

But he has nothing of the salt and savour of Rochester's more serious poetry, and is at best an elegant versifier, who, in his only considerable original poem, the *Essay on Translated Verse*, thinks justly, reasons clearly, and expresses himself with considerable spirit when the subject requires. The most original feature of his literary character is his preference in a rhyming age for blank verse, which he enforces in theory, but is far from recommending by his practice. In his rhymed pieces he is a better versifier than poet, and in his blank verse the contrary. Milton's eyes were just closed ; Shakespeare and Fletcher were still acted ; but the secret of beautiful versification, apart from rhyme, seems to have been entirely lost.

Poetry afforded a subject for verse to another noble writer, John Sheffield, successively Earl of Mulgrave, Marquis of Normanby, and Duke of Buckinghamshire (1649-1721), who achieved real if moderate distinction as soldier, statesman, and scholar. As a poet his reputation rests entirely upon his *Essay on Poetry*, which contains many just thoughts expressed in pleasing numbers, although the author's deference to the conventional dicta of criticism leads him into idolatry, not only of Homer and Virgil, but

John Sheffield, Duke of Buckinghamshire (1649-1721).

of Bossu. To have fostered the genius of Pope by judicious praise is the highest distinction of ' Granville the polite and knowing Walsh.' Congreve, to be treated more fully as a dramatist, stands somewhat higher than these as an inditer of heroic couplets ; but a severer criticism must be passed, if any criticism is needed, upon Pomfret, Duke, Stepney, and the other versifiers of the day who have burrowed their way into the stock collections of poetry.

Andrew Marvell was a virtuous man whose good qualities contrast so forcibly with the characteristic failings of his age, that he appears by contrast even more virtuous than he actually was.

Andrew Marvell
(1621-1678).

His integrity made him the hero of legend, for, although the Court would no doubt have been glad to gain him, it is hardly credible that the prime minister should by the king's order have personally waited upon him ' up two pair of stairs in a little court in the Strand.' But the apocryphal anecdote attests the real veneration inspired by his independence in a venal age. Born in the neighbourhood of Hull on March 31st, 1621, he studied at Cambridge, travelled for some years on the Continent, and settled down about 1650 as tutor to the daughter of Lord Fairfax. At this period he wrote his exquisite poem, *The Garden*, and other pieces of a similar character. He also wrote in 1650 the poem on Cromwell's return from Ireland, which may have gained for him in 1653 the appointment of tutor to Cromwell's ward, William Dutton. Other pieces of a like description followed, and in 1657 Marvell became joint Latin secretary with Milton, an office for which Milton had recommended him four years previously. His poem on the Protector's death in the following year is justly declared by Mr. Firth to be ' the only one distinguished by an accent of sincerity and personal affection.' He was elected for Hull to Richard Cromwell's Parliament, and continued to sit for the remainder of his life. He was the last Member of Parliament who received a salary from his constituents, to whose interests he in return attended so diligently that upwards of three hundred letters from him upon their concerns and general politics are extant in the Hull archives.

Marvell could scarcely be called a republican. He had been devoted to the Protectorate, and would probably have been easily reconciled to the Restoration if the government had been ably and honestly conducted. In wrath at the general maladministration he betook himself to satires, which circulated in manuscript. At first he attacked Clarendon, but eventually concluded that the only remedy would be the final expulsion of the house of Stuart. In 1672 and 1673 he appeared in print as a prose controversialist with *The Rehearsal Transprosed*, a witty attack on a work by Parker, Bishop of Oxford, wherein, in the author's own words, ' the mischiefs and inconveniences of toleration were represented, and all pretences pleaded in behalf of liberty of conscience fully answered.' He silenced his opponent, and escaped being himself silenced through the interposition of Charles II., whose native good sense and easiness of temper inclined him to toleration, and who promoted the freedom of Nonconformists as a means of obtaining liberty for the Church of Rome. Marvell, however, was not to be reconciled, and in 1677 put forth an anonymous pamphlet to prove, what was but too true, that a design had long been on foot to establish absolute monarchy and subvert the Protestant religion. His sudden death on August 18th, 1678, was attributed to poison, but, according to a physician who wrote some years afterwards, was occasioned by that prejudice of the faculty against Peruvian bark which is recorded by Temple and Evelyn.

As a writer of prose, Marvell is both powerful and

humorous, but is not a Junius or a Pascal to impart permanent interest to transitory themes, and make the topics of the day topics for all time. As a poet he ranks with those who have been said to be stars alike of evening and of morning. His earliest and most truly poetical compositions belong in spirit to the period of Charles I., when the strains of the Elizabethan lyric were yet lingering. After passing through a transition stage of manly verse still breathing a truly poetical spirit, but mainly concerned with public affairs, he settles down as a satirist endowed with all the vigour, but, at the same time, with all the prosaic hardness of the Restoration. His most inspired poem, *Thoughts in a Garden*, written under the Commonwealth, and originally composed in Latin, nevertheless rings like a voice from beyond the Civil Wars. Here are the three loveliest of nine lovely stanzas :

'What wondrous life is this I lead !
Ripe apples drop about my head ;
The luscious clusters of the vine
Upon my mouth do crush their wine ;
The nectarine and curious peach
Into my hands themselves do reach ;
Stumbling on melons as I pass,
Ensnared with flowers, I fall on grass.

'Meanwhile the mind, from pleasure less,
Withdraws into its happiness ;
The mind, that ocean where each kind
Does straight its own resemblance find ;
Yet it creates, transcending these,
Far other worlds, and other seas ;
Annihilating all that's made
To a green thought in a green shade.

'Here at the fountain's sliding foot,
Or at some fruit-tree's mossy root,
Casting the body's vest aside
My soul into the boughs does glide :

There, like a bird, it sits and sings,
There whets and claps its silver wings,
And, till prepared for longer flight,
Waves in its plumes the various light.'

'These wonderful verses,' says Mr. Palgrave of the entire poem, 'may be regarded as a test of any reader's insight into the most poetical aspects of poetry.'

As a satirist it is Marvell's error to confound satire with lampoon. He has the *saeva indignatio* which makes the avenger, but spends too much of it upon individuals. Occasionally some fine personification gives promise of better things, but the poet soon relapses into mere personalities. This may be attributed in great measure to the circumstances under which these compositions appeared. They could only be circulated clandestinely, and the writer may be excused if he did not labour to exalt what he himself regarded as mere fugitive poetry. The most celebrated of these pieces are the series of *Advices to a Painter*, in which the persons and events of the day are described to an imaginary artist for delineation in fitting, and therefore by no means flattering, colours. It is to Marvell's honour that he succeeds best with a fine subject. When, in his poems on the events of the Commonwealth, he escapes from mere sarcasm and negation, and speaks nobly upon really noble themes, he soars far above the Marvell of the Restoration, though even here his verse is marred by lapses into the commonplace, and by his besetting infirmity of an inability to finish with effect, leaving off like a speaker who sits down rather from the failure of his voice than the exhaustion of his theme. The panegyric on Cromwell's anniversary, and the poem on his death, abound nevertheless with fine, though faulty passages, of which the following may serve as an example :

'O human glory vain ! O Death ! O wings !
O worthless world ! O transitory things !
Yet dwelt that greatness in his shape decayed,
That still, though dead, greater than death he laid,
And in his altered face you something feign
That threatens Death he yet will live again.
Not much unlike the sacred oak which shoots
To heaven its branches, and through earth its roots,
Whose spacious boughs are hung with trophies round,
And honoured wreaths have oft the victor crowned,
When angry Jove darts lightning through the air
At mortal sins, nor his own plant will spare,
It groans and bruises all below, that stood
So many years the shelter of the wood.
The tree, erewhile foreshortened to our view,
When fallen shows taller yet than as it grew ;
So shall his praise to after times increase,
When truth shall be allowed, and faction cease ;
And his own shadows with him fall ; the eye
Detracts from objects than itself more high ;
But when Death takes from them that envied state,
Seeing how little, we confess how great.'

Marvell's position as the satirist of his era from the Puritan and Republican point of view, was filled upon the Cavalier side by Samuel Butler, who, if general reputation and excellence in his own walk of verse are to be allowed as criterions, may claim to be the third poet of the age after Milton and Dryden. It is true that Butler, though endowed with abundance of fancy, was, strictly speaking, no poet; that he is entirely destitute of the dignity and tenderness which Marvell can display with a congenial theme ; and that he possesses nothing of Dryden's power of exalting unpromising subjects into poetry. But he infinitely surpasses Marvell when they meet on the common ground of satire ; and though he cannot be said to surpass Dryden, their methods are so different that no proper comparison can be drawn. When writing in Dryden's manner

Butler is respectable, but he has the field of burlesque epic entirely to himself. Supremacy in a low style of composition is a surer passport to fame than moderate merit in a high one. With all the defects of Restoration literature, it had a faculty for producing masterpieces, and it must be admitted that Butler's *Hudibras* stands as decidedly at the head of its class as *Paradise Lost*, or *Absalom and Achitophel*, or *Pilgrim's Progress*, or Pepys's *Diary* at the head of theirs.

Samuel Butler was born near Worcester in 1612. His

Samuel Butler (1612-1680).

father, a small farmer, procured him a good education at the Worcester Grammar School. His first employment was that of clerk to a country justice named Jefferys. He afterwards entered the household of Elizabeth, Countess of Kent, at Wrest, in Bedfordshire, and subsequently acted as clerk to various justices of the peace, one of whom, Sir Samuel Luke, of Cople Hoo, near Bedford, served as the original of Hudibras. It is curious to reflect that John Bunyan was at the same time going through his spiritual conflicts in the same county. He seems to have also travelled in France and Holland. He published nothing until 1659, when an anonymous tract in favour of the restoration of the monarchy, entitled *Mola Asinaria*, appeared from his pen. The service was recompensed by the appointment of secretary to the Earl of Carbury, Lord President of Wales, who made him steward of Ludlow Castle, where *Comus* had been performed nearly thirty years before. He resigned this charge upon contracting what seemed a wealthy marriage, but the lady's money was lost, and, notwithstanding the great literary success of *Hudibras*, the remainder of the author's life was spent in poverty. The first part of *Hudibras*, stated in the title to have been written during the Civil War, and if so at least fifteen years old, was published in 1663. Its success was instantaneous, though neither the Puritans nor Mr. Pepys could quite see the joke. The merit of the performance, however, was fully apparent to a better and more influential judge, the king, who encouraged the author by giving numerous copies away, though history does not say at whose expense. But this was all he gave, and the poet who had rendered such essential service to the royalist cause by his writings was as completely neglected by the Court as if he had been John Milton. It is indeed said that he was in receipt of a pension of £100 at his death; but this seems contradicted by the letter, already quoted, of Dryden to the Lord High Treasurer within two years after Butler's death, where he says: ''Tis enough for one age to have neglected Mr. Cowley and starved Mr. Butler.'[1] Oldham's lines, written at the same time, are still more emphatic:

> ' On Butler who can think without just rage,
> The glory and the scandal of the age ?
> Fair stood his hopes when first he came to town,
> Met everywhere with welcomes of renown,
> Courted and loved by all, with wonder read,
> And promises of princely favour fed ;
> But what reward for all had he at last,
> After a life of dull expectance passed ?
> The wretch at summing up his misspent days
> Found nothing left but poverty and praise ;
> Of all his gains by verse he could not save
> Enough to purchase flannel and a grave ;
> Reduced to want, he in due time fell sick,
> Was fain to die, and be interred on tick ;
> And well might bless the fever that was sent
> To rid him hence, and his worse fate prevent.'

These spirited verses are certainly exaggerated. Butler, though, as his biographer says, ' personally known to few,'

---

[1] Mr. Churton Collins, by a clerical error, prints *Waller*.

partook on the same authority of the munificence of
Dorset, and dying on September 25th, 1680, was buried on
September 27th in the churchyard of St. Paul's, Covent
Garden, at the expense of another friend, William Longueville, bencher of the Inner Temple, who had previously
endeavoured to obtain his interment in Westminster
Abbey, where, Atterbury being dean, a tardy monument
was erected to him in 1721 by Alderman Barber. Very
little is known of the latter years of his life, except that
he lived in Rose Street, Covent Garden, and that
he suffered much from the gout. He had. published
a second part of *Hudibras* in 1664, and a third in 1678,
containing many allusions to events much later than the
Civil War. He bequeathed his posthumous papers to
Longueville, by whom they were carefully preserved, and
a large portion eventually came to be published in 1759.
They will be treated of in another place. Not much is
known of Butler's personal character and habits. He
must evidently have been a man of extensive reading, and
versed in several languages and literatures. It seems
natural to attribute the neglect of so popular an author to
some infirmity in his own temper, but the little testimony
we have makes the other way. Wood describes him as ' a
boon and witty companion ; ' and Aubrey says, ' A severe
and sound judgment, a good fellow.' It must be remembered that he was forty-eight at the Restoration, and had
spent almost all his life in the country ; we shall also find
reason to believe that he was neither enough of a churchman nor enough of a loyalist to be entirely agreeable to his
own party.

The defect in *Hudibras* pointed out by Dr. Johnson, the
want of logical sequence in the action, undoubtedly exists,
but is almost inherent in the conception of such a performance. A more serious drawback, the disproportion be-

tween the hero's deeds and his words, probably arises from
the poem having been written at different periods of the
author's life. When he began to write his invention was
lively and vigorous, but it naturally flagged after middle
age, although his wit remained unimpaired. In the first
and part of the second canto disquisition and adventure
are so evenly blended that each supports the other; in the
latter part of the poem the burden falls almost entirely
upon the former. Hence the picturesque and cleverly
varied incident of the bear-baiting, with the varied characters it brings upon the scene, will always be the
favourite passage of the poem, unless an exception be
made for the portraits of Hudibras and Ralpho. There is,
however, considerable inconsistency in the character of
Hudibras. He is represented as a fool, yet half the good
things of the book are, from sheer necessity, put into his
mouth. We are to suppose him a coward, yet he takes
and deals cuffs and bangs in the spirit of a pugilist; and
his attack upon the seven champions of bear-baiting, one
of them an Amazon, is so far from cowardice, that it more
resembles temerity. The more odious traits of his character
hardly seem properly to belong to it; and in fact Butler
probably commenced his poem without too curiously considering how he was to conduct it, or rather where it was
to conduct him, and scribbled away in the spirit of his own
maxim—

> 'One for sense, and one for rhyme,
> Is quite sufficient at one time '—

trusting to the humour ever springing up under his pen to
redeem his verse from the imputation of doggrel. This it
certainly did; for although *Hudibras* as a whole is ram-
bling, ill-compacted, and wordy, the terseness of many individual passages is as remarkable as their humour :

> ' A tool
> That knaves do work with, called a fool.'

> ' Cerberus himself pronounce
> A leash of languages at once.'

> ' Hudibras wore but one spur,
> As wisely knowing, could he stir
> To active trot one side of 's horse
> The other would not hang.'

> ' For as on land there is no beast,
> But in some fish at sea's exprest ;
> So in the wicked there's no vice
> Of which the saints have not a spice.'

> ' Quoth she, There are no bargains driven,
> Nor marriages clapped up in heaven,
> And that's the reason, as some guess,
> There is no heaven in marriages.'

Butler's *Hudibras* may perhaps be best defined as a metrical parody upon *Don Quixote*, with a spice of allusion to the *Faerie Queene*, in which the nobility and pathos of the originals are designedly obliterated, and the humour exaggerated into farce to suit the author's polemic purpose. His design is to kill Presbyterianism and Independency by ridicule, and he is consequently compelled to shut his eyes to everything in them except their occasional tendency to baseness, and their perpetual liability to cant. This is the constant Nemesis of the satirist ; but Butler is even more of a caricaturist than the situation called for. The endurance of his poem to our own times, however, is sufficient proof that, although a caricature, it was not a libel, and amid the enthusiastic reaction of the Restoration it may well have passed for a fair portrait. The machinery is closely modelled upon *Don Quixote*. Presbyterianism is incarnated in the doughty

justice of the peace, Sir Hudibras; Independency and new
light sectarianism in general in his squire, Ralpho; and the
two sally forth in quest of adventure quite in the style of
Don Quixote and Sancho, except that the Don's great aim
is to deliver damsels, and Hudibras's to imprison them.
Though the scene appears to be laid in the west of England,
there is no reason to doubt the tradition that the prototype
of Hudibras's satire was Butler's master, the Bedfordshire
magistrate, Sir Samuel Luke, who is evidently alluded to
where a rhyme to *Mameluke* is left blank to be supplied by
the reader's ingenuity. If, as is more than probable, this
worthy justice was given to suppressing bear-baitings,
Butler would need no more material for his burlesque;
and the first part of the poem, at all events, may well have
been written while he was in Sir Samuel's employment. It
seems, from internal evidence, to have been composed before
Cromwell had ejected the Long Parliament, and its general
atmosphere almost precludes the idea of its having been
written after the execution of Charles I. The second part
has many allusions to later events. The description of
Hudibras, mind and body, is so vivid and precise as to
present internal evidence of having been drawn from a
living model, while Ralpho is in comparison vague. Soon
after sallying forth the pair find themselves at odds with
a crowd about to revel in the amusement of bear-baiting,
which they proceed to interrupt; not, as has been remarked,
out of compassion to the bear, but out of grudge to the
public. This brings on a fight, most amusingly described,
but at somewhat too great length; the 'fatal facility' of
the octosyllabic couplet being nowhere more conspicuous
than in Butler's humorous doggrel. After various turns
of fortune, the knight and squire find themselves in the
stocks, where they sit until Hudibras's lady-love, a frolic-
some widow with a jointure, appears to the rescue:

' No sooner did the Knight perceive her,
But straight he fell into a fever,
Inflam'd all over with disgrace,
To be seen by her in such a place ;
Which made him hang his head, and scowl,
And wink, and goggle like an owl.
He felt his brains begin to swim,
When thus the Dame accosted him,
    This place (quoth she) they say's enchanted,
And with delinquent spirits haunted,
That here are tied in chains, and scourged,
Until their guilty crimes be purged :
Look, there are two of them appear
Like persons I have seen somewhere.
Some have mistaken blocks and posts
For spectres, apparitions, ghosts,
With saucer-eyes, and horns, and some
Have heard the Devil beat a drum :
But if our eyes are not false glasses,
That give a wrong account of faces,
That beard and I should be acquainted,
Before 'twas conjur'd and enchanted ;
For tho' it be disfigured somewhat,
As if 't had lately been in combat,
It did belong t' a worthy Knight,
Howe'er this goblin is come by it.
    When Hudibras the lady heard,
Discoursing thus upon his beard,
And speak with such respect and honour,
Both of the beard, and the beard's owner ;
He thought it best to set as good
A face upon it as he cou'd,
And thus he spoke : Lady, your bright
And radiant eyes are in the right ;
The beard's th' identic beard you knew,
The same numerically true :
Nor is it worn by fiend or elf,
But its proprietor himself.
    Oh Heav'ns ! quoth she, can that be true !
I do begin to fear 'tis you ;
Not by your individual whiskers,

But by your dialect and discourse,
That never spoke to man or beast
In notions vulgarly exprest.
But what malignant star, alas !
Has brought you both to this sad pass ?
   Quoth he, The fortune of the war,
Which I am less afflicted for,
Than to be seen with beard and face
By you in such a homely case.
   Quoth she, Those need not be asham'd
For being honourably maim'd ;
If he that is in battle conquer'd,
Have any title to his own beard,
Tho' yours be sorely lugg'd and torn,
It does your visage more adorn,
Than if 'twere prun'd, and starch'd and lander'd,
And cut square by the Russian standard.
A torn beard's like a tatter'd ensign,
That's bravest which there are most rents in,
That petticoat about your shoulders
Does not so well become a soldier's,
And I'm afraid they are worse handled,
Although i' th' rear, your beard the van led ;
And those uneasy bruises make
My heart for company to ache,
To see so worshipful a friend
I' th' pill'ry set at the wrong end.'

The mischievous lady, nevertheless, only consents to liberate Hudibras upon condition that he shall administer a sound flogging to himself. Hudibras willingly promises this, and is released, but next day he thinks better of it, and consults Ralpho whether he is actually bound by his oath. Ralpho's reply abounds with the pithy couplets so frequent in *Hudibras*, which have become a part of the language :

   ' Oaths were not purposed, more than law,
To keep the good and just in awe,
But to confine the bad and sinful,
Like moral cattle in a pinfold.'

'The Rabbins write, when any Jew
Did make to God or man a vow
Which afterward he found untoward
And stubborn to be kept, or too hard ;
Any three other Jews of the nation
Might free him from his obligation.
And have not two saints power to use
A greater privilege than three Jews ? '

'Does not in Chancery every man swear
What makes best for him in his answer ? '

'He that imposes an oath makes it,
Not he that for convenience takes it ;
Then how can any man be said
To break an oath he never made ? '

'That sinners may supply the place
Of suff'ring saints is a plain case.
Justice gives sentence many times
On one man for another's crimes.
Our brethren of New England use
Choice malefactors to excuse,
And hang the guiltless in their stead,
Of whom the churches have less need :
As lately 't happened in a town,
There liv'd a cobler, and but one,
That out of doctrine could cut use,
And mend men's lives as well as shoes.
This precious brother having slain,
In times of peace, an Indian,
(Not out of malice, but mere zeal,
Because he was an infidel)
The mighty Tottipottymoy
Sent to our elders an envoy ;
Complaining sorely of the breach
Of league, held forth by brother Patch,
Against the articles in force
Between both churches, his and ours,
For which he crav'd the saints to render
Into his hands, or hang th' offender :

> But they maturely having weigh'd
> They had no more but him o' th' trade,
> (A man that serv'd them in a double
> Capacity, to teach and cobble,)
> Resolv'd to spare him; yet to do
> The Indian Hoghgan Moghgan too
> Impartial justice, in his stead did
> Hang an old weaver that was bed-rid.'

Hudibras, however, is but half convinced, or rather, doubts whether conviction can be brought to the minds of others. He bethinks himself of a middle course, and suggests that the whipping shall be inflicted by proxy, and that Ralpho shall be the proxy. To this Ralpho demurs, and an impending rupture is only averted by a new adventure, which seems invented for the purpose. When it is over Hudibras has profited by the interval of reflection to resolve to consult the wizard Sidrophel, who is apparently intended for Lilly. The scene affords Butler an opportunity of venting the dislike to physical science which he shared with so many other literary men, and to which he gave more definite expression in *The Elephant in the Moon*. The interview terminates in a scuffle, in which Hudibras overthrows Sidrophel, and, thinking he has killed him, makes off, leaving Ralpho, as he deems, to bear the brunt. The trusty squire, however, has already gone to the lady with the tale of Hudibras's perjury, which insures the knight a warm reception. Here the action of the story ends, the remainder of the poem being chiefly occupied by 'heroical epistles' between the parties, which do not help it on, and by a digression on the downfall of the Rump, chiefly remarkable for allusions to politics of later date. —One of the most noticeable phenomena in Butler is, that after all this Cavalier poet is little of a Cavalier, and this assailant of Puritanism little of a Churchman. His loyalty is but hatred of anarchy, and his religion but hatred of cant. The genuineness of both these feelings is attested by the detached thoughts found among his papers; otherwise it might fairly have been doubted whether his motive for espousing the royalist cause had been any other than the infinitely greater scope which Puritanism and Republicanism offered to the shafts of a satirist. The follies of the Cavalier party proved that things may be absurd without being ridiculous; those of their opponents demonstrated that ridicule may justly attach to things not intrinsically absurd. It is clear, notwithstanding, from Butler's prose remains, that he was constitutionally hostile to liberty in politics and to the inward light in religion, and that he obeyed his own sincere conviction in attacking them. But it is equally clear that his preference for monarchy was solely utilitarian, and that his preferences in religion were determined simply by taste. The ground of his acquiescence in the Church of England is thus frankly stated by himself in one of his detached thoughts:

'Men ought to do in religion as they do in war. When a man of honour is overpowered, and must of necessity surrender himself up a prisoner, such are always wont to endeavour to do it to some person of command and quality, and not to a mere scoundrel. So, since all men are obliged to be of some church, it is more honourable, if there were nothing else in it, to be of that which has some reputation, than such a one as is contemptible, and justly despised by all the best of men.'

This is not the language of a very fervent churchman; and Butler's royalism is like his religion, a *pis aller*. Nowhere does his aversion for Puritanism kindle into enthusiasm for its contrary, any more than his humour ever rises into poetry. In his verse he is a satirist; in his prose a sceptic; and his satire and his scepticism are alike rooted in a low opinion of human nature, and a disbelief that things can ever be much better than they are. He is a strong spirit, but of the earth, earthy. At the same time he is not one of the satirists who make their readers cynics; on the contrary, his hearty geniality puts the reader into good humour with mankind, and suggests that if there is not much to admire there is also but little to condemn. It is unnecessary to dilate on his peculiar merits, which are of universal notoriety. Few have enriched the language with so many familiar quotations; few have so much fancy along with a total absence of sentiment; few have been so fertile in odd rhymes and quaint illustrations and comparisons; few have so thoroughly combined the characters of wit and humorist.

In 1759 a quantity of MS. compositions of Butler's, which had remained unpublished during his life, and had come into the possession of his friend Longueville, were edited by R. Thyer, librarian of the Chetham Library at Manchester. The most important, his characters in the manner of Theophrastus, and detached thoughts in prose, will be noticed along with the prose essayists. Of the metrical compositions, the most elaborate is *The Elephant in the Moon*, a satire on the appetite for marvels displayed by some of the members of the then infant Royal Society, which exists in two recensions, one in Hudibrastic, the other in heroic verse. The other pieces are also for the most part satirical, with a strong affinity to *Hudibras*, except where they parody the style of some poet of the day. They are always clever, sometimes very humorous and pointed, and, with Marvell's satires, form a transition from the unpolished quaintness of Donne to the weight and splendour of Dryden. Butler in one instance appears a downright plagiarist; in another he would seem, were the thing possible, to have been copied by a later and more illustrious writer. In his satire against rhyme, he writes:

F

> ' When I would praise an author, the untoward
> Damned sense says Virgil, but the rhyme says Howard.'

This is undoubtedly Boileau's 'La raison dit Virgile, et la rime Quinault.' In *Cat and Puss*, on the other hand, an amusing parody of the rhyming tragedy of his day, he observes of the feline Lothario :

> ' At once his passion was both false and true,
> And the more false, the more in earnest grew.'

Can Tennyson, who borrowed and improved so much, have been to Butler for

> ' His honour rooted in dishonour stood,
> And faith unfaithful kept him falsely true ' ?

CHAPTER III.

It is entirely in keeping with the solid and terrestrial character of Restoration literature in general, that no description of poetry should manifest so grievous a lapse from the standard of the preceding age as the lyrical. The decline of the drama has attracted more attention, partly from the violent contrast of two schools which had hardly one principle or one method in common, partly because our own age had but imperfectly realized the exceeding wealth in song of the Elizabethan and Jacobean periods, until Mr. Arthur Bullen showed what unsuspected treasures of poetry were hidden in old music books. Whatever else an Elizabethan or Jacobean lyric may be, it is almost certain to be melodious. The average Restoration lyric is correct enough in scansion, but the melody is conventional, poor and thin. Here and there, and especially in Dryden, we are surprised by a fine exception; but as a rule the Restoration song is deficient alike in the simple spontaneity which inspired such pieces as *Come live with me and be my love*, and in the more intricate harmonies of its predecessors. It was as though a blight had suddenly fallen upon the nation, and men's ears had become incapable of distinguishing between sweetness and smoothness. So, indeed, they had as respected the music of verse; but how little technical music, whether vocal or instrumental, was neglected, even in private circles, we may learn from Pepys's *Diary*, and it is a remarkable proof how little this music and the music of poetry have to do with each other, that this age of degeneracy in the one produced the greatest of all English masters, Purcell, in the other; while the still more hopelessly unmelodious age of the first Georges was the age of Handel. Poetry makes melody, not melody poetry; and the only explanation is, that the age preceding that of the Restoration was poetical, and the Restoration age was prosaic. It could not well have been otherwise if, as all critics agree, the special literary mission of the Restoration period was to prune the luxuriance of English prose, and by introducing conciseness, perspicuity, and logical order, to render it a fit instrument for narrative, reasoning, and the despatch of business.

Such lyric as the age possessed is almost entirely comprehended in Dryden; for Marvell, of whom we must nevertheless speak, belongs in spirit to a former age. The songs in Dryden's plays, to be mentioned shortly, prove that he was by no means destitute of spontaneous lyrical feeling; but he no doubt succeeded best when, having first penetrated himself with a theme sufficiently stirring to generate the enthusiastic mood which finds its natural expression in song, he sat down to frame a fitting accompaniment by the aid of all the resources of metrical art. The principal examples of this lyrical magnificence which he has given us are the elegy on Anne Killigrew and the two odes on St. Cecilia's Day. Of the first of these two latter, Johnson says that 'it is lost in the splendour of the second,' and such is the fact; but had Dryden produced no other lyric, he would still have ranked as a fine lyrical poet. Of the second ode, better known as *Alexander's Feast*, it is needless to say anything, for all readers of poetry have it by heart, and all recognize its claim to rank among the

greatest odes in the language—the greatest, perhaps, until
Wordsworth and Shelley wrote, and little, if at all, behind
even them. Johnson, indeed, prefers the memorial ode on
Anne Killigrew, and if all the stanzas equalled the first
he would be right; but this is impossible; as he himself
remarks, 'An imperial crown cannot be one continued
diamond.' The inevitable falling off, nevertheless, would
have been less apparent if Dryden had shown more judgment in the selection of his topics, or at least more tact in
handling them. The morals of the age were, indeed, bad
enough, as he well knew who had helped to make them
so ; but such frank treatment of a disagreeable theme jars
exceedingly with an ode devoted to the celebration of
chastity and virtue. Notwithstanding this flaw, the entire
ode deserves Mr. Saintsbury's eulogy, 'As a piece of con-
certed music in verse it has not a superior.' The hyper-
bolical praise of Anne Killigrew's now forgotten poems is
explained, and in some measure excused, by the fact that it
was written to be prefixed to them. The first stanza,
appropriate to thousands beside its ostensible subject,
appeals to the general human heart, and indicates the high-
water mark of Restoration poetry :

> ' Thou youngest virgin-daughter of the skies,
>   Made in the last promotion of the blest,
>   Whose palms, new-plucked from Paradise,
> In spreading branches more sublimely rise,
>   Rich with immortal green above the rest :
> Whether, adopted to some neighbouring star,
> Thou roll'st above us in thy wandering race,
>   Or in procession fixed and regular
>   Mov'st with the heavens' majestic pace ;
>   Or, called to more superior bliss,
> Thou tread'st with seraphims the vast abyss :
> Whatever happy region is thy place,
> Cease thy celestial song a little space ;

> Thou wilt have time enough for hymns divine,
>   Since Heaven's eternal year is thine.
> Hear then a mortal Muse thy praise rehearse
>   In no ignoble verse ;
> But such as thy own voice did practise here,
> When thy first fruits of Poesy were given,
> To make thyself a welcome inmate there
>   While yet a young probationer
>   And candidate of heaven.'

The poet who so excelled in majestic artificial harmonies was also the one poet of his day who could occasionally sing as the bird sings. Dryden has never received sufficient praise for his songs, inasmuch as these are mostly hidden away in his dramas, and not always adapted for quotation. The following, with a manifest political meaning, is a good example of his simple ease and melody :

> ' A choir of bright beauties in spring did appear
> To choose a May-lady to govern the year ;
> All the nymphs were in white, and the shepherds in green ;
> The garland was given, and Phyllis was queen :
> But Phyllis refused it, and sighing did say,
> I'll not wear a garland while Pan is away.

> ' While Pan and fair Syrinx are fled from our shore,
> The Graces are vanished, and Love is no more :
> The soft God of Pleasure that warmed our desires,
> Has broken his bow and extinguished his fires ;
> And vows that himself and his mother will mourn
> Till Pan and fair Syrinx in triumph return.

> ' Forbear your addresses and court us no more,
> For we will perform what the Deity swore ;
> But if you dare think of deserving our charms,
> Away with your sheep-hooks, and take to your arms ;
> Then laurels and myrtles your brows shall adorn
> When Pan and his son and fair Syrinx return.'

The following song is from *The Mock Astrologer* :

' You charmed me not with that fair face,
    Though it was all divine ;
To be another's is the grace
    That makes me wish you mine.
The gods and fortune take their part
    Who like young monarchs fight,
And boldly dare invade that heart
    Which is another's right.
First, mad with hope, we undertake
    To pull up every bar ;
But, once possessed, we feebly make
    A dull defensive war.
Now every friend is turned a foe,
    In hope to get our store :
And passion makes us cowards grow
    Which made us brave before.'

The Muse who could mourn to such purpose for Anne Killigrew might have been expected to soar high in celebrating and lamenting Charles II., parts of whose history and character certainly lent themselves to poetry. Whether from haste, indifference, or whatever reason, Dryden was clearly unable to penetrate himself with the subject, and it is perhaps to his honour that his composition should so little simulate an inspiration he was evidently far from feeling. The choice of subjects is judicious, but the treatment is in general inanimate and perfunctory, except when the poet is going to say something absurd, and then his motto is *Pecca fortiter*. There is, perhaps, nothing nearer burlesque in all Dryden's rhyming plays than this couplet :

    ' Ere a prince is to perfection brought,
    He costs Omnipotence a second thought.'

The poet is also weighted by having to flatter Charles and his successor at the same time. The concluding lines, however, eulogizing James's care for the navy, will always echo in the heart of Britain :

'Behold even the remoter shores
A conquering navy proudly spread :
The British cannon formidably roars,
While, starting from his oozy bed,
The asserted Ocean rears his reverend head
To view and recognize his ancient Lord again,
And with a willing hand restores
The fasces of the main.'

This latter fine phrase had occurred already in *Astraea Redux* and *Annus Mirabilis*.

Andrew Marvell, though unequal, is an excellent lyric poet. His best song, *Where the remote Bermudas ride*, is such a household word that we select a less known piece :

'Ye living lamps, by whose dear light
The nightingale does sit so late,
And studying all the summer night,
Her matchless songs does meditate;

'Ye country comets, that portend
No war nor prince's funeral,
Shining unto no other end
Than to presage the grass's fall ;

' Ye glowworms, whose officious flame
To wandering mowers shows the way,
That in the night have lost their aim,
And after foolish fires do stray ;

'Your courteous lights in vain you waste,
Since Juliana here is come ;
For she my mind hath so displaced,
That I shall never find my home.'

In fancy as in melody this and Marvell's other gems belong to the age of Charles I. Apart from Dryden, the Restoration has little to show beside three songs of genuine inspiration in the plays of Crowne, to be mentioned in his place as a middling dramatist; Sir Charles Sedley's charming verses to Chloris ; others, mostly from the same hand

Motteux, and, strange to say, the Dryasdust Rymer, which have found a harbour in Mr. Arthur Bullen's *Musa Proterva*; a few songs of Rochester's and Aphra Behn's; some few carols in Mr. Ebsworth's collections; and the elegant and animated *To all you ladies now at land* of Charles Sackville, Earl of Dorset (1637-1706), less known for his occasional verses, these excepted, than as the arbiter of taste and the benefactor of needy men of letters.

It was but natural that the lyrists, like the dramatists, should endeavour to make up in bombastic extravagance for their deficiencies in simplicity and truth to nature. An appropriate instrument was at hand in the Pindaric ode, the miscreation of a true poet, Cowley. So little were the genuine characteristics of Pindaric versification then understood even by scholars, that it is no wonder that Cowley should have conceived them to be equivalent to absolute irregularity. His own compositions are not within our province; but it may be remarked that they are distinguished from the Pindarics of Charles II.'s time by the preponderance of what was then called wit, which we should describe as a perverse ingenuity in discovering superficial resemblances between dissimilar things. It is impossible not to admire in a measure some of the feats of this kind performed by Cowley, Crashaw, and Donne; but common sense intimates that the real criterion of the merit of a comparison is its justice. The movement, nevertheless, had considerable significance as indicating the exhaustion of the old forms of poetry. It had triumphed in Italy and in Spain in the persons of Marino and Gongora, with most disastrous effects on the literature of those countries. Fortunate it was for England that this fashion arrived late, and before it could take much root was dislodged by the saner methods of France. Pindarics, however, went on existing, but with comparatively little wit, and even less poetry. Sprat, of whom we shall have to speak as the historian of the Royal Society, was perhaps the most conspicuous practitioner. The following lines on Prometheus are a bright example of his amalgam of poetry and wit:

> 'Along he brought the sparkling coal
> From some celestial chimney [1] stole;
> Quickly the plundered stars he left,
>   And as he hastened down,
> With the robbed flames his hands still shone,
> And seemed as if they were burnt for the theft.'

Congreve is equally absurd in his personification of Sleep:

> 'An ancient sigh he sits upon,
> Whose memory of sound is long since gone,
> And purposely annihilated for his throne.'

This poet, nevertheless, who, as pointed out by Dr. Johnson and Mr. Gosse, has the critical merit of having given the English Pindaric a regular structure, was capable of much better things. The opening of the ode which yields the above choice *morceau* (*To Mrs. Arabella Hunt, Singing*) is in a fine strain of poetry:

> 'Let all be hushed, each softest motion cease,
> Be every loud tumultuous thought at peace,
> And every ruder gasp of breath
> Be calm, as in the arms of death:
> And then, most fickle, most uneasy part,
> Thou restless wanderer, my heart,
> Be still; gently, ah gently, leave,
> Thou busy, idle thing, to heave:
> Stir not a pulse; and let my blood,

---

[1] It should be noted that this word is not so absurd as it may appear to the modern reader. Chimney (Fr. *cheminée*) here means the fireplace, not the flue. 'The mantle of the *chimney* in his hall.'—WALTON, *Life of George Herbert.*

That turbulent unruly flood,
Be softly staid :
Let me be all, but my attention, dead.
Go, rest, unnecessary springs of life,
Leave your officious toil and strife ;
For I would hear her voice, and try
If it be possible to die.'

CHAPTER IV.

DRYDEN occupies an unique position as by far the most important representative of a department of literature for which, on his own showing, he had little natural qualification, and in which he had little ambition to excel. Only one of his numerous plays, he tells us, was written to please himself. But he wanted reputation, money, and Court favour, and these inducements directed him to the most popular and lucrative department of the Muses' province. Here, as elsewhere, his progress was slow. His first play, *The Wild Gallant* (1663), has come down to us in an amended version; in its original form it is pronounced by Pepys 'as poor a thing as I ever saw in my life.' Dryden might long have remained an unsuccessful dramatist but for the invention of rhyming tragedy, which, though in itself an objectionable form, suited his talent to perfection. The management of the heroic couplet was and always continued the strongest of all his strong points, and his genius for rhetoric was stimulated to the utmost by the facilities afforded by this sonorous form of metre. Hence *The Indian Emperor* (1665) was a great success, and determined the main course of Dryden's dramatic activity for some years. It necessarily brought him nearer to the French drama, and gave a French character to the drama of the day, not really in harmony with the taste of the

English public, and from which Dryden ultimately freed himself. The opinion of the day was prepared to go in the direction of classicism as far as Jonson, but not as far as Corneille. The French traveller Sorbière having in 1663 censured the irregularity of the English stage, was answered by Sprat, who asserts the superiority of his countrymen, and points out the fundamental difference in the taste of the two nations. 'The French,' he says, 'for the most part take only one or two great men, and chiefly insist upon some one remarkable accident of their story; to this end they admit no more persons than will serve to adorn that: and they manage all in rhyme, with long speeches, almost in the way of dialogues, in making high ideas of honour, and in speaking noble things. The English on their side make their chief plot to consist in a greater variety of actions, and, besides the main design, add many little contrivances. By this means their scenes are shorter, their stage fuller, many more persons of different humours are introduced. And in carrying on of this they generally do only confine themselves to blank verse.' Sprat then proceeds to point out the advantages of the English method; and it is evident that neither he nor the public imagined themselves to be on the eve of such serious modifications of the national drama as actually took place—modifications to be chiefly attributed to the taste of the Court, and the more easily effected from the paucity of theatres.

The inferiority of the Restoration drama to the Elizabethan is one of the commonplaces of criticism, perhaps even one of its platitudes, and cannot be admitted without some qualification. Yet, as the broad general statement of a fact, it is undeniable, and the fact is a proof that the elements which preserve a play as literature for posterity are not those which fit it for the contemporary stage. In every play of serious purpose there is, or should be, an earthly part and a spiritual, dramatic craftsmanship and poetical inspiration. In the former particular the Restoration dramatists compare not unfavourably with their predecessors, always excepting Shakespeare; they fail not as dramatists, but as poets. The whole Elizabethan drama is steeped in an atmosphere of poetry. To say nothing of its chief representatives, take up such satires as *The Return from Parnassus*, or such merely occasional pieces as the academical play on *Timon* which preceded Shakespeare's, and you will not doubt that you are reading the work of a poet. Read through, on the other hand, the best plays of the representative dramatists of the Restoration, and you will generally find the poetical element concentrated in a few brilliant passages. In the Elizabethan age, it is evident, men lived at such a height of heroic and romantic sentiment that the purveyors of public entertainment could not but be poets. In the Restoration era, on the other hand, men habitually lived, breathed, and wrote prose; and when the dramatist would be a poet, he had to set himself to the task. To convince ourselves that the distinction between poetry and prose is not artificial, as Carlyle seemed to think, but essential, we have only to consider the widely different influence of Elizabethan and Restoration drama upon the after world. Both, excepting the works of Shakespeare, are virtually dead as acted drama. But in losing the stage the Restoration drama has lost everything, while the Elizabethan is yet a living and working force. It powerfully co-operated in the splendid revival of English poetry at the end of last century; it is at this moment an inspirer and a nurse of young genius. It is inconceivable that the Restoration drama as a whole should inspire anyone, or that it should count for anything as a factor in future developments of literature. One is a perennial plant, which may die down to the root in ungenial seasons, but will assuredly put forth new flowers; the other is a fossil, curious and in some measure beautiful, but devoid of vital force. And for this, the merely intellectual merits of both being so considerable, no reason can be given but that one is on the whole poetical, and therefore living, the other on the whole prosaic, and therefore inert. Hence we may prophesy of the success of the endeavour of Ibsen, and other men of distinguished talent, to produce dramas conceived in an entirely realistic spirit, and entirely devoted to the problems of modern society. Such competitions will be valuable *pièces justificatives* for the intellectual history of the nineteenth century, but they will be extinct as literary forces long ere the end of the twentieth.

This, nevertheless, is to be said for the Restoration dramatists, that their art is not an imitation of an extinct form of the drama, but is at least something new, really expressive of the sentiments of their generation. The imitation of Shakespeare could only have produced gross unreality, which must have degenerated still further into mere inanity. The playwrights did what the contemporary painters should have done, they fell back, in a measure, upon realism when high imagination was no longer possible. If they had gone further in this direction their works would have possessed more intrinsic merit, and have claimed a more important place in the history of culture. Their tragedies would not so often have been rendered unnatural by the employment of rhyme, and their comedies would have exhibited the manners and the morals of the English nation, and not merely of the playgoing part of it. It cannot be believed that the comedy of that age affords anything like so faithful a picture of the seventeenth century as Fielding's novels do of the eighteenth. The realistic tendency was chiefly conspicuous in the closer approach to the language of common life, and in the more logical character even of appeals to emotion. The extravagant transports of heroes and heroines only betray that true imagination had grown cold; but the manly nervous sense and the almost forensic reasoning so often found in their company show that a new stratum had really been touched.

Another consideration should not be overlooked in the comparison between the Elizabethan and the Restoration drama, that the debasement of the latter is exaggerated from the seeming abruptness of the metamorphosis undergone by the former. Passing from the stage of Shakespeare to the stage of Dryden, we appear to have suddenly entered a new world. The representatives of the drama seem instantaneously transformed by some Circean potion into beings of a lower type. We do not immediately remember that the gradual development which would have interpreted the apparent prodigy was rudely interrupted by the Civil War and the Commonwealth. If the interval between Shirley and Dryden had been continuously occupied by popular dramatists, we should have observed the change slowly coming on, and have watched the older form shading off into the newer by gradations not more violent than those by which the latter subsequently passed into the drama of the eighteenth century. As it is, the poets of Charles II.'s time seem the authors of a revolution of which they were merely the instruments. The younger portion of their audiences, on whose suffrages they had mainly to rely, had scarcely so much as seen a play. (The spells of authority and tradition were broken, or at least so grievously impaired as to be unable to withstand the seduction of French example.) Honest Samuel Pepys would not have so easily pronounced the *Midsummer Night's Dream* 'a mean thing' if the romantic drama had not been absolutely extinct for him. And, taking a broad

view of the revolution in popular taste, we must admit
that, however deplorable in itself, it had some good sides.
It tended to bring England more into harmony with the
general current of European taste and thought, and re-
pressed the tendency of our noble literature to fanciful
and eccentric insularity. In the long run, moreover, it was
serviceable to the English drama by providing a substitute,
however inferior, for the old vein now unproductive. The
want of such a resource killed the drama of Spain.
Spanish dramatists, until the nineteenth century, were
unable to accommodate themselves to any dramatic form
but the national one, every phase of which had been completely exemplified before the end of the seventeenth
century. In consequence, the Spanish theatre of the
eighteenth century did not produce a single tolerable piece
until, near the termination of the epoch, a playwright
arose who was capable of profiting by French example.

Another extenuation of the departure of the Restoration
dramatists from the better traditions of the English stage
is the strength as well as the suddenness of the new influence to which they were subjected. It came from the
Court, and the Court dispensed the playwright's daily
bread. There is sufficient evidence that even Shakespeare
was by no means indifferent to the good opinion of Elizabeth and James, but neither of these sovereigns was sufficiently the drama's patron to be the drama's legislator. It
was otherwise with Charles II., a man of wit, taste, and
polish, inaccessible to the deeper emotions of humanity,
and without a grain of poetry in his composition. Such a
man must have found the Elizabethan drama intolerable.
He no doubt honestly agreed with his laureate, who coolly
says : 'At his return he found a nation lost as much in
barbarism as in rebellion ; and, as the excellency of his
nature forgave the one, so the excellency of his manners

reformed the other. The desire of imitating so great a pattern first awakened the dull and heavy spirits of the English from their natural reservedness.' With every allowance for adulation, there can be no doubt that Dryden in a considerable measure believed himself a reformer. Charles had his Paladins in the field of letters. 'The favour,' says Dryden elsewhere, 'which heroic plays have lately found upon our theatres has been wholly derived to them from the countenance and approbation they have received at Court.' We may well feel thankful that the experiment of Gallicizing the native genius of England should have been tried so fairly, and have broken down so utterly, under such patronage as Charles's and in such hands as Dryden's. We have not quite seen the last of it, but where Corneille and Molière failed Goncourt and Zola are not likely to succeed.

This may at least be said for Dryden, that the romantic drama was for a time in a state of suspended animation, and that the only question was what successor should fill its place. For a short time two foreign schools seemed contending for the prize. Dryden's own allegiance in his first piece, *The Wild Gallant*, was given to the Spanish drama, a form exceedingly attractive from its brisk action, sudden vicissitudes, and dexterous development of intrigue. But the Spanish drama cannot be naturalized in England for two reasons, one creditable to English genius, the other the reverse. A play of intrigue is necessarily a play of incident, and allows little room for the development of character; but Englishmen are 'humoursome,' and enjoy the discrimination of character to the nicest shades. If we judged the two nations solely by their dramas, we should say that all Spaniards were exactly alike, and no two Englishmen. The other reason is that Englishmen do not particularly excel in the contrivance of incident, and

that few even of our best dramatists could rival the ingenuity of third-rate Spanish playwrights. The Anglo-
Spanish drama soon disappeared, and its place in serious
dramatic literature was taken by a *genre* most intimately
associated with the name of Dryden, its most brilliant
practitioner, and upon whose desertion it crumbled into
dust.

Dryden himself has told us in few words what he understands by an heroic play, and the definition exempts him
from much of the criticism to which he might otherwise
have been held liable: 'An heroic play ought to be an
imitation, in little, of an heroic poem.' In other words, it
must have an epical element as well as a dramatic. The
experiment was worth making, as it proved that neither
branch of the poetic art gained anything by invading the
other's territory. Compared with the art of Shakespeare
or of Sophocles, the art of Dryden in this department
seems a tawdry caricature. All the higher qualities of
the dramatist are absent, being, in fact, inconsistent with
the demands of epic poetry, while epic dignity is equally
sacrificed to the exigencies of drama. Without constant
hurry and bustle, such pieces would be intolerable. They
require, as Dryden tacitly admits by the quotation from
Ariosto, which he adduces as expressive of his guiding
principle, a constant succession of adventures. Such in-
cessant agitation leaves no place for the development of
character; the actors come on the stage ready labelled; or
if, like Nourmahal in *Aurengzebe*, they disclose a new trait,
the sudden novelty produces the effect of complete metamorphosis. The pieces could only be regarded as splendid
puppet-shows, were not the failings of the dramatist so
frequently redeemed by the poet. It so chanced that the
Coryphæus of this unnatural style was the most splendid
poetical declaimer (unless Byron be excepted) that England

ever produced, and his pieces resound with tirades not merely brilliant in diction and sonorous in versification, but now fiery with mettlesome spirit, now weighty with manly sense. And these qualities were aided by the otherwise objectionable form selected by the poet. His blank-verse plays, far superior as works of art, contain few such eloquent passages as his rhyming tragedies. Rhyme helped him on, as a riderless runaway horse is spurred by the thunder of his own hoofs. Even where his thought is poor, its poverty is veiled by the brilliancy of the diction—a brilliancy which he could hardly have attained by the use of any other form; and if the employment of rhyme seems, as it is, unnatural, the form at least harmonizes with the substance, and they produce between them an illusive effect of a species of art which may possibly be legitimate, as the ordinary rules evidently do not apply. We must also remember how this subornation of the judgment, not imperceptible or ineffective in the closet, was aided on the stage by the most potent appeals to the senses.

Tyrannic Love, Dryden's first considerable attempt in 'heroic tragedy,' is very remarkable as a proof of to what extraordinary absurdities a vigorous intellect may be liable, and also how these may be dignified by energy of expression. ' The rants of Maximin,' says Johnson, ' have long been the sport of criticism;' but so spirited and sonorous is the diction, that, inconsistent as seems the alliance of admiration with derision, such actually is the mingled feeling which they excite in the quiet of the closet. On the stage they must have passed off much better by the aid of scenery, costume, and emphatic declamation; and success on the boards, it must be remembered, was invariably Dryden's first object. The same consideration which explains, though it does not excuse, his indecency, palliates his bombast. He wrote to live, and could not afford to produce unactable dramas.

A much more interesting performance than *Tyrannic Love* is his *Conquest of Granada* (1669-1670). It is a touchstone of ' heroic tragedy,' a crucial test of what it can and what it cannot do. It renounces all pretence to nature, reason, and probability; on the other hand, it delights with a crowd of striking sentiments and images, and enchains the attention with perpetual bustle and variety. It is to one of Shakespeare's plays as a bit of shining glass is to a plant of which every fibre is the creation of a natural law. Yet the glass is not a displeasing object, neither is the play.

The worst offence of *The Conquest of Granada*, after all, is not its bombast, but its bathos. It is true that both spring from the same root, that want of genuine creative imagination which in attempting the great only achieves the big, which a small oversight easily converts into the laughable. But apart from this failing, which Dryden shares with most epic poets of the second rank, it is difficult to acquit him of a singular insensibility to the ridiculous. This is evinced among other things by the entire conception of one of his most serious and elaborate works, *The Hind and the Panther*, and it requires all the gravity and obvious conviction of his preface to *The Conquest of Granada* to convince us that he did not occasionally mean to burlesque his own principles. The rapid changes of fortune, the constant fallings into and out of love,—the odd predicaments in which heroes and heroines continually find themselves, frequently produce the effect of the broadest comedy—an effect much assisted by the extraordinary rants of the principal speakers; as when Lyndaraxa desires the personage who has first stabbed her and then himself to

'Die for us both, I have not leisure now;'

or Almahide threatens to send her ghost to fetch back

Almanzor's scarf, as if she and her ghost were different beings; or Almanzor's astounding menace to his mother's spirit:

> ' I'll squeeze thee like a bladder there,
> And make thee groan thyself away in air.'

So unequal is Dryden's genius that the second of these monstrosities occurs in close proximity to the exquisite verses:

> ' What precious drops are those
> Which silently each other's track pursue,
> Bright as young diamonds in their infant dew?'

and the burlesque threat to the ghost is immediately succeeded by the noble couplet:

> ' I am the ghost of her who gave thee birth,
> The airy shadow of her mouldering earth.'

The beauties which are thickly sown throughout *The Conquest of Granada* owe, perhaps, something of their effect as poetry to the utter want of nature in the characters and of reason in the conduct of the play. In a drama aiming at the delineation of real men and women they would frequently have appeared absurdly inappropriate, but when it is once understood that the personages are the puppets and mouthpieces of the author, the question of dramatic propriety becomes irrelevant. Yet *The Conquest of Granada* is something more than a heap of glittering morsels of sentiment and wit. It possesses a unity of feeling which serves as cement for these scattered jewels. The 'kind of generous and noble spirit animating it,' to employ Mr. Saintsbury's just description, maintains the reader at a level above the pitch of ordinary life. When he opens the book he rises, as he closes it he descends. He may laugh, but his amusement is unmingled with contempt; and ever and anon he comes upon the genuine heroic, unsuspected of sham, unspoiled by bombast. The soul of chivalry inspires the lines quoted with just applause by both Scott and Saintsbury:

> 'Fair though you are
> As summer mornings, and your eyes more bright
> Than stars that twinkle on a winter's night;
> Though you have eloquence to warm and move
> Cold age and fasting hermits into love;
> Though Almahide with scorn rewards my care;
> Yet than to change 'tis nobler to despair.
> My love's my soul, and that from fate is free,
> 'Tis that unchanged and deathless part of me.'

Aurengzebe (1675), Mr. Saintsbury considers 'in some respects a very noble play.' We should rather have called it an indifferent play with some noble passages more remarkable for eloquence than dramatic propriety. The characters, though by no means subtle or even natural, are better discriminated than in *The Conquest of Granada;* there is much less rant and bustle, yet quite enough to make one cordially echo Indamora's naïve inquiry:

> 'Are there yet more Morats, more fighting kings?'

Nor are choice examples of bathos wanting. Aurengzebe finely says:

> 'I need not haste the end of life to meet,
> The precipice is just beneath my feet.'

Nourmahal replies:

> 'Think not my sense of virtue is so small,
> I'll rather leap down first and break your fall.'

The first act opens with a striking couplet:

> 'The night seems doubled with the fear she brings,
> And o'er the citadel now spreads her wings.'

To which immediately succeeds:

> ' The morning, as mistaken, turns about,
> And all her early fires again go out.'

Dryden was probably betrayed into these lapses, not so much by mere haste and carelessness, as by the trick of the heroic metre, which in dialogue almost enforces balanced antithesis.

Nearly all *Aurengzebe* is composed in this brilliant snip-snap, where the ball of a fine sentiment, tossed from one character to another, comes back in a retort, to be returned in a repartee. Of dramatic art as Shakespeare or the Greeks understood it there is not a trace; the pivot of the action is the property, fitter for a fairy tale than a tragedy, possessed by Indamora, of compelling every one who sees her to fall in love with her. Neither pity nor terror can be excited on such terms; if Aristotle's criterion be sound, *Aurengzebe* is no tragedy at all. If, however, we are content to regard it as a medley of fine things, a model of spirited declamation and sonorous versification, it claims high praise. Great must have been the intellectual strength which could thus thunder and dazzle through five acts of unabated energy: and the sentiments, considered merely as such, lose nothing of their effect from being placed in the mouths of puppets, and misplaced even there. Take, for instance, the most famous passage in the play, one of the finest in all Dryden:

> ' When I consider life, 'tis all a cheat ;
> Yet, fooled with hope, men favour the deceit ;
> Trust on, and think to-morrow will repay ;
> To-morrow's falser than the former day ;
> Lies worse, and while it says, we shall be blest
> With some new joys, cuts off what we possest.
> Strange cozenage !   None would live past years again,
> Yet all hope pleasure in what yet remain ;

And from the dregs of life think to receive
What the first sprightly runnings could not give.'

This potent quintessence of the experience of age is ill assigned to Aurengzebe, a young prince at the outset of a splendid career; but the word remains while the lip is forgotten, and has taken its place among the treasures of English poetry. Among other claims to notice, *Aurengzebe* is remarkable as one of the few English dramas in which a living foreign potentate is brought upon the stage, and, less exceptionally, for its entire perversion of the truth of history. The generous and filial part here ascribed to the unnatural and cold-blooded Aurengzebe was really performed by his unfortunate brother Dara. To have crowned Dara, however, would have involved an equal violation of historical truth, to have killed him a violation of what the dramatists of Dryden's day considered more important, poetical justice.

Marriage à la Mode (1673), the first fair example of Dryden's comedy, is a more satisfactory exhibition of his power as a dramatist, if a piece adding little to his fame as a poet. Mr. Saintsbury justly remarks that 'Scott's general undervaluing of Dryden's comic pieces is very evident' in his prefatory notice. Mr. Saintsbury himself, though warmly appreciative of 'Dryden's only original excursion into the realms of the higher comedy,' might, we think, have said even more in its favour. The situation of the spouses, fancying themselves tired of each other while their affection only needs the fillip of jealousy, is comic in a high degree, and the brisk intricacy of the action, with only four actors to sustain it, manifests great ingenuity and deftness in dramatic construction. The serious section of the play is certainly much less meritorious than the comic, to which it is a mere appendage. Written in most slovenly blank verse, it entirely wants the fire and energy of Dryden's heroic plays. Its fault is rather sterility than extravagance; with some exceptions, it appears tame and bald. But these exceptions are very fine. The scene between Leonidas and Palmyra (act ii., sc. 1) is like a morsel of Theocritus, allying the charm of pastoral innocence to the wit and point of an accomplished court-poet. It is remarkable how surely, at this period of his career, Dryden rises when he resorts to rhyme; but even the careless blank verse of this play, in general merely a foil to the comic part, sometimes sparkles with strokes worthy of a great poet :

> ' *Pol.* He is a prince, and you are meanly born.
> *Leon.* Love either finds equality, or makes it.'

> ' For this glory, after I have seen
> The canopy of state spread wide above
> In the abyss of heaven, the court of stars,
> The blushing morning, and the rising sun,
> What greater can I see ? '

—a thought borrowed from Menander.

Continuing our survey of Dryden's plays, rather according to subject than to chronological order, we arrive at the tragi-comedy of *The Spanish Friar* (1681), one of the most esteemed of his lighter pieces, but whose praise, we must agree with Mr. Saintsbury, has outstripped its desert. The comic portion is certainly very drastic, but it is not comedy of a high order. It exhibits a distinct declension from *Marriage à la Mode*, where the quartette of *Mitschuldiger* are well individualized personages. The sinners in *The Spanish Friar* are of the most ordinary type —a stage rake, a stage coquette, a stage miser, and a stage friar. Dominick is, indeed, exceedingly amusing, but is more farcical than truly comic. He is painted in broad, staring colours, without delicacy of gradation, with the same brush as the author's Morats and Almanzors, only dipped into a different paint. Like so many of Dryden's personages, he is better adapted for the stage than the closet. Every word and gesture would tell in the hands of a good actor, and in Dryden's time the stage was richer in first-class performers than it ever was before, and probably than it has ever been since. Dryden himself, it must be recorded, attached a high value to his piece, and Dryden was an excellent critic of himself as well as of others. The merit on which he lays chief stress, however, is the ingenious blending of the tragic and comic action. 'The tragic part,' says Mr. Churton Collins, 'helps out the comic, and the comic relieves naturally and appropriately the tragic. In this work, tragi-comedy, from an artistic point of view, has achieved perhaps its highest success.' This, however, is the achievement of a playwright; in one passage alone do we find the poet. It is the highly imaginative series of descriptions of the distant noises from the Moorish camp, boding assault to the beleaguered city, of the panic in the city itself, and of the far-off, uncertain battle:

> 'From the Moorish camp, an hour and more,
> There has been heard a distant humming noise,
> Like bees disturbed, and arming in their hives.'

> 'Never was known a night of such distraction;
> Noise so confused and dreadful, jostling crowds,
> That run, and know not whither; torches gliding,
> Like meteors, by each other in the streets.'

> 'From the Moors' camp the noise grows louder still:
> Rattling of armour, trumpets, drums, and atabals;
> And sometimes peals of shouts that rend the heavens,
> Like victory; then groans again, and howlings,
> Like those of vanquished men, but every echo
> Goes fainter off, and dies in distant sounds.'

The next play of Dryden's which it is necessary to notice here might have ranked among his masterpieces if it had been entirely or even principally his own. It is sufficient praise for him to have followed Plautus and Molière with no unequal steps, and while borrowing, as he could not help, the substance of his piece from them, to have enriched their groundwork with original conceptions of his own. The plot of *Amphitryon* may be considered common property. A better subject for the comic theatre cannot be conceived than the equivocations occasioned by Jupiter's assumption of Amphitryon's appearance, doubled, and, as it were, parodied over again by the comic poet's happy thought of introducing Mercury in the disguise of Amphitryon's valet. It is surprising that the theme should not have attracted the best poets of the Athenian Middle Comedy. So far as we know, however, it was only treated by a single author, and he not one of the highest reputation, Archippus. How far Plautus translated Archippus must remain a question, but considering that the Greek play attained no especial reputation, while the Latin is one of the best we have, it is only fair to give Plautus credit for having introduced a good deal of his own. His comedy has unfortunately reached us in a mutilated condition, wanting, probably, not less than three hundred verses in the fourth act, but enough remains to show how the action was conducted. Molière, the greatest of comic poets, could not fail to improve upon his model. The substance of the piece admitted of no material alteration, but Molière has greatly enriched and embellished it—first by the happy idea of the prologue between Mercury and Night, for which, however, he is as much indebted to Lucian as he is to Plautus for the rest—and even more by the amusing scene between Sosia and Cleanthis. His play, unlike most of his other performances, is written in a lyrical metre, and the language is a model of elegance, harmony, and polish. Dryden, writing in prose or negligent blank verse, could not rival Molière in this respect; but while losing nothing of the *vis comica* of either of his predecessors, he has heightened the humour of the piece by a still further elaboration of the hints given by Molière. He was himself well acquainted with Lucian, from whom he has borrowed several additional strokes; and he has doubled the entertainment of the situation between Sosia and Cleanthis by the creation of Phædra, whose intrigue with Mercury makes the comedy of errors absolutely complete.

We have now to consider the two plays of Dryden's on which his fame as a dramatist principally rests, and which, if in some respects less interesting than his other dramatic writings, as less intensely characteristic of the man and his age, are for that very reason better equipped for competition for a place among the dramas of all time.

All for Love (1678) is, Dryden tells us, the only play he wrote entirely to please his own taste, and composed professedly in imitation of 'the divine Shakespeare.' He did not, as in his unfortunate alteration of *Troilus and Cressida*, select a piece of Shakespeare's which, not understanding, he rashly thought himself able to improve, but, in a spirit of true reverence, set himself to copy one which he held in high esteem. It should be remembered, to the honour of Dryden's critical judgment, that the two plays of Shakespeare's most warmly commended by him, *Antony and Cleopatra* and *Richard the Second*, were generally underrated even by Shakespeare's most devoted worshippers, until Coleridge taught us better. In *All for Love* he found a subject suitable to his genius, and, in our opinion, achieved very decidedly his best play. It is, indeed, almost as good as a play on the French model can be, inferior to its prototypes only from the lack of brilliant declamation, scarcely practicable without rhyme, but more than compensating this inferiority by the greater freedom and flexibility of its blank verse. Its defects are mainly those of its species, and would be less apparent if it did not so directly court comparison with one of the greatest examples of Shakespeare's art. It would have been impossible for a greater genius than Dryden to have done justice to his theme within the confines prescribed by the classical drama. The demeanour of Antony during the period of his downfall, as recorded by history, is below the dignity of tragedy. Some weakness may be forgiven in a hero, but the heroism of the real Antony is swallowed up in weakness. We can but pity, and pity is largely leavened with contempt. There is but one remedy, to create a Cleopatra so wondrous and fascinating as fairly to counterbalance the empire which Antony throws away for her sake. Shakespeare's art is equal to the occasion; his Cleopatra is dœmonic, and at the same time so intensely feminine that the purest and meekest of her sex may see much of themselves in her. She is at once an epitome and an encyclopædia, and the reader can hardly despise Antony for being the slave of a spell which he feels so strongly himself. Dryden's Cleopatra wants this character of universality, which, indeed, none but Shakespeare could have given, and Shakespeare himself could not have given if in bondage to the unities. She is a fine, passionate, sensuous woman, a kind of Mary Stuart, interesting, but not to the point at which it could be felt that the world were well lost for her. The inferiority of Cleopatra reacts grievously upon Antony. Shakespeare's Cleopatra is so grand that her lover is exalted by the admiration which, in spite of her perfidies, she manifestly feels for him. The beloved of such a woman must be heroic, an impression skilfully assisted by the effect Antony

produces upon the prudent and politic Augustus. Dryden's
Cleopatra can bestow no such patent of distinction. By
so much as the chief personages are inferior to their exemplars, by so much also is the puny, starved action of
Dryden's tragedy, restricted to one day and seven characters, inferior to the opulence of Shakespeare's, ranging
over the Roman world, crowded with personages, and
gathering up every trait from Plutarch that could contribute picturesqueness to its prodigality of incident and
sentiment. Nor is Dryden entirely successful in the conduct of his plot. The introduction of Octavia is a happy
idea, but she appears at too late a period of Antony's
history. The implication that his return to her could
have availed him in so desperate an extremity is more
contrary to historical truth and common reason than any
of the anachronisms for which Dryden derides Elizabethan
poets. The intrigue by which Dolabella is made to excite
Antony's jealousy is more worthy of comedy than of heroic
tragedy, besides being inconsistent with the manly character of its promoter, Ventidius. This gallant veteran is
indeed a fine creation; too fine, for he sometimes seems to
eclipse Antony and Cleopatra both, and assumes more
prominence in the action than Shakespeare would have
allowed him. Alexas is the hasty and much marred outline of a character which might have been hardly less
impressive had Dryden been at the pains to work out the
conception adumbrated in the first act. When all these
imperfections are admitted, and they should not be passed
over in silence after Scott's ill-judged parallel of Dryden's
performance with Shakespeare's, it remains true that *All
for Love* is a very fine play, energetic, passionate, and
steeped in that atmosphere of nobility which half redeems
the literary defects of *The Conquest of Granada*. The
poetry is frequently very fine, as in Octavia's speech

to Antony, remarkable as perhaps the sole instance of genuine pathos throughout the entire range of Dryden's dramatic writings:

> ' Look on these ;
> Are they not yours ? or stand they thus neglected
> As they are mine ? Go to him, children, go ;
> Kneel to him, take him by the hand, speak to him ;
> For you may speak, and he may own you, too,
> Without a blush ; and so he cannot all
> His children.   Go, I say, and pull him to me,
> And pull him to yourselves, from that bad woman.
> You, Agrippina, hang upon his arms ;
> And you, Antonia, clasp about his waist :
> If he will shake you off, if he will dash you
> Against the pavement, you must bear it, children,
> For you are mine, and I was born to suffer.'

Antony's sarcasms upon Augustus reveal the ripening satirist of *Absalom and Achitophel*:

> ' *Ant.* Octavius is the minion of blind chance,
> But holds from virtue nothing.
> *Vent.*   Has he courage ?
> *Ant.* But just enough to season him from coward.
> O, 'tis the coldest youth upon a charge,
> The most deliberate fighter ! if he ventures,
> (As in Illyria once, they say, he did,
> To storm a town) 'tis when he cannot choose ;
> When all the world have fixt their eyes upon him ;
> And then he lives on that for seven years after ;
> But, at a close revenge he never fails.
> *Vent.* I heard you challenged him.
> *Ant.*   I did, Ventidius.
> What think'st thou was his answer ?   'Twas so tame !—
> He said, he had more ways than one to die ;
> I had not.
> *Vent.*   Poor !
> *Ant.*   He has more ways than one ;
> But he would choose them all before that one.

Vent. He first would choose an ague, or a fever.

Ant. No; it must be an ague, not a fever;
He has not warmth enough to die by that.

Vent. Or old age and a bed.

Ant.   Ay, there's his choice.
He would live, like a lamp, to the last wink,
And crawl upon the utmost verge of life.
O, Hercules! Why should a man like this,
Who dares not trust his fate for one great action,
Be all the care of heaven? Why should he lord it
O'er fourscore thousand men, of whom each one
Is braver than himself?

Vent.   You conquer'd for him:
Philippi knows it; there you shared with him
That empire, which your sword made all your own.

Ant. Fool that I was, upon my eagle's wings
I bore this wren, till I was tired with soaring,
And now he mounts above me.
Good heavens, is this,—is this the man who braves me?
Who bids my age make way? drives me before him
To the world's ridge, and sweeps me off like rubbish?'

Don Sebastian (1690) is generally regarded as Dryden's
dramatic masterpiece. It did not please upon its first
appearance, owing to its excessive length. Dryden in-
genuously confesses that he was obliged to sacrifice twelve
hundred lines, which he restored when the play was printed.
Mr. Saintsbury more than hints a preference for *All for
Love*, which we entirely share. Were even the serious part
of the respective dramas of equal merit, the scale would be
turned in favour of *All for Love* by the wretchedness of the
comic scenes which constitute so large a portion of the rival
drama. They are at best indifferent farce, and cannot be
even called excrescences on the main action, inasmuch as
they do not grow out of it at all. In unity of action, therefore, and uniformity of literary merit, *All for Love* excels
its competitor, and its personages are more truthful and

more interesting. Sebastian, though a gallant, chivalrous figure, takes no such hold on the imagination as Antony and Ventidius; and Almeyda, one of the least interesting of Dryden's heroines, is a sorry exchange for Cleopatra. Muley Moloch and Benducar are wholly stagey. Nothing, then, remains but Dorax, and his capabilities are chiefly evinced in one great scene. Even this is in some respects inartificially conducted. The spectator is insufficiently prepared for it. The special ground of Dorax's resentment comes upon us as a surprise; and his repentance is too hasty and sudden. A similar defect may be alleged against the whole of the tragic action. The centre of interest is gradually shifted, not intentionally, but from the author's omission to foreshadow the events to come after the fashion of a masterpiece he must have studied, the *Œdipus Tyrannus.* At first all our interest is enlisted for Sebastian's life, and it is with a sort of puzzlement that we feel ourselves at last listening to a story of incest. Muley Moloch and Benducar have disappeared, and their place is occupied by a new character, Alvarez. In every respect, therefore, regarded as a work of art, *Don Sebastian* fails to sustain comparison with *All for Love,* and there is no countervailing superiority in the diction, whose general nobility and spirit occasionally swell into bombast. The worst fault remains to be told: Dorax's ludicrous escape from death by reason of being poisoned by two enemies at once. If either the Emperor or the Mufti would have let him alone he would never have lived to be reconciled to Sebastian, but the fiery drug of the one is neutralized by the icy bane of the other, and *vice versâ.* Dryden thinks it sufficient excuse that a similar incident is vouched for by Ausonius, but really there is nothing so farcical in the *Rehearsal.* On the whole, we cannot but consider *Don Sebastian* a very imperfect play, redeemed from mediocrity by the general vigour and anima-

tion of the diction, and the loftiness of soul which seldom
forsakes Dryden, except when he wilfully panders to the
popular taste.

But little space can here be devoted to Dryden's other
plays. Some are not worth criticism. *The Mock Astrologer*,
largely borrowed from French and Spanish sources, contains some of his best lyrics. Many parts of *Cleomenes*
are very noble, but it is somewhat heavy as a whole. *King
Arthur*, a musical and spectacular drama, is an excellent
specimen of its class. Dryden's portion of *Œdipus*, written
in conjunction with Lee, shows how finely he, like his
model Lucan, could deal with the supernatural. This
is by no means the case with his *State of Innocence and
Fall of Man*, which is, nevertheless, one of his pieces most
worthy of perusal. It measures the prodigious fall from
the age of Cromwell to the age of Charles; while Dryden
yet displays such fine poetical gifts as to command respect
amid all the absurdities of his unintentional burlesque of
Milton.

Dryden undeniably took up the profession of playwright
without an effectual call. He became a dramatist, as clever
men in our day become journalists, discerning in the
stage the shortest literary cut to fame and fortune. He
can hardly be said to have possessed any strictly dramatic
gift in any exceptional degree, but he had enough of all to
make a tolerable figure on the stage, and was besides a
great poet and an admirable critic. His poetry redeems
the defects of his serious plays, if we except such a mere
pièce de circonstance as *Amboyna*. The best of them have
very bad faults, but even the worst are impressed with the
stamp of genius. It is only in comedy that his failure is
sometimes utter and irretrievable; yet a perception of the
humorous cannot be denied to the author of *Amphitryon*.
But we nowhere find evidence of any supreme dramatic

faculty, anything that would have constrained him to write plays if plays had not happened to be in fashion. As he was not born a dramatic poet he had to be made one, and he became one mainly in virtue of his eminent critical endowment. His prefaces are a most interesting study. They exhibit the steady advance of a slow, strong, sure mind from rudimentary conceptions to as just views of the requisites of dramatic poetry as could well be attained in an age encumbered with venerable fallacies. Dryden's manly sense, homely sagacity, and piercing shrewdness, break through many trammels, as when, in the preface to *All for Love*, he vindicates his breach of the conventions of the French stage. In that to *Troilus and Cressida* he compares Shakespeare with Fletcher, and pronounces decidedly in favour of the former, a preference far from universal in his day. The preface to *The Spanish Friar* is the most remarkable of any, and shows how much he had learned and unlearned. We shall, nevertheless, find his special glory in his character as the most truly representative dramatist of his time. Otway might have been an Elizabethan, Dryden never could. If we seek for the dramatic author to whom he is on the whole nearest of kin, we may perhaps find him in Byron. Byron had no more genuine dramatic vocation than Dryden had, but, like Dryden, produced memorable works by force and flexibility of genius. From the theatrical point of view Dryden's plays are greatly superior to Byron's; if the latter's rank higher as literature the main cause is the existence of more favourable conditions. Dryden's worst faults would have been impossible in the nineteenth century; and his treatment of the supernatural, his frequent visitations of speculation, and the lofty tone of his heroic passages, prove that he could have drawn a Manfred, a Cain, or a Myrrha, if he had lived like Byron in a renovated age.

CHAPTER V.

DRAMATIC POETS AND PLAYWRIGHTS.

AFTER Dryden, the metrical dramatists of the Restoration, as of other epochs, may be accurately divided into two classes, the poets and the playwrights. As was to be expected in an age when even genuine poetry drooped earthward, and prose seldom kindled into poetry, the latter class was largely in the majority. Only three dramatists can justly challenge the title of poet—Dryden, Otway, and Lee. In Dryden a mighty fire, half choked with its own fuel, struggles gallantly against extinction, and eventually evolves nearly as much flame as smoke. In Otway a pure and delicate flame hovers fitfully over a morass; in Lee the smothered fire breaks out, as Pope said of Lucan and Statius, 'in sudden, brief, and interrupted flashes.' Dryden was incomparably the most vigorous of the three, but Otway was the only born dramatist, and the little of genuine dramatic excellence that he has wrought claims a higher place than the more dazzling productions of his contemporary.

Thomas Otway, son of the vicar of Woolbeding, was born at Trotton, near Midhurst, in Sussex, March 3rd, 1651. He was educated at Winchester and Christchurch, but (perhaps driven by necessity, for he says in the dedication to *Venice Preserved*, 'A steady faith, and loyalty to my prince was all

Otway (1651-1685).

the inheritance my father left me ') forsook the latter ere
his academical course was half completed to try his fortune
as a performer on the stage, where he entirely failed.   His
first play, *Alcibiades* (1675), a poor piece, served to introduce
him to Rochester and other patrons; and in the following year
Don Carlos, founded upon the novel by Saint Réal, obtained,
partly by the support of Rochester, with whom Otway soon
quarrelled, a striking success, and is said to have produced
more than any previous play.   Two translations from the
French followed; next (1678) came the unsuccessful comedy
of *Friendship in Fashion*, and in 1680 *Caius Marius*, an
audacious plagiarism from *Romeo and Juliet*.   In the interim Otway had made trial of a military career, but the
regiment in which he had obtained a commission was
speedily disbanded, his pay was withheld, and he had to
support himself by plundering Shakespeare.   In the same
year in which he had stooped so low he proved his
superiority to all contemporary dramatists by his tragedy
of *The Orphan*, in which he first displayed the pathos by
which he has merited the character of the English Euripides.   Johnson remarks that Otway ' conceived forcibly,
and drew originally, by consulting nature in his own breast; '
and it is known that he experienced the pangs of a seven years'
unrequited passion for the beautiful actress, Mrs. Barry.   In
1681 he produced *The Soldier's Fortune*, a comedy chiefly
interesting for its allusions to his own military experiences.
According to Downes, its success was extraordinary, and
brought both profit and reputation to the theatre.   If it
brought any of the former to the author, this must have been
soon exhausted, since in the dedication to *Venice Preserved*
(1682) he speaks of himself as only rescued from the direst
want by the generosity of the Duchess of Portsmouth.   For
this great play, as well as for *The Orphan*, he is said to have
received a hundred pounds.   *The Atheist*, a second part of

The Soldier's Fortune (1684), was probably unproductive;
and in April, 1685, Otway died on Tower Hill, undoubtedly
in distress, although, of the two accounts of his death, that
which ascribes it to a fever caught in pursuing an assassin,
is better authenticated than the more usual one which represents him as choked by a loaf which he was devouring
in a state of ravenous hunger. Such a story, nevertheless,
could not have obtained credit if his circumstances had not
been known to have been desperate. It is not likely that
he had much conduct or economy in his affairs, or was
endowed in any degree with the severer virtues. The tone
of his letters to Mrs. Barry, however, and the constancy of
his seven years' affection for her, seem to indicate a natural
refinement of feeling, and if there is truth in the dictum,

'He best can paint them, who can feel them most,'

the creator of Monimia and Belvidera must have been
endowed with a heart tender in no common degree. 'He
was,' we are told, 'of middle size, inclinable to corpulency,
had thoughtful, yet lively, and as it were speaking eyes.'

Otway's reputation rests entirely on his two great performances, *The Orphan* and *Venice Preserved.* His other
plays deserve no special notice, although *Don Carlos*, which
is said to have for many years attracted larger audiences
than either of his masterpieces, might have been a good
play if it had not been written in rhyme. The action is
highly dramatic, and the characters, though artless, are
not ineffective; but the pathos in which the poet excelled
is continually disturbed by the bombastic couplets, ever
trembling on the brink of the ridiculous. The remorse of
Philip after the murder of his wife and son is as grotesque
an instance of the forcible feeble as could easily be found,
and is a melancholy instance indeed of the declension of
the English drama, when contrasted with the demeanour

of Othello in similar circumstances.   Otway, however, was
yet to show that his faults were rather his age's than his
own.   The fashion of rhyme must have had much to do
with the bombast of *Don Carlos*, for in *The Orphan*, his
next effort in serious tragedy, there is hardly any rant, even
when the situation might have seemed to have excused the
exaggerated expression of emotion.   The central incident
of this admirable tragedy—the deception of a maiden beloved by two brothers, through the personation of the
favoured one by his rival—seems now to be held to ex-
clude it from the stage.   The objection would probably
prove to be imaginary, for the play was performed as late
as 1819, when no less an actress than Miss O'Neill represented Monimia, and the diction is in general of quite
exemplary propriety for a play of the period.   Its principal
defect as a work of art is that the pathos springs almost
solely from the situation, and that the personages have
hardly any hold upon our sympathies except as sufferers
from an unhappy fatality.   So powerful is the situation,
nevertheless, that the sorrows of Castalio and Monimia can
never fail to move; the poet's language, too, is at its best,
simpler and more remote from extravagance than even in
Venice Preserved.   The description of the old hag is justly
celebrated:

> ' I spied a wrinkled hag, with age grown double,
> Picking dry sticks, and mumbling to herself;
> Her eyes with scalding rheum were galled and red;
> Cold palsy shook her head, her hands seemed withered,
> And on her crooked shoulders had she wrapt
> The tattered remnant of an old striped hanging,
> Which served to keep her carcase from the cold;
> So there was nothing of a piece about her;
> Her lower weeds were all o'er coarsely patched
> With different coloured rags, black, red, white, yellow,
> And seemed to speak variety of wretchedness.'

There are also delightful touches of poetry:

> ' Oh, thou art tender all :
> Gentle and kind as sympathizing nature !
> When a sad story has been told, I've seen
> Thy little breasts, with soft compassion swelled,
> Shove up and down and heave like dying birds.'

The opening speech of act iv., sc. 2, also reveals a feeling for nature unusual in Restoration poetry, and may be taken to symbolize Otway's regrets for the country. The items of the description are in no way conventional, and would not have occurred to one without experience of rural life :

> ' Wished morning's come !   And now upon the plains
> And distant mountains, where they feed their flocks,
> The happy shepherds leave their homely huts,
> And with their pipes proclaim the new-born day.
> The lusty swain comes with his well-filled scrip
> Of healthful viands, which, when hunger calls,
> With much content and appetite he eats,
> To follow in the fields his daily toil,
> And dress the grateful glebe that yields him fruits.
> The beasts that under the warm hedges slept,
> And weathered out the cold bleak night, are up,
> And looking towards the neighbouring pastures, raise
> Their voice, and bid their fellow-brutes good-morrow.
> The cheerful birds, too, on the tops of trees
> Assemble all in quires, and with their notes
> Salute and welcome up the rising sun.
> There's no condition here so cursed as mine.'

Venice Preserved, Otway's most memorable work, though inferior in mere poetry and unstudied simplicity to *The Orphan*, surpasses it in tragic grandeur, in variety of action, and in intensity of interest. It has the further great advantage that the interest does not entirely arise from the situation, but that at least one of the characters is a skilful piece of painting from the life, and very probably from the author. In Jaffier we have a vivid portrait of the man who is entirely governed by the affections, and who sways from ardent resolution to a weakness hardly distinguishable from treachery, as friendship and love alternately incline him. The little we know of Otway warrants the impression that he was such a man, and assuredly he could not have excited such warm interest in a character so feeble in his offence, so abject in his repentance, and in general so perilously verging on the despicable, without a keen sympathy with the subject of his portrait. *Tout comprendre c'est tout pardonner.* Pierre, though an imposing figure, is much less subtly painted than his friend ; and Belvidera, her husband's evil genius, interests only through her sorrows. The 'despicable scenes of low farce' which eke the drama out, are a grievous blot upon it. M. Taine may be right in deeming some comic relief allowable, but such trash is neither relief nor comedy. The language of the serious portion of the play, however, is in general dignified and tragic. Perhaps the best conducted, as it is the best known, is that in which Pierre spurns the remorseful Jaffier :

> ' *Jaff.* I must be heard, I must have leave to speak.
> Thou hast disgraced me, Pierre, by a vile blow :
> Had not a dagger done thee nobler justice ?
> But use me as thou wilt, thou canst not wrong me,
> For I am fallen beneath the basest injuries ;
> Yet look upon me with an eye of mercy,
> With pity and with charity behold me ;
> Shut not thy heart against a friend's repentance,
> But, as there dwells a godlike nature in thee,
> 'Listen with mildness to my supplications.
>   *Pier.* What whining monk art thou ? what holy cheat,
> That wouldst encroach upon my credulous ears,
> But cant'st thus vilely ?   Hence ! I know thee not.

Dissemble and be nasty: leave me, hypocrite.

Jaff. Not know me, Pierre?

Pier.   No, know thee not: what art thou?

Jaff. Jaffier, thy friend, thy once loved, valued friend,
Though now deservedly scorned, and used most hardly.

Pier. Thou Jaffier! thou my once loved, valued friend?
By Heavens, thou liest!   The man so called, my friend,
Was generous, honest, faithful, just, and valiant,
Noble in mind, and in his person lovely,
Dear to my eyes and tender to my heart:
But thou, a wretched, base, false, worthless coward,
Poor even in soul, and loathsome in thy aspect;
All eyes must shun thee, and all hearts detest thee.
Pr'ythee avoid, nor longer cling thus round me,
Like something baneful, that my nature's chilled at.

Jaff. I have not wronged thee, by these tears I have not,
But still am honest, true, and hope, too, valiant;
My mind still full of thee: therefore still noble.
Let not thy eyes then shun me, nor thy heart
Detest me utterly: oh, look upon me,
Look back and see my sad, sincere submission!
How my heart swells, as even 'twould burst my bosom,
Fond of its goal, and labouring to be at thee!
What shall I do—what say to make thee hear me?

Pier. Hast thou not wronged me?   Dar'st thou call thyself
Jaffier, that once loved, valued friend of mine,
And swear thou hast not wronged me?   Whence these chains?
Whence the vile death which I may meet this moment?
Whence this dishonour, but from thee, thou false one?

Jaff. All's true, yet grant one thing, and I've done asking.

Pier. What's that?

Jaff.   To take thy life on such conditions
The Council have proposed: thou and thy friends
May yet live long, and to be better treated.

Pier. Life! ask my life? confess! record myself
A villain, for the privilege to breathe,
And carry up and down this cursèd city
A discontented and repining spirit,
Burthensome to itself, a few years longer,

To lose it, may be, at last in a lewd quarrel
For some new friend, treacherous and false as thou art!
No, this vile world and I have long been jangling,
And cannot part on better terms than now,
When only men like thee are fit to live in't.

Jaff. By all that's just—

Pier.　　　　　　　Swear by some other powers,
For thou hast broke that sacred oath too lately.

Jaff. Then, by that hell I merit, I'll not leave thee,
Till to thyself, at least, thou'rt reconciled,
However thy resentments deal with me.

Pier. Not leave me!

Jaff.　　　　　No; thou shalt not force me from thee.
Use me reproachfully, and like a slave;
Tread on me, buffet me, heap wrongs on wrongs
On my poor head; I'll bear it all with patience,
Shall weary out thy most unfriendly cruelty:
Lie at thy feet and kiss them, though they spurn me,
Till, wounded by my sufferings, thou relent,
And raise me to thy arms with dear forgiveness.

Pier. Art thou not—

Jaff.　　　　　What?

Pier.　　　　　　　A traitor?

Jaff.　　　　　　　　　　Yes.

Pier.　　　　　　　　　　　A villain?

Jaff. Granted.

Pier.　　　　A coward, a most scandalous coward,
Spiritless, void of honour, one who has sold
Thy everlasting fame for shameless life?

Jaff. All, all, and more, much more: my faults are number-
　　less.

Pier. And wouldst thou have me live on terms like thine?
Base as thou'rt false—

Jaff.　　　　　No; 'tis to me that's granted.
The safety of thy life was all I aimed at,
In recompense for faith and trust so broken.

Pier. I scorn it more, because preserved by thee:
And as when first my foolish heart took pity
On thy misfortunes, sought thee in thy miseries,

Relieved thy wants, and raised thee from thy state
Of wretchedness in which thy fate had plunged thee,
To rank thee in my list of noble friends,
All I received in surety for thy truth
Were unregarded oaths ; and this, this dagger,
Given with a worthless pledge thou since hast stolen,
So I restore it back to thee again ;
Swearing by all those powers which thou hast violated,
Never from this cursed hour to hold communion,
Friendship, or interest with thee, though our years
Were to exceed those limited the world.
Take it—farewell !—for now I owe thee nothing.
 Jaff. Say thou wilt live then.
 Pier.   For my life, dispose it
Just as thou wilt, because 'tis what I'm tired with.
 Jaff. O Pierre !
 Pier.   No more.
 Jaff.   My eyes won't lose the sight of thee,
But languish after thine, and ache with gazing.
 Pier. Leave me.—Nay, then thus, thus I throw thee from
  me,
And curses, great as is thy falsehood, catch thee ! '

**Nathaniel Lee
(1653-1691).**
The only tragic dramatist of the age, after Dryden and Otway, who had any pretension to rank as a poet, was Nathaniel Lee, and his claims are not very high. Notwithstanding his absurd rants, however, there are fire and passion in his verse which lift him out of the class of mere playwrights. After receiving a Cambridge education, Lee came up to town to seek his fortune. Thrown on the world, it is said, by the failure of the Duke of Ormond to redeem his promises of patronage, Lee became an actor, but obtained no success, although celebrated for the beauty of his elocution as a dramatic reader. The transition from actor to author was easy. Lee produced three bad rhyming plays in the taste of the time, and in 1677 did himself

more justice in *The Rival Queens*, a tragedy on the history
of Alexander the Great, which kept the stage for nearly a
century and a half. *Mithridates* (1678) was also successful, and Dryden thought sufficiently well of Lee to combine
with him in the production of an *Œdipus*, which continued
to be acted until 1778, when the situation, rather than the
diction, was found unendurable. Kemble wished to revive
it so late as 1802, but was prevented by the reluctance of
Mrs. Siddons. It is true that on a modern stage the piece
must want the religious consecration which accompanied it
on the Greek. Lee wrote on, enjoying the notoriety of the
prohibition by authority of his *Lucius Junius Brutus*, in
which allusions, merely imaginary, to the vices of Charles
II., were discovered by the Court, and regaining his lost
favour by the tragedy of *The Duke of Guise* (1682), a play
full of political allusions, in which also Dryden had a
hand. In 1684 he was disabled by an attack of insanity,
brought on, it is alleged, by his intemperate habits; and
although he recovered sufficiently to be released from confinement, he wrote no more, his last two published plays
being compositions of an earlier date. He died miserably
in returning from the tavern on a winter's night, fallen
down and stifled in the snow.

That Lee was a poet, a passage quoted by Mr. Saintsbury
would prove, had he written nothing else :

> ' Thou coward ! yet
> Art living? canst not, wilt not, find the road
> To the great palace of magnificent death,
> Though thousand ways lead to his thousand doors,
> Which day and night are still unbarred for all? '

A variation of this thought in Lee's *Theodosius* might well
have inspired Beckford with the conception of his Hall of
Eblis, nor would it be difficult to find other impressive
passages. Lee's rants of mere sound and fury are unfor-

tunately much more frequent, and his pre-eminence above all competitors in this line is so indisputable, that it is no wonder if he is remembered by his gigantic faults rather than by his comparatively tame and temperate merits. The following speech of Roxana in *The Rival Queens*, for instance, is quite an average specimen of her conversation:

> ' And shall the daughter of Darius hold him?
> That puny girl? that ape of my ambition,
> That cried for milk when I was nursed in blood?
> Shall she, made up of watery element,
> Ascend, shall she embrace my proper God,
> While I am cast like lightning from his hand?
> No, I must scorn to prey on common things.
> Though hurled to earth by this disdainful Jove,
> I will rebound to my own orb of fire,
> And with the wrack of all the heavens expire.'

Even when the thought is dignified and noble, it frequently loses dramatic propriety from want of keeping with the speaker or the situation:

> ' Therefore, my friend,
> Let us despise the torrent of the world,
> Fortune, I mean, and dam her up with fences,
> Banks, bulwarks, all the fortresses which virtue,
> Resolved and manned like ours, can raise against her:
> That, if she does o'erflow, she may at least
> Bring but half ruin to our great designs;
> That being at last ashamed of her own weakness,
> Like a low-baséd flood, she may retire
> To her own bounds, and we with pride o'erlook her.'

Into what Cato's mouth has Lee put this deliverance of Stoic dignity? Truly, into Cæsar Borgia's. Machiavelli having been privy to all Borgia's villainies, is selected to pronounce the moral of the play:

'No power is safe, nor no religion good,
Whose principles of growth are laid in blood.'

A proposition supposed to have been irrefragably established by five acts full of poniards and poisons.   This
childish want of nature Lee shares with most of the tragic
dramatists of the Restoration period.   He is mainly glare
and gewgaw, and seldom succeeds but in those scenes of passion and frenzy where extravagant declamation seems a
natural language.   There is little to remark on his dramatic
economy, which is that of the French classical drama.   His
characters are boldly outlined and strongly coloured, but
transferred direct from history to the stage, or wholly
conventional.   His merit is to have been really a poet.
'There is an infinite fire in his works,' says Addison, 'but
so involved in smoke that it does not appear in half its
lustre.'   The following scene from *Mithridates* is a fair
example of the mingled beauties and blemishes of his tragic
style :

        '*Ziph.* Farewell, Semandra ;   O, if my father should
   Fall back from virtue, ('tis an impious thought !)
   Yet I must ask you, could you in my absence,
   Solicited by power and charming empire,
   And threaten'd too by death, forget your vows ?
   Could you, I say, abandon poor Ziphares,
   Who midst of wounds and death would think on you ;
 ⸰ And whatsoe'er calamity should come,
   Would keep his love sacred to his Semandra,
   Like balm, to heal the heaviest misfortune ?
        Sem. Your cruel question tears my very soul :
   Ah, can you doubt me, Prince ? a faith, like mine,
   The softest passion that e'er woman wept ;
   But as resolv'd as ever man could boast :
   Alas, why will you then suspect my truth ?
   Yet since it shews the fearfulness of love,
   'Tis just I should endeavour to convince you :

Make bare your sword, my noble father, draw.

Arch. What would'st thou now?

Sem.   I swear upon it, oh,
Be witness, Heav'n, and all avenging pow'rs,
Of the true love I give the Prince Ziphares:
When I in thought forsake my plighted faith,
Much less in act, for empire change my love;
May this keen sword by my own father's hand
Be guided to my heart, rip veins and arteries;
And cut my faithless limbs from this hack'd body,
To feast the ravenous birds, and beasts of prey.

Arch. Now, by my sword, 'twas a good hearty wish;
And, if thou play'st him false, this faithful hand
As heartily shall make thy wishes good.

Ziph. O hear mine too. If e'er I fail in aught
That love requires in strictest, nicest kind;
May I not only be proclaim'd a coward,
But be indeed that most detested thing.
May I, in this most glorious war I make,
Be beaten basely, ev'n by Glabrio's slaves,
And for a punishment lose both these eyes;
Yet live and never more behold Semandra.   [*Trumpets.*

Arch. Come, no more wishing; hark, the trumpets call.

Sem. Preserve him, Gods, preserve his innocence;
The noblest image of your perfect selves:
Farewell; I'm lost in tears. Where are you, Sir?

Arch. He's gone. Away, my lord, you'll never part.

Ziph. I go; but must turn back for one last look:
Remember, O remember, dear Semandra,
That on thy virtue all my fortune hangs;
Semandra is the business of the war,
Semandra makes the fight, draws every sword;
Semandra sounds the trumpets; gives the word.
So the moon charms her watery world below;
Wakes the still seas, and makes 'em ebb and flow.'

The remaining dramatists of the Restoration, with the exception of the brilliant group of comic authors near the end of the century, who demand a separate notice, un-

I

doubtedly belong to the class of playwrights. The most characteristic playwright of all, taking the term in the sense of a steady competent workman destitute of originality, was perhaps John Crowne. Crowne was the man to supply

John Crowne (1640-1703 ?).

the playhouses with a regular output of respectable work, and, as he had no other object than to suit his market, we perhaps learn better from him and his like than from writers of genius what the public of the day required. It seems rather extraordinary that such heavy tragedies as Crowne's should have been marketable in any age; but it must be considered that the tragic stage had to be kept going for the sake of the actors, and that if people would not have Shakespeare they must take what they could get. Indifferent plays, moreover, may make fine spectacles; and Crowne's Julianas, Reguluses, and Caligulas served the purpose of habitual playgoers, that is, of playgoers from the force of habit, as well as better pieces.[1] The success of Crowne's comedies is less difficult to understand. Here he really gave the public a fair reflection of itself, and exhibited contemporary manners with truth, if with no great brilliancy. On one occasion he soared higher, and (1685) created a real type in the exquisite coxcomb, Sir Courtly Nice. The rest of the play is partly imitated from the Spanish, but the character of Nice is Crowne's own. The humour is considerably overdone, but is still a genuine piece of comedy, which culminates at the end, when the

---

[1] Crowne himself assigns another reason, which may have had weight in some quarters: " I presume your ladyship nauseates comedies. They are so ill-bred, and saucy with quality, and always crammed with our odious sex. At tragedies the house is all lined with beauty, and then a gentleman may endure it,'—a confirmation of the statement that modest women avoided the comic theatre, or went masked.

infuriated fop rushes from the stage, vowing to be avenged, 'as far as my sword and my wit can go.' *The English Friar* (1689), a satire on the Tartufes of the Roman Catholic persuasion, is also a remarkable piece, the parent of a long line of imitations. In *City Politics* (1673), Crowne's first comedy, the Whig party in the City is held up to obloquy in the transparent disguise of a Neapolitan rabble, and the satire is keen and vivid. *The Married Beau* (1694) is remarkable as a reversion towards the style of Fletcher and Shirley. *Calisto* is an interesting attempt to revive the ancient masque. The only one of Crowne's serious dramas entitled to much attention is *Darius*, where the poetry is frequently fine, but the characters are tame. Not much is known of his life. He appears to have been taken in youth to America, and to have returned by 1665, when he published a romance entitled *Pandion and Amphigenia*. His connection with the stage commenced in 1671 with *Juliana*, and terminated with *Caligula* in 1698. He would seem to have been a precise and matter-of-fact man, and is ridiculed by Rochester as 'Little starch Johnny Crowne with his ironed cravat.' He was fond of accompanying his plays with long prefaces and dedications, which throw some light on his opinions and private history, and, so far as they go, exhibit his disposition in an advantageous light. From one of them it appears that he suffered in his latter days from 'a distemper seated in my head.' His tantalizing gleams of talent as a lyrist have been already mentioned.

Thomas Southern undoubtedly belonged to the genus playwright, and has none of the flashes of poetry which occasionally seem to exalt Crowne to a higher rank. His distinction rather arises from the financial success of his pieces, which was such that he died 'the richest of all our

Thomas Southern (1660-1746).

poets, a very few excepted.' For this, however, he is said to have been indebted not so much to the actual vogue of his pieces as to his assiduity in soliciting tickets. It is to be wished that he had been equally assiduous in collecting facts about Shakespeare, if, as is somewhat doubtfully asserted, his father came from Stratford-on-Avon. He was born at Dublin in 1660, and is said to have been a servitor at Oxford and a student at the Middle Temple. This he forsook for the army, but his service cannot have been of long duration. His first play, *The Loyal Brother* (1682), was designed to compliment the Duke of York upon the failure of the Exclusion Bill. He was not a very industrious writer, producing only ten plays down to 1726, and of these only two, *The Fatal Marriage* (1694) and *Oroonoko* (1696), had any considerable reputation even in his own day. Both, however, kept the stage until an advanced period of the nineteenth century. The diction of both pieces, though never rising into poetry, and interlarded with dull scenes intended to be comic, is by no means contemptible ; the main strength, however, consists in the situations, which are really powerful, and in the writer's art in arousing an interest both in his innocent and his mixed characters. Respected as a relic of the past, a decorous church-goer with silver hair, Southern lived far into the eighteenth century, and came sufficiently under its influence to repent of his mingling of tragic and comic action in the same piece ; which indeed he had reason to regret, not because he had done it, but because he had not done it better.

Thomas Shadwell is remarkable as the leading Whig votary of *belles lettres* after the death of Marvell, a distinction which secured him the laureateship upon the cashiering of Dryden. To call him poet would be a gross misapplication

Thomas Shadwell (1640-1692).

of the term, and Dryden's withering couplet might seem
justified if he had nothing but his serious verse to rely
upon :

> ' With all his bulk, there's nothing lost in Og,
> For every inch that is not fool is rogue.'

His title to recollection, however, rests upon things as
remote from poetry as possible—his coarsely indecent, but
humorous comedies, which are undoubtedly of value as
reflecting the manners of the time.   Shadwell, in imitation
of Ben Jonson, laid himself out to study ' humours,' so
well defined by Ben himself :

> ' When some peculiar quality
> Doth so possess a man that it doth draw
> All his affects, his spirits, and his powers
> From their complexions all to run one way,
> This may be truly said to be a humour.'

We have seen the like in Dickens, who, possessing little
delicacy of psychological observation, laid himself out to
study obvious eccentricities of character, the more grotesque the better, and frequently made the entire man the
incarnation of an attribute.   This is certainly not very
high art, but has recommendations for the stage which
it lacks in the novel ; it is easy to write, easy to act, and
gives genuine entertainment to the crowd of spectators.
Shadwell valued himself so much upon his performances
in this way as to declare in his preface to *The Virtuoso*
that he trusted never to have less than four new humours
in any comedy.   Shadwell's plays, though poorly written,
might still be read for their humour, were it not for their
obscenity ; his chief merit, however, is to bring the society
of his time nearer to us than any other writer.   No other
records such minute points of manners, or enables us to
view the actual daily life of the age with so much clear-

ness. This is especially the case in his *Epsom Wells*
(1675), *Squire of Alsatia* (1688), and *Volunteers* (1692).
From Dryden's satire, which must have had a basis of
truth, he would seem to have been just the boisterous
corpulent *bon vivant* we might expect. 'If,' said Rochester,
'Shadwell would burn all he writes and print all he says,
he would have more wit and humour than anybody.' His
friend, Dr. Nicholas Brady, vouches for the openness and
friendliness of his temper; and further describes him as
'a complete gentleman.' But this was in a funeral sermon.
The regard for Otway, imputed to him by Rochester, is
creditable to him.

The violent death of Archbishop Abbot's gamekeeper
would have passed unnoticed if the poor man had been
shot by anybody but the archbishop himself; and Elkanah
Settle (1648-1724) would have slipped away in the crowd
of poetasters if Rochester had not taken it into his head
to pit him against Dryden. In the sense in which the
mysterious W. H. was 'the only begetter of Shakespeare's
sonnets,' he may hence claim to be the parent of one of
the most scathing pieces of invective in the language.
Although, however, Doeg is undoubtedly Settle, Settle is
not wholly Doeg. Miserable as his lampoons are, a line
here and there is not destitute of piquancy; and if his
Empress of Morocco (1673) has no literary pretensions, it
is important in literary history for having so moved the
wrath of Dryden, and in the history of the drama for
having been issued with plates which contribute greatly
to our knowledge of the internal arrangements of the
Restoration Theatre. By a singular irony of fortune, his
fate bears some analogy to that of his mighty antagonist.
Settle lost caste by changing his politics at the wrong
time, as Dryden his religion; but while Dryden bore up
against the storm of adversity, Settle sunk into obscurity,

and ultimately into the Charter House. Of his twenty plays none but *The Empress of Morocco* is now ever mentioned, unless an exception be made in favour of *Ibrahim, the Illustrious Bassa* (1676), noticeable, as Professor Ward remarks, for being founded upon one of the voluminous French romances of the day.

Some other playwrights would deserve extended notice in a history of the drama, but are only entitled to the barest mention in a general literary survey. Among these are Sir Robert Howard, Dryden's brother-in-law, and joint-author with him of *The Indian Queen*, the most important of whose plays is *The Committee* (printed 1665), a satire on the Commonwealth, described by Sir Roger de Coverley as 'a good old Church of England comedy:' John Wilson, Recorder of Londonderry, author of three comedies and a tragedy of more than average merit; Roger Boyle, Earl of Orrery; Sir Charles Sedley, Major Thomas Porter, and John Lacy, all very mediocre as dramatists; Thomas D'Urfey, better known than any of the above, but not by his writings, which are below mediocrity. The ten plays of Edward Ravenscroft procured him no other reputation than that of a plagiarist. Some female dramatists will be mentioned in another place.

Before passing to the opulent comedy of the latter part of the century, two writers remain to be mentioned, one of whom stands alone in the drama of the period, while the other forms the transition to the comedy of Wycherley and Congreve. In describing George Villiers, second Duke of Buckingham, as one standing apart, we refer to the character of his solitary work, and not to his share in it; for, though passing solely under his name, there can be little doubt that it was the production of a junto of wits, of whom he was not the wittiest. Butler, Sprat, and Martin Clifford are named as his coadjutors. Buckingham, who must be credited with a keen sense of the ridiculous, had already resolved to satirize rhyming heroic plays in the person of Sir Robert Howard, when the latter's retirement diverted the blow to Dryden, whom Butler, as we shall see, did not greatly relish, and against whose device of rhyme, Sprat, as we have seen, had committed himself by anticipation. The play chiefly selected for parody is *The Conquest of Granada*, which certainly invited it. Dryden appears as Bayes, in allusion to his laureateship; and, although his perpetual use of 'egad' seems derived from the usage by one of his *dramatis personae* rather than his own, we cannot doubt that his peculiarities of speech and gesture were mostly copied to the life. Within a week the town were unanimously laughing at what they had been unanimously applauding; and, scurrilous and ill-bred as the mockery of *The Rehearsal* was, it must be allowed to have been neither uncalled for nor unuseful. The machinery of the piece is sufficiently indicated by its title. Bayes entertains the dissembling Johnson and the unsympathetic Smith with a rehearsal of *The Two Kings of Brentford*, commenting meanwhile and explaining, vaunting beauties and extenuating miscarriages with a verve that still amuses, notwithstanding the far superior treatment of the same theme in Sheridan's *Critic*. Some of the scenes are highly farcical; and some of the passages are very fair hits at the bombast and other extravagances of the writers of heroic plays, for Dryden is by no means the sole object of satire:

' The blackest ink of fate was sure my lot,
And when she writ my name, she made a blot.'

' Durst any of the Gods be so uncivil,
I'd make that God subscribe himself a Devil.'

' The army's at the door, and in disguise
Demands a word with both your majesties.'

'Yes, I think, for a dead person, it is a good way enough of making love, for being divested of her terrestrial part, and all that, she is only capable of these little, pretty, amorous designs that are innocent, and yet passionate.'

One of Bayes's precepts may be commended to the attention of any who may think of reviving rhyming tragedy. It also shows the cramped condition of the theatre in Dryden's day:

'*Bayes*. Gentlemen, I must desire you to remove a little, for I must fill the stage.

Smith. Why fill the stage?

Bayes. O sir, because your heroic verse never sounds well but when the stage is full.'

Sir George Etheredge is neither an edifying nor an attractive writer of comedy, but his plays are of considerable historical importance as prototypes of the comedy of manners afterwards so brilliantly developed by Congreve. They are *Love in a Tub* (1664), *She Would if She Could* (1668), and *The Man of Mode* (1676). The last is celebrated for the character of Sir Fopling Flutter, who is said to have been the image of the author, though it is added on the same authority that his intention had been to depict himself in the character of the heartless rake Dorimant, whom others took for Rochester. All the plays suffer from a deficiency of plot, a deficiency of wit, and a superfluity of naughtiness, but cannot be denied to possess a light airy grace, and to have imbibed something of the manner, though little of the humour, of Molière. By his own account the author was lazy, careless, and a gamester. Little, except that 'he was knighted for marrying a fortune,' is known of his history until 1685, when, unexpectedly to himself, he was appointed envoy to Ratisbon, and

Sir George Etheredge (1634-1691).

details become copious from the accidental preservation of his letter-book, now in the British Museum. The general tone of his correspondence is good-natured and easy; he seems to have made just the kind of ambassador to be expected from an idle man of fashion without diplomatic experience; while he may well have merited his friends' description of him as 'gentle George,' and his repute as easy and generous. The Revolution deprived him of his post; he seems to have refused allegiance to William, and to have died at Paris in 1691.

CHAPTER VI.

ETHEREDGE's comedies serve to introduce one of the most brilliant schools of English comic writing—faulty, in that so far from correcting the manners of its age, it did not even portray them, but eminent above the English comedy of every other period for wit. So great is the family likeness between its chief representatives, that it will be advisable to consider their lives and their writings together. The connecting link among them all is that all were fine gentlemen whose code was the fashionable morality of the day. Any conclusions as to the state of contemporary manners which may be deduced from their writings must be confined to this small, though conspicuous section of English society.

William Wycherley was the son of a Shropshire gentleman of good estate. His father, disliking the management of public schools under the Commonwealth, sent the youth to France, where he became a Roman Catholic, but recanted upon his return. He entered at the Temple, and for some years led the life of a gay young man about town. According to his own statement, all his four comedies were written about this period, but Macaulay has shown clearly that they must have, at all events, undergone very considerable revision, and that it is not probable that any but *Love in a Wood* were in existence when this was

William Wycherley
(1640-1715).

acted in 1672. *The Gentleman Dancing Master, The Country Wife,* and *The Plain Dealer,* appeared in 1673, 1675, and 1677 respectively; and the last of these was the termination of the author's brief and brilliant career as a dramatist. It was also the term of his prosperity. A secret marriage with a lady of rank offended the king, by whom Wycherley had been entrusted with the tuition of one of his natural children, and eventually involved him in debt. He was thrown into the Fleet, where he remained several years. At last James II., chancing to witness a representation of *The Plain Dealer,* was led to inquire for the author, and, a piece of munificence towards letters most unusual with him, to pay his debts and grant him a pension of two hundred a year, which, as Wycherley straightway reverted to the Roman Catholic faith, was probably withdrawn by William. He had, however, come into possession of the family estate, and existed for the rest of his life respectably as regarded his means of subsistence, though much the reverse as regards the licentious verses which he went on writing, and published at the age of sixty-four. Macaulay and Mr. Gosse, however, attribute to him a tract in defence of the stage against Jeremy Collier, not devoid of merit; and his later poems enjoyed the advantage of revision by Pope, whose hand, Macaulay thinks, is everywhere discernible. Comedy he never essayed again. He died in 1715, having ten days before his death married a young girl to injure his nephew. This Macaulay considers the worst of his actions; but we do not know that the nephew did not deserve to be injured. A contemporary poet dubs the uncle, " generous Wycherley."

William Congreve (1670-1729).

William Congreve, a scion of a good Staffordshire family, was born at Bardsey, near Leeds, in 1670. His father, an officer in the army, obtained a command in Ireland, where a branch of the family is still settled, and Congreve received his education at Kilkenny and at Trinity College, Dublin. In 1691 he came to London, and at once found admission to the best literary circles. A novel by him, *Incognita*, was published anonymously at the beginning of 1692. Later in the year he co-operated in a translation of Juvenal by various hands, and submitted his *Old Bachelor* to Dryden, who declared that he had never seen such a first play, and lent his aid in adapting it for the stage. It was produced with great success in January, 1693. In November of the same year *The Double-Dealer* appeared, but, though preferred by the judicious, was less popular with the town. It was published with an elegant preface by the author, and a noble panegyric from Dryden. 'Perhaps,' says Mr. Gosse, 'there is no other example of such full and generous praise of a young colleague by a great old poet.' Dryden's notions of architecture, indeed, seem borrowed from the churches of his time, where we not uncommonly see a spire in one style clapped upon a body in another :

> ' Fine Doric pillars found your solid base,
> The fair Corinthian crowns the higher space,
> Thus all below is strength and all above is grace.'

But the lines in which he adjures Congreve to protect his own memory are an unparalleled blending of pathos and compliment :

> ' Be kind to my remains, and O, defend,
> Against your judgment, your departed friend,
> Let not the insulting foe my fame pursue,
> But shade those laurels which descend to you.'

Shortly after the performance of *The Double Dealer*, dissensions broke out between the patentees of the Theatre Royal and their *corps dramatique*, and the majority of the latter seceded to Lincoln's Inn Fields. Congreve followed them, and, in consideration of receiving a stipulated share of the profits, agreed to write for them a play annually, should his health permit. In pursuance of this agreement, _Love for Love_, generally considered the best of his comedies, was brought out in April, 1695. It was a signal success; as was Congreve's solitary tragedy, _The Mourning Bride_, produced in 1697, which, indeed, is believed to have produced him more than any of his comedies. The last, and, in the opinion of some, the best of these, _The Way of the World_ appeared in 1700, and its failure disgusted Congreve with the stage. He had always rather affected to condescend to be a dramatist, as Monsieur Jourdain condescended to be a haberdasher; and he was probably hurt at the rough handling he had received from Jeremy Collier, to whose _Short View of the Immorality and Profaneness of the Stage_ he had unsuccessfully endeavoured to reply. Collier's victory, indeed, proved that the licentiousness of the stage was a mere fashion, rather tolerated than approved by the majority of the playgoing public, and Congreve may have felt that his wings would be clipped by the reformation which public opinion was evidently about to demand. Whatever the cause, he was lost to the stage at thirty, and his occasional poetical productions, the most important of which have been already noticed, were far from qualifying him to sit in the seat of Dryden. He enjoyed, nevertheless, supremacy of another kind. Regarded as an extinct volcano, he gave umbrage to no rivals; his urbane and undemonstrative temper kept him out of literary feuds; all agreed to adore so benign and inoffensive a deity, and the general respect of the lettered world fitly culminated in Pope's dedication of his _Homer_ to him, the most splendid literary tribute the age could bestow. Sinecure Government places made his circumstances more than easy, but he suffered continually from gout, the effect of free living, and he became blind, or nearly so, in his latter years. His death (1729) was hastened by a carriage accident. He had a splendid funeral in Westminster Abbey, and a monument erected by the Duchess of Marlborough (Marlborough's daughter, not his widow), whom he had capriciously made his principal legatee.

It is, as Mr. Gosse remarks, difficult to form any very distinct notion of Congreve as a man. We must be content with knowing that he was a fine gentleman before all things, convivial in his habits, witty in conversation, extremely sensitive to criticism, otherwise placid; able to keep on good terms with both Pope and Dennis throughout his life; and that Pope thought him, Garth, and Vanbrugh, 'the three most honest-hearted real good men of the poetical members of the Kit-cat Club.'

Sir John Vanbrugh, the next of the quartette of illustrious comic writers, occupies a remarkable position in literature. Few other distinguished architects have gained renown in elegant letters, and these have not attempted the drama. As, however, Angelo is more celebrated for St. Peter's than for his sonnets, so Vanbrugh is better remembered by Blenheim, which most have beheld, than by his plays, which are never seen on the stage, and yet connoisseurs have found infinitely more to censure in the former. The faults of the plays are those of the author's age and his school; the faults imputed to his buildings, if they exist, which is a question for architects, are personal to the Fleming, who shared his countryman Rubens's taste for the massive and substantial, and whose epitaph was couched in the adjuration:

Sir John Vanbrugh (1664-1726).

> ' Lie heavy on him, earth, for he
> Laid many a heavy load on thee.'

Though born an English subject, Vanbrugh was of Flemish descent. His first profession was the army. His *début* as a dramatist was made in 1697 by two sparkling comedies, *The Relapse* and *The Provoked Wife*, followed by *The False Friend* (1702), *The Confederacy*, and *The Mistake* (1705), some imitations of the French, and an unfinished play, *A Journey to London*, completed by Cibber, and produced in 1728 as *The Provoked Husband*. All these plays seem to have been successful; certainly none were in any peril of damnation on the ground apprehended by Orrery:

> ' This play, I'm horribly afraid, can't last ;
> Allow it pretty, 'tis confounded chaste,
> And contradicts too much the present taste.'

Latterly he became somewhat careless in the composition of his plays, which may be reasonably attributed to the demands made upon him by the laborious profession of architecture, which he took up, apparently without a regular education, about the end of the seventeenth century, and which he may have been the more inclined to pursue on account of the serious loss entailed upon him by his dramatic speculations. Interest or ability made him successful; he was entrusted with no less a task than the erection of Blenheim ; and Castle Howard and other celebrated country mansions were built after his designs. He died in 1726. The little known of his personal character is to his credit.

George Farquhar was born at Londonderry in 1678, and is believed to have been the son of an George Farquhar (1678-1707). Irish clergyman. He forsook Trinity College for the stage, where he made some figure, but renounced his calling out of compunction for having accidentally wounded a fellow-actor. Coming to London with ten guineas lent to him by the manager, he achieved renown by his comedy of *Love and a Bottle* (1699). *The Constant Couple* (1701) was even more successful. Other plays followed, and from allusions in one of the principal, *The Recruiting Officer* (1706), as well as reminiscences and traditions, he is believed to have held a commission in the army. According to tradition, he was induced to sell his commission to pay his debts by the Duke of Ormond's promise to procure him another, and the disappointment of this expectation so deeply mortified him as to occasion his death. His last and best comedy, *The Beaux' Stratagem*, was written on his deathbed. He is a sympathetic figure among the literary men of the day, gallant and witty, nor incapable of serious feeling. According to his own account he was, like Liston and others who have contributed to the mirth of mankind, by nature a melancholy man. 'As to the mind, which in most men wears as many changes as their body, so in me 'tis generally drest like my person, in black. Melancholy is its everyday apparel, and it has hitherto found few holidays to make it change its clothes.' He adds: 'I am seldom troubled by what the world calls airs and caprices; and I think 'tis an idiot's excuse for a foolish action to say, 'twas my humour. I hate all little malicious tricks of vexing people; and I can't relish the jest that vexes another in earnest. If ever I do a wilful injury, it must be a very great one. I have so natural a propensity to ease, that I cannot cheerfully fix to any study which bears not a pleasure in the application; which makes me inclinable to poetry above anything else. I have very little estate but what lies under the circumference of my hat; and should I by mischance come to lose my head, I should not be worth a groat; but I ought to thank Providence that I can by three hours' study live one-and-twenty with satisfaction to myself, and contribute to the maintenance of more families than some who have thousands a year. I have something in my outward behaviour which gives strangers a worse opinion of me than I deserve; but I am more than recompensed by the opinion of my acquaintance, which is as much above my desert.'

This, which is only part of a much longer character, addressed to a lady, is remarkable as the most detailed self-estimate of any man of letters of the period we possess, until we come to Steele.

Although there are undoubtedly considerable distinctions between the works of these four dramatists, such a fundamental unity nevertheless prevails among them that they may be advantageously considered together. They may be compared to a jewel with four facets, each casting a separate ray, but with little diversity in their cold brilliant glitter. Wit, gaiety, heartlessness, and profligacy are the common notes of them all, save that Congreve has tragic power, and, as well as Farquhar, real feeling. How far they painted, or intended to paint, the manners of their age, is a difficult question. Lamb thought that the world they depict was merely conventional, a Lampsacene Arcadia. Not even the indulgent Leigh Hunt, much less the austere Macaulay, can concur in this judgment, which is assuredly much too absolute. Yet it is indisputable that the manners they portray were not those of a nation that devoured *Pilgrim's Progress*, brought up children and domestics by the *Whole Duty of Man*, and deposed a king who meddled with the Church. Were they even the manners of the gay world? To some extent this is true; but there is evidence enough that even fashionable men thought of something else than seducing their neighbours' wives and daughters; that the slips even of fashionable

women were by no means inordinately frequent or mere
matters of course; and that the standard of personal
honour was much higher than would appear from the
comedies. We may be assisted to comprehend the real
state of the matter by observing the condition of the
French literature of fiction at this very moment. Anyone who should form his opinion of French people
entirely from their novels could come to no other conclusion than that they were entirely given up to the pursuit of
illicit love, and deemed nothing else worthy of the attention
of a rational creature. Yet we know that as a matter of
fact the French nation does think of very different things;
that a ridiculously small corner of actual life is conven-
tionally made to stand for the whole of it; that the novels
which profess to depict manners, while accurate in their
delineation of certain characters and certain phases, would
entirely mislead those whose notions should be solely
derived from them. It would be nearer the truth, though
still erroneous, to take the reverse view, and maintain that
works composed for the sake of amusement are more likely
to usher the reader into an ideal world than to weary him
with familiar scenes and incidents. So far as this is the
case, the English society of the seventeenth century must
be acquitted at the expense of the dramatists, who incur
the obloquy of missing both the two great ends of comedy,
for they neither delineate nor correct it. Possibly the
unsatisfactory position which writers of so much wit and
sense thus came to occupy may be partly accounted for
by the influence of Ben Jonson. We have seen Dryden
almost hesitating to avow his preference for Shakespeare
to Jonson, we shall see that Butler has no hesitation in
asserting the superiority of Jonson to Shakespeare as an
obvious thing; nor could it well be otherwise in so essentially prosaic an age. This implies the triumph of the

comedy of types over the comedy of nature. Jonson, like
Menander, impersonates particular characteristics, or situations in life; Shakespeare paints human nature as large
as it really is. We have seen how the exhibition of these
so-called 'humours' forms the staple of the comedy of
Shadwell. The handling of Congreve and his associates,
who had the example of Molière before them, is far
superior, but the principle is at bottom the same. A
characteristic is incarnated in a personage, and often indicated by his very name. Instead of the names bestowed
by fancy, or borrowed from romance, the Benedicts, Rosa-
linds, Imogens, Mirandas, we have Witwoulds, Maskwells,
Millamants, and Gibbets. Each character being thus more
or less conventional, the *tout ensemble* is necessarily conventional too; and to this extent the world of these dramatists
may be fairly regarded as ideal; while it is not true that
they had any definite purpose of creating such a world, or
that it was so dissimilar to actual society as to interfere
with the appreciation of the audience. Their works may be
compared to the novels of Mr. George Meredith, who would
have been a great comic writer if he had lived in the days
of Congreve. No one would call Mr. Meredith's novels
unnatural; yet his works will convey but little notion of
the English society of the nineteenth century to posterity,
who will only need to turn to George Eliot and Anthony
Trollope to realize it as no bygone age was ever realized
before.

Wycherley has been characterized by Professor Ward as
the Timon of his stage, and the description is excellent, if
not understood of one animated by moral indignation at
its immorality, but of one impelled by temperament to
insist upon and exaggerate its most disagreeable features.
The two most important of his plays, *The Country Wife*
and *The Plain Dealer*, are rather tragi-comedies than

comedies, especially the latter, of which Professor Ward justly observes, 'Working within the limits of his own horizon, with nothing perceptible to him but a vicious world hateful on account of the palpable grossness of its outward pretences, Wycherley must be allowed to have worked with vigour and effect, and to have produced what is indisputably one of the most powerful dramas of its age.' Its unpardonable sin is to be to a great extent an adaptation of Molière's *Misanthrope*, and to pervert and brutalize whatever is most admirable in that masterpiece. *Love in a Wood* and *The Gentleman Dancing Master* are comparatively slight performances, but there is great humour in the representation in the latter of the disguised lover helped out of all his scrapes by the self-complacent credulity of the young lady's father and his own rival, whose business it is to detect him. The delineation of the father as a merchant returned from long residence in Spain, enamoured of Spanish manners, and quoting the language at every second sentence, is one of those which justify Aubrey's remark that the dramatists of his age would be soon forgotten, because their ephemeral 'humours' would have ceased to be intelligible. The character, if still possible in Wycherley's time, ceased to be so very soon afterwards. It must, however, have been popular if it gave or helped to give the nickname of Don Diego to the Spaniards, which survives to this day in 'dago,' the familiar appellation of South Americans in the United States. One characteristic of all Wycherley's comedies should be mentioned, their length, which confirms the impression that he composed with slowness. 'When,' says Hazlitt, ' he got hold of a good thing, or sometimes even of a bad one, he was determined to make the most of it, and might have said with Dogberry, "Had I the tediousness of a king, I could find it in my heart to bestow it all upon your worships."'

If Wycherley is the satirist of Restoration comedy, Congreve is its wit ; but at the same time he betrays a vein of much deeper feeling than Wycherley, and, notwithstanding the contrary opinion of Hazlitt, his characters appear to us more easily appreciated and more readily remembered. His insight into women in particular is so considerable that it is a real loss that he never attempted to paint a noble one, who would indeed have looked strangely amid the crowd of his heartless, or frivolous, or absurd people, but whom he might have rendered a true dramatic success. Both *The Double Dealer* and *The Way of the World* border upon tragedy, and suggest how much finer things Congreve might have written had the taste of his time allowed of tragedy in prose; or if, by treating ordinary domestic life in a serious spirit, even though in verse, he could have taken the step that was afterwards taken by Lillo. He evidently felt conscious of innate tragic power, and essayed heroic tragedy in *The Mourning Bride*, where, hampered by the conventionalities he dared not transgress, he broke down with a romantic plot, romantic characters, and stilted blank verse, all things most repugnant to his genius. Johnson's praise of a passage in this play as ' the most poetical paragraph in the whole mass of English poetry,' and which is actually fine enough to survive such extravagant laudation, is well known. It will be instructive to set it side by side with a still finer passage in a modern tragedy, as examples of the classic and romantic schools of composition. It is the strength and weakness of Congreve that his thoughts are such as would naturally have occurred to any one in the situation of his personages, and that his sole part is to afford them dignified expression; while Beddoes' thoughts are the thoughts of a poet, and as such might well appear fantastic and overstrained to an average audience :

'*Almeria.* It is a fancied noise, for all is hushed.
Leonora. It bore the accent of a human voice.
Almeria. It was thy fear, or else some transient wind
Whistling through hollows of this vaulted aisle.
We'll listen.
Leonora. Hark!
Almeria. No, all is hushed and still as death.   'Tis dreadful.
How reverend is the face of this tall pile,
Whose ancient pillars rear their marble heads
To bear aloft its arched and ponderous roof,
By its own weight made steadfast and immovable,
Looking tranquillity! It strikes an awe
And terror on my aching sight; the tombs
And monumental caves of death look cold,
And shoot a chillness to my trembling heart.
Give me thy hand!
Oh, speak to me! nay, speak! and let me hear
Thy voice; my own affrights me with its echoes.'

Mourning Bride, act ii., sc. 3.

' *Duke.* Deceived and disappointed vain desires!
Why laugh I not, and ridicule myself?
'Tis still, and cold, and nothing in the air
But an old grey twilight, or of eve or morn
I know not which, dim as futurity,
And sad and hoary as the ghostly past   ·
Fills up the space.   Hush! not a wind is there,
Not a cloud sails over the battlements,
Not a bell tolls the hour.   Is there an hour?
Or is not all gone by which here did hive
Of men and their life's ways?   Could I but hear
The ticking of a clock, or someone breathing,
Or e'en a cricket's chirping, or the grating
Of the old gates amid the marble tombs,
I should be sure that this was still the world.
Hark! Hark! Doth nothing stir?
No light, and still no light, besides this ghost
That mocks the dawn, unaltered? Still no sound?
No voice of man? No cry of beast? No rustle

Of any moving creature? And sure I feel
That I remain the same: no more round blood drops
Roll joyously along my pulseless veins:
The air I seem to breathe is still the same:
And the great dreadful thought that now comes o'er me
Must remain ever as it is, unchanged.
This moment doth endure for evermore;
Eternity hath overshadowed time;
And I alone am left of all that lived.'

Death's Jest Book, act iii., sc. 3.

The writer of these lines might have been a great tragic
poet, if he could have achieved the construction of a cohe-
rent plot. Congreve might have been a greater, but for the
conventions of an age that required his *dramatis personae*
to be remote by a thousand years or a thousand miles.

The dazzle of Congreve's wit has perhaps blinded critics
to his more serious powers, and it may be that its brilliancy
has been even exaggerated. What is chiefly admirable is
perhaps not so much the occasional flashes and strokes,
felicitous as they are, as the unflagging verve, energy, and
gaiety. His plays are not of the kind that keep the
audience in a roar from first to last, but they never cease
to stimulate the spirits ; the fire does not always blaze, but
it never burns low: there is not a dull scene, or a tiresome
or useless character. The general tone of good breeding, if
it does not purify the pervading atmosphere of profligacy,
at any rate prevents it from becoming offensive. In verbal
impropriety and *double entendre* Congreve is even worse
than Wycherley, but his plays are far from giving the same
impression of a thoroughly obnoxious state of society. It
is true that the pursuit of women seems the sole business
of the men, and the pursuit of men the business of half the
women ; but the universal passion is so pleasantly varie-
gated with extraneous humours and oddities that it is far

from producing the monotony of a modern French novel.
Thus, there is an amourette between Brisk and Lady
Froth in *The Double Dealer*, but the pair are æsthetic
as well as amorous, and the blue-stocking is more conspicuous than the unfaithful wife. The scene where
Brisk corrects Lady Froth's poetry, imitated but not ser-
vilely copied from one in *Les Femmes Savantes*, is a good
specimen of the humour and sparkle of Congreve's
dialogue:

'*Lady Froth.* Then you think that episode between Susan,
the dairy-maid, and our coachman, is not amiss; you know I
may suppose the dairy in town as well as in the country.

Brisk. Incomparable, let me perish!—But then being an
heroic poem, had not you better call him a charioteer? charioteer
sounds great; besides, your ladyship's coachman having a red
face, and you comparing him to the sun; and you know the sun
is called heaven's charioteer.

Lady Froth. Oh, infinitely better! I am extremely beholden
to you for the hint; stay, we'll read over those half a score lines
again. [*Pulls out a paper.*] Let me see here, you know what
goes before,—the comparison, you know. [*Reads.*

> For as the sun shines every day,
> So, of our coachman I may say—

Brisk. I'm afraid that simile won't do in wet weather;—
because you say the sun shines every day.

Lady Froth. No, for the sun it won't, but it will do for the
coachman; for you know there's more occasion for a coach in
wet weather.

Brisk. Right, right, that saves all.

Lady Froth. Then, I don't say the sun shines all the day, but
that he peeps now and then; yet he does shine all the day too,
you know, though we don't see him.

Brisk. Right, but the vulgar will never comprehend that.

Lady Froth. Well, you shall hear.—Let me see. [*Reads.*

> For as the sun shines every day,
> So, of our coachman I may say,

> He shows his drunken fiery face,
> Just as the sun does, more or less.

Brisk. That's right, all's well, all's well!—More or less.
Lady Froth. [*Reads.*]

> And when at night his labour's done,
> Then too, like heaven's charioteer the sun—

Ay, charioteer does better.

> Into the dairy he descends,
> And there his whipping and his driving ends;
> There's he's secure from danger of a bilk,
> His fare is paid him, and he sets in milk.

For Susan, you know, is Thetis, and so—
Brisk. Incomparably well and proper, egad!—But I have one exception to make:—don't you think *bilk* (I know it's good rhyme), but don't you think *bilk* and *fare* too like a hackney-coachman?
Lady Froth. I swear and vow, I am afraid so.—And yet our Jehu was a hackney-coachman when my lord took him.
Brisk. Was he? I'm answered, if Jehu was a hackney-coachman.—You may put that in the marginal notes though, to prevent criticism.—Only mark it with a small asterism, and say, Jehu was formerly a hackney-coachman.
Lady Froth. I will; you'd oblige me extremely to write notes to the whole poem.
Brisk. With all my heart and soul, and proud of the vast honour, let me perish!'

Congreve excels not only in dialogue, but in painting a character by a single speech. How thoroughly we realize the inward and outward man of old Foresight the omen-monger, from a single passage in *Love for Love:*

'*Nurse.* Pray heaven send your worship good luck! marry and amen with all my heart; for you have put on one stocking with the wrong side outward.
Fore. Ha! hm? faith and troth I'm glad of it. And so I have; that may be good luck in troth, in troth it may, very good luck:

nay I have had some omens : I got out of bed backwards too this
morning, without premeditation ; pretty good that too ; but then
I stumbled coming down stairs, and met a weasel ; bad omens
these, some bad, some good, our lives are chequered ; mirth and
sorrow, want and plenty, night and day, make up our time.   But
in troth I am pleased at my stocking ; very well pleased at my
stocking.'

Or Mr. Bluffe, the *miles gloriosus* of *The Old Bachelor :*

'You must know, sir, I was resident in Flanders the last cam-
paign, had a small part there, but no matter for that.   Perhaps,
sir, there was scarce anything of moment done but an humble
servant of yours that shall be nameless, was an eye-witness of—
I won't say had the greatest share in it ; though I might say that
too, since I name nobody, you know.   Well, Mr. Sharper, would
you think it ? in all this time this rascally gazette writer never so
much as once mentioned me—not once, by the wars !—took no
more notice than as if Nol. Bluffe had not been in the land of the
living !
Sharper. Strange !
Bluffe. Ay, ay, no matter.—You see, Mr. Sharper, that after
all I am content to retire—live a private person—Scipio and
others have done it.'

Vanbrugh has less individuality than his eminent contemporaries, and has consequently produced less impression
than they upon the public mind, has added fewer typical
characters to comedy, and stands some steps nigher to
oblivion.   Yet he is their equal in *vis comica*, and their
superior in stage workmanship.   'He is no writer at all,'
says Hazlitt, 'as to mere authorship; but he makes up for
it by a prodigious fund of comic invention and ludicrous
description, bordering upon caricature.   He has none of
Congreve's graceful refinement, and as little of Wycherley's
serious manner and studious insight into the springs of
character ; but his exhibition of it in dramatic contrast and
unlooked-for situations, where the different parties play

upon one another's failings, and into one another's hands, keeping up the jest like a game of battledore and shuttle-cock, and urging it to the utmost verge of breathless extra-vagance, in the mere eagerness of the fray, is beyond that of any other of our writers.' In Hazlitt's opinion, Van-brugh did not bestow much pains upon the construction of his pieces, and their excellent dramatic effect is mainly to be attributed to his promptness in seizing upon the hints for powerful situations which continually arose as he went along. He has nothing of the passion which some-times raises Congreve so near to the confines of tragedy, nor has he the airy gaiety of Farquhar; but his animal spirits are abundant and unforced, and his humour has a true Flemish exuberance. His characters are always lively and well discriminated, but the only type he can be said to have created is the model fop, Lord Foppington in *The Relapse*, and even he is partly borrowed from Etheredge's Sir Fopling Flutter. He is nevertheless a most perfect portrait, and gives real literary distinction to what would otherwise have been a mere comedy of intrigue. The powerful though disagreeable character of Sir John Brute lends force to *The Provoked Wife;* and the un-finished *Journey to London* is grounded on an idea which might have been very fruitful, the country senator who has gone into Parliament as a speculation, but who, upon taking up his residence in London, finds that he loses more by the extravagance of his wife than he can gain by the prostitution of his vote. Vanbrugh's other plays are mere comedies of intrigue, written without moral or immoral purpose for the sake of amusement, of which they are abundantly prolific for readers not repelled by a disregard of virtue so open and unblushing that, being too gay for cynicism, it almost seems innocence. The scene be-tween Flippanta and her pupil in *The Confederacy* is an excellent specimen of Vanbrugh's spirited comedy. It might be headed, *Malitia supplet aetatem.*

'*Flip.* Nay, if you can bear it so, you are not to be pitied so much as I thought.

Cor. Not pitied! Why, is it not a miserable thing for such a young creature as I am should be kept in perpetual solitude, with no other company but a parcel of old fumbling masters, to teach me geography, arithmetic, philosophy, and a thousand useless things? Fine entertainment, indeed, for a young maid at sixteen! Methinks one's time might be better employed.

Flip. Those things will improve your wit.

Cor. Fiddle, faddle! han't I wit enough already? My mother-in-law has learned none of this trumpery, and is not she as happy as the day is long?

Flip. Then you envy her I find?

Cor. And well I may. Does she not do what she has a mind to, in spite of her husband's teeth?

Flip. [*Aside.*] Look you there now! If she has not already conceived that as the supreme blessing of life!

Cor. I'll tell you what, Flippanta; if my mother-in-law would but stand by me a little, and encourage me, and let me keep her company, I'd rebel against my father to-morrow, and throw all my books in the fire. Why, he can't touch a groat of my portion; do you know that, Flippanta!

Flip. [*Aside.*] So—I shall spoil her! Pray Heaven the girl don't debauch me!

Cor. Look you: in short, he may think what he pleases, he may think himself wise; but thoughts are free, and I may think in my turn. I'm but a girl, 'tis true, and a fool too, if you'll believe him; but let him know, a foolish girl may make a wise man's heart ache; so he had as good be quiet.—Now it's out.

Flip. Very well, I love to see a young woman have spirit, it's a sign she'll come to something.

Cor. Ah, Flippanta! if you would but encourage me, you'd find me quite another thing. I'm a devilish girl in the bottom; I wish you'd but let me make one amongst you.

Flip. That never can be till you are married. Come, examine your strength a little. Do you think you durst venture upon a husband?

Cor. A husband! Why, a—if you would but encourage me. Come, Flippanta, be a true friend now. I'll give you advice when I have got a little more experience. Do you in your conscience and soul think I am old enough to be married?

Flip. Old enough! why, you are sixteen, are you not?

Cor. Sixteen! I am sixteen, two months, and odd days, woman. I keep an exact account.

Flip. The deuce you are!

Cor. Why, do you then truly and sincerely think I am old enough?

Flip. I do, upon my faith, child.

Cor. Why, then, to deal as fairly with you, Flippanta, as you do with me, I have thought so any time these three years.

Flip. Now I find you have more wit than ever I thought you had; and to show you what an opinion I have of your discretion, I'll show you a thing I thought to have thrown in the fire.

Cor. What is it, for Jupiter's sake?

Flip. Something will make your heart chuck within you.

Cor. My dear Flippanta!

Flip. What do you think it is?

Cor. I don't know, nor I don't care, but I'm mad to have it.

Flip. It's a four-cornered thing.

Cor. What, like a cardinal's cap?

Flip. No, 'tis worth a whole conclave of 'em. How do you like it?   [*Showing the letter.*

Cor. O Lard, a letter! Is there ever a token in it?

Flip. Yes, and a precious one too. There's a handsome young gentleman's heart.

Cor. A handsome young gentleman's heart! [*Aside.*] Nay, then, it's time to look grave.

Flip. There.

Cor. I shan't touch it.

Flip. What's the matter now?

Cor. I shan't receive it.

Flip. Sure you jest.

Cor. You'll find I don't. I understand myself better than to take letters when I don't know who they are from.

Flip. I'm afraid I commended your wit too soon.

Cor. 'Tis all one, I shan't touch it, unless I know who it comes from.

Flip. Heyday, open it and you'll see.

Cor. Indeed I shall not.

Flip. Well—then I must return it where I had it.

Cor. That won't serve your turn, madam. My father must have an account of this.

Flip. Sure you are not in earnest?

Cor. You'll find I am.

Flip. So, here's fine work! This 'tis to deal with girls before they come to know the distinction of sexes!

Cor. Confess who you had it from, and perhaps, for this once, I mayn't tell my father.

Flip. Why then, since it must out, 'twas the Colonel. But why are you so scrupulous, madam?

Cor. Because if it had come from anybody else—I would not have given a farthing for it.

[*Snatching it eagerly out of her hand.'*

Farquhar has what Vanbrugh wants—individuality. He seems to identify himself with his favourite characters, the heedless, dissolute, but gentlemanly and good-hearted sparks about town whom he so delights to portray, and hence wins a firmer place in our affections than his wittier and in every way stronger rival, who might have been a comic automaton for any idea of his personality that we are able to form. Whether the inevitable conception of Farquhar is really correct may be doubted; it is not in harmony with the few particulars which we possess of his manners and personal appearance. While reading him, nevertheless, one feels no doubt of the applicability to the author of the character of his Sir Harry Wildair, 'entertaining to others, and easy to himself, turning all passion into gaiety of humour.' The plays answer the description of the personage; they are lively, rattling, entertaining, and the humour is certainly much in excess of the passion. Serjeant Kite, in *The Recruiting Officer*, has become proverbial, otherwise no character has been recognized as an absolute creation, though almost all are natural and unaffected. *The Beaux' Stratagem*, his last play, is by common consent his best; it is assuredly admirable, from the truth and variety of the characters, and the pervading atmosphere of adventurous gaiety. The separation between Mr. and Mrs. Sullen is a good specimen of Farquhar's *vis comica*:

' *Mrs. Sul.* Hold, gentlemen, all things here must move by consent, compulsion would spoil us; let my dear and I talk the matter over, and you shall judge it between us.

Squire Sul. Let me know first who are to be our judges. Pray, sir, who are you?

Sir Chas. I am Sir Charles Freeman, come to take away your wife.

Squire Sul. And you, good sir?

Aim. Charles Viscount Aimwell, come to take away your sister.

Squire Sul. And you, pray, sir?

Arch. Francis Archer, esquire, come——

Squire Sul. To take away my mother, I hope. Gentlemen, you're heartily welcome. I never met with three more obliging people since I was born!—And now, my dear, if you please, you shall have the first word.

Arch. And the last, for five pound!

Mrs. Sul. Spouse!

Squire Sul. Rib!

Mrs. Sul. How long have we been married?

Squire Sul. By the almanac, fourteen months; but by my account, fourteen years.

Mrs. Sul. 'Tis thereabout by my reckoning.

Count Bel. Garzoon, their account will agree.

Mrs. Sul. Pray, spouse, what did you marry for?

Squire Sul. To get an heir to my estate.

Sir Chas. And have you succeeded?

Squire Sul. No.

Arch. The condition fails of his side.—Pray, madam, what did you marry for?

Mrs. Sul. To support the weakness of my sex by the strength of his, and to enjoy the pleasures of an agreeable society.

Sir Chas. Are your expectations answered?

Mrs. Sul. No.

Count Bel. A clear case! a clear case!

Sir Chas. What are the bars to your mutual contentment?

Mrs. Sul. In the first place, I can't drink ale with him.

Squire Sul. Nor can I drink tea with her.

Mrs. Sul. I can't hunt with you.

Squire Sul. Nor can I dance with you.

Mrs. Sul. I hate cocking and racing.

Squire Sul. And I abhor ombre and piquet.

Mrs. Sul. Your silence is intolerable.

Squire Sul. Your prating is worse.

Mrs. Sul. Have we not been a perpetual offence to each other? a gnawing vulture at the heart?

Squire Sul. A frightful goblin to the sight?

Mrs. Sul. A porcupine to the feeling?

Squire Sul. Perpetual wormwood to the taste?

Mrs. Sul. Is there on earth a thing we could agree in?

Squire Sul. Yes—to part.

Mrs. Sul. With all my heart.

Squire Sul. Your hand.

Mrs. Sul. Here.

Squire Sul. These hands joined us, these shall part us.— Away!

Mrs. Sul. North.

Squire Sul. South.

Mrs. Sul. East.

Squire Sul. West—far as the poles asunder.

Count Bel. Begar, the ceremony be vera pretty!'

Farquhar is fuller of allusions to contemporary events

L

and humours than any of the other dramatists, and these
are sometimes very happy; as when a promising scheme
is said to be in danger of 'going souse into the water, like
the Eddystone lighthouse,' or when an alarm is given by
shouting, 'Thieves! thieves! murder! *popery!*' Another
peculiarity of all these dramatists, but especially Farquhar,
is the constant use in serious passages of a broken blank
verse, which continually seems upon the point of becoming
regular ten-syllabled iambic, but never maintains this
elevation for any considerable space. The extremely
powerful scene between the two Fainalls, in Congreve's
Love for Love, for example, which borders closely upon
tragedy, is all but regular blank verse, which, if perfectly
finished, would be much better than the verse of *The
Mourning Bride*. It is difficult to determine whether this
was intentional or accidental. Possibly the exigencies of
the performers had something to do with it. It is by no
means unlikely that prose, as well as verse, was then
declaimed with more attention to rhythm than is now the
custom. In estimating the merits of these dramas it must
never be forgotten, as a point in their favour, that they
were written for the stage, and that success in the closet
was quite a secondary consideration with the authors; on
the other hand, that they had the advantage of being
produced when the histrionic art of England was probably
at its zenith.

This notice of the later Restoration comedy may be completed by the mention of three ladies who cultivated it with
success during the latter part of the seventeenth century.
How much of this success, in the case of one of them, was
due to merit, and how much to indecency, is a difficult,
though not in every sense of the term a nice or delicate
question. Despite the offensiveness of her writings,
Aphra Behn (1640-1689), whose maiden name was John-

son, is personally a sympathetic figure. She was born in
1640, and as a girl went out with her family to Surinam,
then an English possession. She there made the acquaintance of the Indian chief Oroonoko and his bride Imoinda,
afterwards celebrated in the novel by her upon which
Southern founded his popular play. Returning to England, she married a Dutch merchant of the name of Behn,
and after his death was sent as a spy to Antwerp. A
young Dutchman to whom she was engaged died; she was
wrecked and nearly drowned upon her return to England;
and, probably from necessity, as the English government
appears to have refused to recompense or even to reimburse
her, turned novelist and playwright. Her novels will be
noticed in another place; her eighteen plays have, with
few exceptions, sufficient merit to entitle her to a respectable place among the dramatists of her age, and sufficient
indelicacy to be unreadable in this. It may well be
believed, on the authority of a female friend, that the
authoress 'had wit, humour, good-nature, and judgment;
was mistress of all the pleasing arts of conversation; was
a woman of sense, and *consequently* a woman of pleasure.'
She was buried in Westminster Abbey, but not in Poets'
Corner. The plays of Mrs. Manley (1672-1724), though
moderately successful, need not detain us here, but we
shall have to speak of her as a writer of fiction. She was
the daughter of a Cavalier knight, but became the mistress of Alderman Barber, and was concerned in several
doubtful transactions. Swift, nevertheless, speaks of her
as a good person 'for one of her sort'—fat and forty, it
seems, but *not* fair. Mrs. Susannah Centlivre (1667-1723)
appears to have had her share of adventures in her youth,
but survived to contract one of the most respectable unions
imaginable, namely, with the queen's cook. She was a
wholesale adapter from the French, and her lively comedies

possess little literary merit, but so much dramatic instinct that three of them, *The Busy Body*, *The Wonder*, and *A Bold Stroke for a Wife*, remained long upon the list of acting plays, and might be represented even now.

CHAPTER VII.

CRITICISM.

THE age of the Restoration possessed many men qualified
to shine in criticism, but their acumen is in general only
indicated by casual remarks, and, setting aside the metrical
prolusions of Roscommon and Sheffield, nearly all the
serious criticism it has bequeathed to us proceeds from
the pen of Dryden. No other of our poets except Coleridge and Wordsworth has given us anything so critically
valuable, but Dryden's principal service is one which they
could not render; for, even if their style had equalled
his—and this would be too much to say even of Wordsworth's—it could not have exerted the same wide and
salutary influence. Dryden is entitled to be considered
as the great reformer of English prose, the writer in whom
the sound principles of the Restoration were above all
others impersonated, and who above all others led the
way to that clear, sane, and balanced method of writing
which it was the especial mission of Restoration literature
to introduce. We need only compare his style with
Milton's to be sensible of the enormous progress in the
direction of perspicuity and general utility. Milton is a
far more eloquent writer, but his style is totally unfit
for the close reasoning and accurate investigation which
the pressure of politics and the development of science

and philosophy were soon to require, and the rest of the prosaists of the time are, with few exceptions, either too pedantic or too commonplace. Dryden is lucid, easy, familiar, yet he can be august and splendid on occasion, and if he does not emulate Milton's dithyrambic, the dignity of English prose loses nothing in his hands. Take the opening of his *Dialogue on Dramatic Poesy:*

'It was that memorable day, in the first summer of the late war, when our navy engaged the Dutch; a day wherein the two most mighty and best appointed fleets which any age had ever seen, disputed the command of the greater half of the globe, the commerce of nations, and the riches of the universe: while these vast floating bodies, on either side, moved against each other in parallel lines, and our countrymen, under the happy conduct of his royal highness, went breaking, by little and little, into the line of the enemies; the noise of the cannon from both navies reached our ears about the city, so that all men being alarmed with it, and in a dreadful suspense of the event, which they knew was then deciding, every one went following the sound as his fancy led him; and leaving the town almost empty, some took towards the park, some across the river, others down it; all seeking the noise in the depth of silence.

'Amongst the rest, it was the fortune of Eugenius, Crites, Lisideius, and Neander, to be in company together; three of them persons whom their wit and quality have made known to all the town; and whom I have chose to hide under these borrowed names, that they may not suffer by so ill a relation as I am going to make of their discourse.

'Taking then a barge, which a servant of Lisideius had provided for them, they made haste to shoot the bridge, and left behind them that great fall of waters which hindered them from hearing what they desired: after which, having disengaged themselves from many vessels which rode at anchor in the Thames, and almost blocked up the passage towards Greenwich, they ordered the watermen to let fall their oars more gently, and then, every one favouring his own curiosity with a strict silence, it was not long ere they perceived the air to break about them like the noise of distant thunder, or of swallows in a chimney: [1] those little undulations of sound, though almost vanishing before they reached them, yet still seeming to retain somewhat of their first horror, which they had betwixt the fleets. After they had attentively listened till such time as the sound by little and little went from them, Eugenius, lifting up his head, and taking notice of it, was the first who congratulated to the rest that happy omen of our nation's victory: adding, that we had but this to desire in confirmation of it, that we might hear no more of that noise, which was now leaving the English coast.'

This fine induction can hardly have formed part of the original essay, which, Dryden tells us, was written in the country in 1665, since the naval battle, which was fought on June 3rd, 1665, is described as having taken place in 'the first summer of the late war.' One extraordinary passage must have been left uncorrected by oversight, at least we cannot well suppose that Dryden would have printed 'Blank verse is acknowledged to be too low for a poem' after the appearance of *Paradise Lost*, which was published on the day after the conclusion of the Peace of Breda, not then known in England. The essay has two objects not very compatible: to defend the English stage against the French, and to advocate the use of rhyme in tragedy, which necessarily gives the piece a French air, and makes it appear imitative, when it is in truth original. Dryden points out with considerable force the restrictions which French dramatists of the classical school impose upon themselves by servile adherence to the unities of time and place, and in a well-known passage which does honour to his taste sets Shakespeare above Ben Jonson. His criticism of *Troilus and Cressida*, in his essay on *The Grounds of Criticism in Tragedy* (1679), is instructive as

[1] An instance of the observation of nature as unusual with Dryden as chimneys of the size required are unusual with us.

illustrating by force of contrast that enlarged view of Shakespeare for which we are indebted to Goethe and Coleridge. He justly censures *Troilus and Cressida* as a play; it does not occur to him that Shakespeare may have intended a satire. All his essays, which consist principally of prefaces and dedications to his own works, are worth reading; none more so than his defence of Virgil in the dedication to his translation of his poems, and the remarks on Horace and Juvenal in his *Essay on Satire*. Everywhere we must admire his sanity, penetration, and massive common sense; his chief defects are conventional prejudice, negligence (as when he ascribes the invention of blank verse to Shakespeare), and the parade of secondhand learning. It may be said of his criticisms, as truly as of his poems or plays, that his merits are his own, his faults those of his age.

Another critic of the stage only deserves notice in this capacity from his connection with Dryden. Thomas Rymer (1639-1714) will be mentioned again as a meritorious antiquary. As a critic he is remarkable for having by his *Trage-dies of the Last Age* (1673) drawn some judicious remarks from Dryden, and for having analyzed *Othello* as a pattern of a bad play. He has consequently been unanimously hooted by his countrymen, for it passes belief that Pope should have praised him to Spence, though Spence affirms it. It was his misfortune to be an Englishman; in France at the time his views would have been thought very correct; in fact, he criticises Shakespeare much in the style of Voltaire. He is a votary of decorum and dignity, and would no more than Voltaire have let a mouse into a tragedy. He discusses with imperturbable gravity, ' Who and who may kill one another with decency ? ' and decides, ' In poetry no woman is to kill a man, except her quality gives her the advantage above him. Poetical decency will not suffer death to be dealt to each other by such persons, whom the laws of duel allow not to enter the lists together.' And Rymer would have been content to have dwelt in such decencies for ever.

Jeremy Collier, a Nonjuring clergyman (1650-1726), attained fame, not as the advocate of decencies, but of decency. His *Short View of the Immorality and Profaneness of the English Stage* (1698) occasioned a great sensation, and was efficacious in abating the evils against which it was directed, although it is probable that Addison's mild rebuke and better example accomplished even more. As the adversary of men of wit and genius, Collier has become obnoxious to their representatives, and has been unfairly reviled as a sour fanatic. In fact he is very moderate, admits that the stage may be a valuable medium of instruction, and only denounces its abuse. Scott and Macaulay have done him justice, and Mr. Gosse gives an excellent analysis of his work in his biography of Congreve. His wit is as unquestionable as his zeal, but his argument is not everywhere equally cogent. On the chapter of profaneness he is fantastic and straitlaced, and so tender of dignities that he will not allow even the god Apis to be disrespectfully mentioned. On that of immorality he is unanswerable, and unless the incriminated dramatists were prepared to say, 'Evil, be thou my good,' they could but own

'Pudet haec opprobria nobis
Et dici potuisse, et non potuisse refelli.'

Congreve and Vanbrugh attempted to reply, but to little purpose. Dryden kissed the rod. Collier's volume is said to have been 'conceived, disposed, transcribed, and printed in a month.' He had previously achieved notoriety as a Jacobite pamphleteer, and in his old age became the official head of the decaying sect of the Nonjurors.

Although Richard Bentley (1662-1743) belongs mainly to the eighteenth century, his dissertation upon the *Epistles of Phalaris* (1699) falls within the seventeenth, and an account of the literary criticism of this age would be incomplete without some mention of the one epoch-making critical work it produced. There is no need to tell again the story of the Bentley-Boyle controversy, so admirably narrated by Macaulay and Jebb; but it may be observed here that it marks an era in criticism as the first example of the testimony of antiquity being irretrievably overthrown by internal evidence. It was not the first time that the genuineness of attested ancient writings had been disputed. Valla had waged war upon the forged donation of Constantine, but his case was so very clear that he had not been answered, but as far as possible ignored. Phalaris had found defenders, and this controversy was perhaps the first in which tradition and authority were fairly vanquished in a pitched battle. Bentley's extraordinary powers of mind were almost equally evinced in his *Boyle Lectures*, also a production of the seventeenth century, which will be noticed in their place.

CHAPTER VIII.

PHILOSOPHY.

FROM the criticism of books we pass, by no violent transition, to the criticism of principles—moral science. The latter half of the seventeenth century is a distinguished period in the history of English philosophy, for in it the most distinctively national of all systems which have obtained currency in this country was fully formulated. It is remarkable that while both empirical and transcendental views in philosophy found supporters, the champions of the latter comprised several illustrious names, and that of the former only one, while nevertheless empiricism obtained as complete a triumph as has ever been recorded in the history of opinion. The principal reason, no doubt, is the natural attractiveness to the solid homely understanding of the Englishman of conclusions based on experience and common sense;[1] but partly also to the fact that the illustrious man by whom the empirical philosophy was mainly upheld carried his speculations into practical life, and became foremost among the defenders of civil and religious liberty. If Locke, like his forerunner Hobbes, had employed his acuteness in defence of absolute power, he

---

[1] Coleridge told Crabb Robinson that he 'considered Locke as having led to the destruction of metaphysical science, by encouraging the unlearned public to think that with mere common sense they might dispense with disciplined study.'

would, like Hobbes, have been caressed by the court, but his doctrines would have been slighted by the nation.

John Locke was born at Wrington in the north of Somerset, August 29 (N.S.), 1632, the same year that gave birth to Spinoza. His father, an attorney, was a man of independent character and strong principle, which he proved by accepting a commission in a Parliamentary regiment. Locke was elected to a foundation scholarship at Westminster in 1647, and to a studentship at Christ Church in 1652. He became M.A. in June, 1658, was appointed Greek Lecturer in 1660, and held other college offices. He wrote about this time two treatises as yet unpublished, one upon the Roman commonwealth, the other on the right of the civil magistrate to regulate indifferent matters touching the exercise of religion, which, under the influence of the hopes which moderate men entertained of the Restoration government, he was at the time inclined to allow. Having determined to study medicine, he obtained in 1666 a dispensation to enable him to hold his studentship, and in the same year the decisive bias was given to his life by his acquaintance with Shaftesbury, of whose family he became virtually a member in the following year. Shaftesbury was as yet neither the Shaftesbury of the Cabal nor the Shaftesbury of the Popish Plot, and there was no reason why Locke should hesitate in attaching himself to a statesman, who, whatever his astuteness and versatility, possessed by far the most enlightened and comprehensive mind of any public man of his day. The main bond which united the two was their agreement on the principle of toleration, for which Chillingworth had been denounced and Roger Williams persecuted, and which scarcely any one would then have subscribed as an abstract proposition, though Cromwell had gone a long way towards reducing it to prac-

John Locke
(1632-1704).

tice. Influenced probably by Shaftesbury, Locke drew up in 1667 an *Essay on Toleration*, the first draft of his subsequent celebrated work, and which has itself been retrieved from oblivion by Mr. Fox Bourne. Considering the circumstances of the times, it can excite neither surprise nor censure that he should have argued in favour of denying the privileges of toleration to those who denied them to others, *i.e.*, to Roman Catholics. Two years later he drew up, at Shaftesbury's instance, a constitution for the colony of Carolina, in which Shaftesbury was largely interested. His medical skill was exerted in relieving Shaftesbury from the effects of a serious complaint; and he acquitted himself successfully in a yet more delicate undertaking, the choosing a wife for his son. He also attended professionally at the birth of Shaftesbury's grandson, the future author of *Characteristics*. These services were fitly recompensed by secretaryships, both at the Great Seal and at the Board of Trade, but there is not the slightest proof of his having participated in any of his patron's plots; while it is not too much to say that the steady regard entertained for Shaftesbury by a man like Locke affords the strongest of all presumptions that this enigmatical personage was, after all, a patriot. During three and a half stormy years Locke was in France for the benefit of his health, making observations on the culture of the vine and olive, and noting, under the external splendour of Louis XIV.'s reign, symptoms of that distress among the industrial classes which was to issue in the Revolution. Returning, he found his patron just liberated from the Tower, and their intimate relations continued until Shaftesbury's flight to Holland in November, 1682, followed by his death in the succeeding January. Locke was thus a mark for the suspicions and animosities of the triumphant Court party. His usual place of residence was now Oxford, where he still enjoyed his Christ Church studentship, and curious letters are extant from Dean Prideaux, avowing practices akin to espionage, but admitting that John Locke is so close a man, and his servant such a phœnix of discretion, that nothing can be made out. Locke wisely withdrew to Holland about the autumn of 1683, and in November, 1684, was arbitrarily rejected from his studentship by a royal mandate. He employed his exile in forming friendships with Limborch, Le Clerc, and other distinguished men, in composing his famous *Letter on Toleration*, published anonymously in 1689, and in active communication with William and Mary when the Deliverer's expedition was finally determined upon. He came to England with Mary in 1689, and received the most flattering offers of important diplomatic posts, which he declined on account of the weakness of his health. He accepted, however, a small appointment, but his principal public services were rendered as a referee on the various important questions submitted to him by Government; and as a man of letters, having nearly reached the age of sixty without publishing anything of importance, he produced within ten years the series of unadorned tracts which have made him, alike in the regions of philosophy and of politics, the most conspicuous representative of masculine, unimaginative, English common sense.

The *Letter on Toleration*, as already mentioned, had appeared anonymously in Holland in 1689. In 1690 the *Essay on the Human Understanding* was published, and also the two *Treatises on Government*; the first, a reply to Filmer, the advocate of divine right, composed, in Professor Fowler's opinion, between 1680 and 1685; the second written during the last years of Locke's residence in Holland. The *Letter on Toleration*, the authorship of which was not acknowledged during Locke's lifetime, was followed by three defences against assailants, two of which appeared respectively in 1690 and 1692, the third was posthumous. The *Essay on the Human Understanding*, adopted from the first as a text-book at Trinity College, Dublin, but ineffectually proscribed in the writer's own university, called forth criticisms from Norris of Bemerton, to which Locke replied in two essays allowed to remain unpublished during his life, 'for,' he said, ' I love not controversy.' He could not, however, avoid a controversy with John Edwards and Bishop Stillingfleet, on his *Reasonableness of Christianity* (1695). After writing five pamphlets, Locke ultimately remained in possession of the field, the drift of opinion being entirely in his favour, though few of the official ministers of religion ventured to come forward openly in his defence. The *Treatise on Education* (1693), written at the request of William Molyneux, excited comparatively little controversy. Another very important class of the productions of his affluent maturity were those on trade and finance, by which he rendered the utmost service to the state. By his *Considerations on the Value of Money* (1691), and other tracts, he contributed largely to the reform of the currency, the condition of which had become intolerable, but was in great danger of being corrected by remedies worse than the disease. Several other publications contributed to disseminate enlightened views on trade, manufactures, and the interest of money. He could not always be right; it is both painful and ludicrous to find so wise and good a man obliged *ex officio* as a Commissioner of Trade to find reasons for discouraging the woollen manufacture in Ireland; which Swift seems to ridicule in describing the Laputan philosophers who had devised means to remove the wool from a sheep's back, and hoped shortly to propagate the breed of naked sheep over the kingdom. This, nevertheless, is but a slight inconsistency with the general tenor of Locke's views on economical subjects, which, no less than his political and religious convictions, tended irresistibly towards unrestricted freedom. In 1700 he was released from public life, and spent his few remaining years undisturbed by controversy, in the society of the amiable family of Sir Francis Masham, of High Laver, Essex, of whose house he had long been an inmate. Lady Masham, singularly enough, was the daughter of Ralph Cudworth, the great English champion of the ideal school of philosophy, and therefore as far removed as possible from Locke in opinion. He died on October 28, 1704.

Locke's intellectual character must be considered along with his writings; of his moral character it may justly be said, that no English writer of equal eminence stands so high. Butler and Berkeley may have been equally faultless, and the latter, no doubt, possessed more of the spell of personal fascination; but neither was, like Locke, exposed to the storms of a corrupt and factious age; neither was called upon to encounter such perils and make such sacrifices; neither had the same opportunity of exercising fortitude in adversity and moderation in success. Whether as public patriot or private friend, Locke appears 'a spirit without spot,' and his resolute temper, his intellectual ardour, and his brilliant achievements, effectually preserve him from the insipidity which so frequently mars the moral physiognomies of good men. His countenance, indeed, is not illumined by the spirituality of a Channing; but the robuster virtues stand forth in even bolder relief, and his apparent exemption from the minor failings which beset even a Newton, is the more remarkable as he wanted neither for enemies nor biographers.

Locke's great work as a philosopher is the *Essay on the Human Understanding*, 'the best chart of the human mind,' says Hallam, one of the great representative books of the world. In Locke, as in his predecessor Hobbes, were united two endowments rarely combined, the sturdy prosaic common sense of the man of the world and the dexterity and subtlety of the practised logician. In his utter antipathy to everything in the slightest degree illumined, or, as he would have thought, distorted, by the glamour of imagination or fancy, Locke was the true representative of his age, and no subsequent change of mental attitude, as the world sweeps on into new and more genial climates of thought, can deprive his work of its representative historical importance. Nor is this all. Locke's treatise was almost the first investigation of the mind which took note of facts, and was not purely metaphysical. It was also the first in which this study took a leading place. 'The science which we now call Psychology, or the study of mind,' says Dr. Fowler, ' had hitherto, amongst modern writers, been almost exclusively subordinated to other branches of speculation. Locke was the first of modern writers to attempt at once an independent and a complete treatment of the phenomena of the human mind, of their mutual relations, of their causes and limits. This task he undertakes, not in the dogmatic spirit of his predecessors, but in the critical spirit which he may be said almost to have inaugurated. And the effect of his candour on his first readers must have been enhanced by the fact, not always favourable to his precision, that, as far as he can, he throws aside the technical terminology of the schools, and employs the language current in the better kinds of ordinary literature and the well-bred society of his time.' In fact, as was said of Socrates, he brought philosophy down from heaven to earth; and this service, and the great influence which his work produced upon the future development of philosophy, are perhaps stronger claims to permanent distinction

M

than the merits of a theory which can never be overlooked, but can never again command the almost universal assent which it received in its own day. For the application of physiology to psychological research, implicitly, at all events, advocated by Locke, has produced results of which neither he nor his opponents dreamed. The central point of his philosophy is the denial of innate ideas; the mind is to him a *tabula rasa*, a sheet of blank paper, and all the ideas which have been thought inherent in it are the result of experience. In a sense we now know this to be true; but we also know this experience not to be the experience of the individual, but of the race, or rather say of sentient existence for ages inconceivably remote. It follows that although Locke may be abstractedly right in denying the possibility of the acquisition of ideas except through experience, yet practically everyone comes into the world with a host of ideas derived from his ancestors, connate if not innate; and that, so far from the human mind resembling a sheet of blank paper, it is more like a palimpsest inscribed and reinscribed *ad infinitum*. It also follows that the discrepancies of mankind respecting points of morality do not, as Locke thought, disprove the existence of an ideal rule of right, for everyone must necessarily be born with inherited instincts by which such a rule is more or less deflected or obscured. In fact, Locke and his adversaries were both partly right and partly wrong—one party in denying intuition, the other in defining it. Neither had found, or at that period could have found, the real key to the difficulty; but it is to the immortal honour of Locke that all real advance in psychology has been effected by working in his spirit of observation and induction, rather than by the *à priori* method of his opponents. The third and fourth books of the essay, *On Words* and *On Knowledge*, contain but little controversial matter, and are chiefly devoted to illustrating the imperfection of human faculties, especially language, the necessity for clear and definite conceptions, and the countless impediments in the way of truth.

Three others among Locke's writings are regarded as classical: *On the Reasonableness of Christianity*, and *On Education*, and his *Letters on Toleration*. The *Reasonableness of Christianity* (1695) is from one point of view an endeavour to render Christianity reasonable by eliminating its corruptions; from another an attempt to establish it on the basis of fulfilled prophecy and miracle. In both respects it was admirably adapted to the prevalent sentiment of Locke's own day, and, although warmly attacked by Stillingfleet, exerted a great influence upon the theology of the eighteenth century. In our time the point of view has shifted so far as to expose Locke to the full weight of Dr. Martineau's terse criticism, 'The affidavit has become the brief.' Its historical importance, however, can never be impaired, any more than that of the admirable *Letters on Toleration*, which seem commonplace because they are now esteemed irrefragable. It was otherwise in his own time, and for long afterwards. Their principal literary defects are that they are too polemical, and too long. Of all Locke's works, *Some Thoughts concerning Education* is perhaps the most universally approved, and it is in truth a golden treatise, the very incarnation of good sense and right feeling; and more useful in its own time than it can be now that the errors which Locke especially assailed have become contrary, instead of congenial, to the general spirit of the age. The prevailing tone, the confidence in human nature rightly treated, the abhorrence of the merely arbitrary and despotic, render the work an epoch in the history of culture, and, compared with the coarse maxims of a Defoe, or even the *Whole Duty of Man's* exclusive reliance upon authority, show how greatly Locke was beyond his contemporaries in enlightenment and the genuine spirit of humanity. The insight and penetration into children's characters are surprising in a man who had no children of his own, or much direct concern with the education of the children of others. They prove that Locke must have been a most careful and accurate observer. If there is a fault in the treatise, it is that the range of view is not always sufficiently wide, and that the author's precepts are too exclusively propounded with reference to the individual, and too little with a view to the general advantage of society. The disuse of Latin composition, for example, would have done little personal harm to the majority of the individual boys of whom Locke is thinking; but, in his day at all events, would have lowered the standard of culture throughout Europe. In general, however, Locke's remarks are characterized by the soundest common sense; and there is perhaps no other production of the age so thoroughly in harmony with its pervading spirit.

In sharp contrast to Locke and his school stand the small knot of Cambridge Platonists and their allies— Cudworth, Henry More, Culverwell, Cumberland, Glanvil, and Whichcote, which last may indeed be regarded as a connecting link between the rival thinkers. His place is rather with the divines, and Henry More (1614-1657) belongs more properly to the period of Vaughan in virtue of his poetry, though continuing to write to a late date. Culverwell and Cumberland scarcely rank in a literary history; so that the school is chiefly represented by Ralph Cudworth (1617-1688). Cudworth's life was uneventful. One of those moderate men whom the excesses of party provoke to opposi-

tion, he sided mainly with the Puritans during the
Civil War, but was no Puritan himself, and protested
energetically against Puritan disparagement of sweetness
and light. He had no difficulty in conforming to the
Restoration, and accepting a living from Archbishop
Sheldon, but his life was mainly spent in his study, in the
production of vast folios, where the ingots of philosophy
lay stored while Locke's current coin passed nimbly from
hand to hand. The contrast between the men and the
systems is complete at every point; and it is assuredly
one of the strangest ironies of fate that Cudworth's
daughter should have become the good angel of Locke's
old age. Cudworth is no doubt by much the more attractive figure to imaginative minds; but it must be conceded
as an indisputable truth that his way of thinking could
not possibly have produced nearly so much good, have so
profoundly leavened men's ideas on legislation and education, or have so contributed to build up the national character for sound common sense. This admitted, Cudworth
may be heartily praised as a sublime and refined thinker,
epithets inappropriate to Locke. His great work is *The
Intellectual System*, published in 1678, only the first part
of which ever appeared. A *Treatise on Immutable Morality*
remained in manuscript until 1731. Cudworth's purpose
may briefly be defined as the expulsion of all materialistic
and mechanical notions from theology, metaphysics, and
ethics. He wages war upon atheism, fatalism, utilita-
rianism, whatsoever is opposed to elevating and poetical
conceptions of the order of things. His erudition is only
too extensive, and he is very candid. Dryden thought
that he had stated the atheistic objections more powerfully than he had answered them; and his doctrine of
plastic force in nature verges upon Pantheism, as indeed
religious philosophies usually do. He is finely analyzed

in the *Types of Ethical Theory* of Dr. Martineau, who says of his philosophy :

> 'Embodied as it is in unfinished books, and buried in massive erudition, it has been distantly respected rather than closely studied; and has left upon few readers an adequate impression of the depth of the author's penetration, the comprehensiveness of his grasp, the subtlety of his analysis, and the happy flashes of expression by which he flings light upon real though unsuspected relations.'

Joseph Glanvil, although an Oxford man, practically belonged to the group of Cambridge Plato-nists, and was especially connected with Henry More. He is the author of two very dissimilar books, *The Vanity of Dogmatizing* (1660), and *Saducismus Triumphatus* (1681), published after his death with additions by More, Horneck, and others. The former book, though containing no evidence of original power of thought, is remarkable as an evidence of the influence of Bacon in overthrowing the authority of Aristotle ; for its idolatry of Descartes; for its many curious anticipations (not originating with Glanvil) of modern discoveries ; above all, for its testimony of the ardent scientific curiosity then fermenting in England, and about to issue in the establishment of the Royal Society. 'Methinks,' Glanvil says, 'this age seems resolved to bequeath posterity something to remember it.' The following is a remarkable passage to have been written six years before Newton's great discovery: 'That heavy bodies descend by gravity, is no better an account than we might expect from a rustic ; and again, that gravity is a quality whereby a heavy body descends, is an imperti-nent circle, and teacheth nothing.' The other and much more celebrated work, on the other hand, is a most melancholy example of superstitious credulity, but full of striking

Joseph Glanvil (1636-1680).

stories of the supernatural. The contrast between the styles of the two books is instructive; the earlier might have been written in the days of James I.; the later, though still antiquated, is much nearer modern English prose.

CHAPTER IX.

THE hinge of the controversies on government which agitated England in the seventeenth century, and produced the great treatises of Locke and Algernon Sidney, was a feeble book by Sir Robert Filmer, a Cavalier, written about the end of the Civil War, but published at a period which brings it within the scope of this volume. Filmer, though not a man of conspicuous mental power, was able to discern that the right of the nation to resist the arbitrary encroachments of Charles I. could not well be disputed so long as it continued to be held that 'Mankind is naturally endowed and born with freedom from all subjection, and at liberty to choose what form of government it please, and that the power which any one man hath over others was at first bestowed according to the discretion of the multitude.' This opinion, which he admits to be that generally held, he endeavours to overthrow by the argument that no man was ever born in a state of freedom, for everyone comes into the world subject to the authority of his parents. 'Not only Adam, but the succeeding patriarchs had, by right of fatherhood, royal authority over their children.' How they came to have royal authority over the children of other patriarchs Filmer does not explain; and it seems obvious on his own showing that either this latter authority does not exist, in which case there must be as many monarchies as families, or that it exists in virtue of a mutual contract among individual families ; so that royal authority derives from the people after all. Illogical, however, as Filmer might be, his views were too agreeable to the Court and to the supporters of absolute power not to find much encouragement, and men of first-rate powers found it necessary to take the field against them. Seldom indeed has a writer of such slender abilities made so much stir, or unintentionally laid the cause of liberty and reason under such deep obligations. As a measure of his own qualifications, it is sufficient to state that he seriously takes Samuel's dissuasion of the Israelites from setting up a monarchy on the ground of the oppressions to which they would subject themselves, for a luminous exposition of the rights of the sovereign and the duties of the subject.

Filmer was answered by three writers of great distinction—Locke, Algernon Sidney, and the Rev. George Johnson, a memorable pamphleteer who scarcely vindicates a place for himself in literature. The merit of their polemic, and the obligation under which it has placed posterity, must of necessity be ill appreciated by an age which finds it difficult to believe that Filmer could ever be thought to require an answer. The propositions that the first man was invested by Heaven with monarchical privileges, and that these privileges had in some manner devolved on King Charles I., seem to us so palpably absurd that Locke himself appears chargeable with folly for having spent his time in refuting them. The steady intellectual upheaval which has been going on ever since the revival of letters has lifted us into a region where the conceptions of divine right and non-resistance cannot live ; and we are inclined to attribute to the improvement of our understandings what really proceeds from the alteration of our environment. Ideas as baseless as Filmer's are now daily advanced, and daily combated by opponents whose services will one day be requited by the neglect that has overtaken Locke. Had Locke been a wit, he might indeed have immortalized himself and his antagonist together; but although he can and does make the latter ridiculous, he cannot make him amusing. There is more vitality in the second of his two *Tracts on Government*, for this in part deals with speculative questions regarding the origin of civil society as yet unsettled, and therefore not as yet commonplace. Locke deduces the mutual relations and obligations of rulers and ruled from a contract which he supposes to have been entered into in the infancy of society. The theory was highly salutary for the age, abolishing all superstitious notions of divine right, and providing sufficient justification for popular resistance to evil rulers. It must be owned, however, that it lacked the only safe basis of theory, the historical ; the constitutions of uncivilized man were little known in Locke's day, and the better known they have become the less affinity they have seemed to present to the parliament which his imagination transported back from Westminster to Shinar. His essay nevertheless represents a necessary phase in the development of opinion, and exerted the most beneficial influence in generating the enlightened political sentiment of the eighteenth century. It is amusing to remark that, in spite of the Israelites, Locke stoutly refuses his imaginary society the right to contract itself out of its freedom by establishing an absolute monarchy, the only form of government which, according to his opponents, could be legitimate in any sense.

Algernon Sidney's *Discourse on Government* has attracted less attention than Locke's, mainly because it claims more. So elaborate and ambitious a work was not required to crush Filmer, who had in fact been crushed by Locke some

years before the appearance of Sidney's belated refutation.
It is nevertheless a more interesting work than Locke's,
partly from the fineness of the style, a noble specimen of
dignified though vehement English prose, partly from the
reflection of the striking personality of the author, 'a
Roman in un-Roman times.' Though a patrician both on
the father's and the mother's side, Sidney was theoretically
a republican. Born in 1622, second son of the Earl of
Leicester, he had served the Commonwealth in the Civil
War, and distinguished himself afterwards by his resistance to what he deemed the usurpation of Cromwell. The
Restoration found him envoy to the northern courts.
Exchanging embassy for exile, he remained abroad until
1677, when he returned under an engagement to live
quietly. Whether he had any actual concern in the Rye
House plot is one of the problems of history; certain it is
that no good evidence was produced, and that he was
iniquitously condemned on the testimony of one witness of
infamous character, and of papers in his handwriting
written years before. These seem to have formed part of
a brief reply to Filmer, never published; the stately work
that has come down to us was written after the publication
of Filmer's manuscript in 1680, and was evidently
prompted by the debates on the Exclusion Bill. The
style precisely corresponds to the author's character,
haughty, fiery, and arrogant; but thrilling with conviction, and meriting the highest praise as a specimen of
masculine, nervous, and at the same time polished English.
Much additional zest is imparted to the author's argument
by his continual strokes at the political abuses and the
unworthy characters of his own day, from Charles II.
downwards. He had the advantage of writing under the
stimulus of fiery indignation kindled and maintained by
the actual existence of a tyranny. He is thus never tame,

and depicts himself as one of that remarkable class of men of whom Alfieri is perhaps the most characteristic type— aristocrats by temperament, champions of democracy by intellectual conviction.[1] Although the controversy in which he engaged now belongs entirely to the past, he is often modern in sentiment as well as in style; sometimes we are reminded of Shelley, at other times, and more frequently, of Landor. It certainly indicates some want of good sense to have written so grandiose a reply to a tract so diminutive in every point of view, and most will be contented with his biographer's, Miss Blackburne's, excellent analysis. As a fine writer, however, Sidney has a right to a place in any collection of Restoration prose:

'No man can be my judge, unless he be my superior; and he cannot be my superior, who is not so by my consent, nor to any other purpose than I consent to. This cannot be the case of a nation, which can have no equal within itself. Controversies may arise with other nations, the decision of which may be left to judges chosen by mutual agreement; but this relates not to our question. A nation, and especially one that is powerful, cannot recede from its own right, as a private man, from the knowledge of his own weakness, and inability to defend himself, must come under the protection of a greater power than his own. The strength of a nation is not in the magistrate, but the strength of the magistrate is in the nation. The wisdom, industry, and valour of a prince may add to the glory and greatness of a nation, but the foundation and substance will always be in itself. If the magistrate and people were upon equal terms, as Caius and Sejus, receiving equal and mutual advantages from each other, no man could be judge of their differences, but such

---

[1] Sidney and his friends are frequently taxed with having accepted money from France. It is worth noting that their conduct in so doing is vindicated by so powerful and, in this instance, so unprejudiced a reasoner as Warburton, in an unpublished letter to Balguy now before us.

as they should set up for that end. This has been done by
many nations. The ancient Germans referred the decision of
the most difficult matters to their priests; the Gauls and Britons
to the Druids; the Mahometans for some ages to the caliphs of
Babylon; the Saxons in England, when they had embraced the
Christian religion, to their clergy. Whilst all Europe lay under
the popish superstition, the decision of such matters was frequently assumed by the pope: men often submitted to his
judgment, and the princes that resisted were for the most part
excommunicated, deposed and destroyed. All this was done for
the same reasons. These men were accounted holy and inspired,
and the sentence pronounced by them was usually reverenced as
the judgment of God, who was thought to direct them; and all
those who refused to submit were esteemed execrable. But no
man or number of men, as I think, at the institution of a magistrate, did ever say, if any difference happen between you or
your successors and us, it shall be determined by yourself, or by
them, whether they be men, women, children, mad, foolish, or
vicious. Nay, if any such thing had been, the folly, turpitude,
and madness of such a sanction or stipulation must necessarily
have destroyed it. But if no such thing was ever known, or
could have no effect, if it had been in any place, it is most
absurd to impose it upon all. The people therefore cannot be
deprived of their natural rights upon a frivolous pretence to
that which never was, and never can be. They who create
magistracies, and give to them such name, form, and power, as
they think fit, do only know, whether the end for which they
were created be performed or not. They who give a being to
the power which had none can only judge, whether it be employed to their welfare, or turned to their ruin. They do not
set up one or a few men, that they and their posterity may live
in splendour and greatness, but that justice may be administered,
virtue established, and provision made for the public safety.
No wise man will think this can be done, if those who set themselves to overthrow the law are to be their own judges.'

Sir William Temple, in an essay on government written
in 1672, arrives at substantially the same conclusion as
Sidney by a different path. Fletcher of Saltoun, the illus-

trious Scottish patriot, wrote *An Account of a Conversation for a right Regulation of Governments* (1704).

The development of the English periodical press during the Restoration epoch is a matter of such moment that the two men principally connected with it cannot be left unnoticed, although, at least in one instance, their claim to rank as men of letters is very slender. Marchamont Needham (1620-1678) had scarcely any other character than that of a pamphleteer who only escaped the designation of hired scribbler by his political infidelities and a certain rough effectiveness in his ephemeral writings. This 'most seditious, mutable, and railing author's' position in the history of the press is nevertheless important; for if not the first strictly professional journalist, he is the first whose name has descended to posterity. Having from 1641 to 1647 made war against the king in his *Mercurius Britannicus,* he changed sides and wrote as a royalist in *Mercurius Pragmaticus,* recanted again and supported Cromwell as the conductor of *Mercurius Politicus;* and, after a short exile, ultimately made his peace with the Restoration. He had already excited the animosity of the stricter Puritans, one of whom thus anticipated and refuted the best plea that could be made for him: 'He is a man of parts, and hath a notable vein of writing. Doubtless so hath the Devil; must therefore the Devil be made use of?' He subsequently made war upon schoolmasters and physicians, and died suddenly as he was about returning to his old trade of political pamphleteer. Roger L'Estrange (1616-1704) was a man of much higher character, being a consistent royalist. His connection with the periodical press in Charles II.'s day was brief, lasting only from 1663 to 1666, when his *Intelligencer* and *News* were extinguished by the appearance of an official journal, the *Oxford,* afterwards the *London Gazette.* But he has a permanent place in history as the first 'able editor,' who not only made his journal the vehicle for political discussions, and availed himself of regular news-letters, but employed a regular staff of assistants to collect news. He was no friend to his own trade, for he says in a prospectus: 'Supposing the press in order, the people in their right wits, and news or no news to be the question, a public Mercury should never have my vote, because I think it makes the multitude too familiar with the actions and counsels of their superiors, too pragmatical and censorious, and gives them not only a wish but a kind of colourable right and licence to the meddling with the government.' A man who thought thus must have seemed admirably qualified for the office of licenser of the press, which he held from 1663 to the Revolution, and in the discharge of which he inevitably accumulated the odium which even now somewhat undeservedly rests upon his memory. In 1681 he returned to newspaper editing, and successfully carried on *Heraclitus Ridens* and *The Observator* until March, 1687, when James II., who was enacting liberty of conscience to serve his own ends, silenced the old Cavalier just as the latter was demonstrating this liberty to be 'a paradox against law, reason, nature, and religion.' L'Estrange's prose style is bad, but he was the author of several useful translations, of which those from Æsop, Josephus, Quevedo, and Erasmus are the best known. He was a courtly and well-bred man, of considerable culture, and would be mentioned with more respect if he had not exercised a function detestable to the entire republic of letters. Dr. Johnson regarded him as the first writer upon record who regularly enlisted himself under the banners of a party for pay, and fought for it through right and wrong. This is probably correct as a mere statement of fact, but unjust if it was intended to imply any doubt of the purity of

L'Estrange's motives in serving the high monarchical party, or of the sincerity of his advocacy of its principles.

The *Political Arithmetic* of Sir William Petty (1623-1687), and the *Discourse of Trade* of Sir Josiah Child (1630-1699), take high rank among economic publications, but can scarcely be regarded as literature.

CHAPTER X.

HISTORY is one of the departments of literature in which it is easiest to approach the unsurpassable perfection of antiquity. Poets must in general be accepted as inspiring influences rather than as models; but the methods of historians may be studied and even copied without undue servility. This was soon perceived by the Latin races, and by the middle of the seventeenth century the vernacular literatures of Italy, Spain, and Portugal possessed many truly classical historians. It is difficult to understand why England should have been so backward. The Restoration found its historical literature in an intermediate stage, half way between the artless old chroniclers and the consummate examples of historical style and construction which the next century was to produce. It left historical composition, however, much more advanced than it had found it. The chief history of the age, though far from perfect, at all events was a history and not a chronicle. Clarendon's great work, it is true, belongs to the preceding generation in everything but the date of its composition; and will, accordingly, be found to be treated in a previous section of this history. His successor, Burnet, on the other hand, was in literary matters a perfect representative of his own day, a man of his times;

N

and their works taken together, while illustrating the mutations of taste and the gradual popularization of culture, may be regarded as the Iliad and Odyssey of the period, the former a high epical treatment of a tragic theme, decreed by the Fates and directed by the Gods; the second a bustling tragi-comedy true to human nature and crowded with domestic incident. The writers, moreover, have these things in common: that both are men of original and marked character, whose personality is vividly embodied in their productions; that both had been busy actors in many of the events which they detail; that both, therefore, had unusual means of information, and the narrative of neither could miss the liveliness imparted by actual contact with the transactions they relate. Both were inevitably prejudiced, but both were high-minded and conscientious; and the bias against which they vainly contended is too visible and too much a matter of course to detract seriously from the value of their histories.

Gilbert Burnet, Bishop of Salisbury, was born at Edinburgh, September 18th, 1643. By the wish of his father he selected the Church as his profession, which placed him in the invidious position of an Episcopalian ministering amid a nation of Presbyterians. His moderation, nevertheless, gained the confidence of the dissidents, and his great influence with Lauderdale, the ruler of Scotland, was exerted in favour of the most conciliatory measures and the widest toleration possible. When at length Lauderdale had become hopelessly committed to a violent course, Burnet withdrew from Scotland, and settled in London as preacher at the Rolls and at St. Clement Danes. During Charles's reign, though an object of great suspicion to the court, he maintained his ground, but at the accession of James found it expedient to go abroad. After travelling in France, and proceeding as far as Rome, he settled in Holland, returning with William III. in 1688. William's proclamation was drafted by him, and he drew up the engagement signed by the nobility who joined the prince.   These and many other services were rewarded by the bishopric of Salisbury, where, by the confession of his adversaries, he proved as charitable and exemplary a prelate as the Church had ever seen.   He is especially memorable in this capacity as the author of the scheme for the augmentation of poor livings commonly known as Queen Anne's Bounty.   He died in 1715.   His moral character was of the highest; his intellectual character was disfigured by some foibles, unimportant in themselves, but which, not being of the kind usually found in conjunction with first-rate abilities, have occasioned his powers to be considerably under-valued.   The man, however, who was respected by the cynical Charles and trusted by the jealous William, cannot have been of ordinary mould; nor can it be said of many authors that they have produced three books which, after the lapse of two centuries, are still regarded as standard authorities.   The *History of the Reformation* was published in 1679-1714; the *Exposition of the Articles* in 1699; the *History of his Own Times* in 1723-34.

Burnet's *History of his Own Times* actually deserves the character which Clarendon incorrectly gives of his own; it is rather the material for history than history itself.   This is not a consequence of crude treatment, for all is well arranged and lively, nor from the encumbrance of original documents, of which it is nearly destitute.   It arises rather from the predominance of the autobiographic tone, much more marked than in Clarendon, though Clarendon also relates as an eyewitness, which almost brings the book down to the level of personal memoirs.   It must neverthe-

less be classed with histories, and, if not one of the most
dignified, it is undoubtedly one of the most entertaining.
Burnet's deep interest in the events in which he had taken
so large a share insures vivacious and effective treatment;
his personages breathe and move, and impress themselves
indelibly upon the reader's imagination, though he usually
abstains from set efforts at the depicting of character. The
defects of his method are no less apparent; in relating
what he has not himself heard or seen, he relies upon
hearsay, and sinks into a gossip. The extent, nevertheless,
to which he speaks as an eyewitness, renders his work
very valuable. Well acquainted with Charles and James,
admitted to the favour of William and the full confidence
of Mary, he is able to introduce us into their presence, and
summon them as it were from the dead. His point of
view, being so largely personal, is inevitably partial; he
can tell us, for example, of the defects in Shaftesbury's
character, which he discovered from actual acquaintance,
but nothing of the surprising enlightenment of the statesman, which could only be learned from speeches which he
never heard and documents which he never saw. Impartiality is the last virtue to be expected from a busy actor
in a troubled age, but Burnet approaches it as nearly as
can with any reason be demanded. It is hardly in human
nature that he should be entirely fair to adversaries by
whom he had himself been maligned, but his intention of
being so is very apparent. The most impartial and generally the most valuable portion of his work is his narrative
up to the Revolution. When he wrote this, animosities
had become mellowed by time; when he lived it his contact
with affairs had been more intimate as the political agent
than afterwards as the spiritual peer. Disappointment
with the course of events colours his account of Anne's
reign, and renders him splenetic and querulous. His per-

picuous and animated diction does not always attain the
dignity of history; he hardly ever attempts eloquence,
except in the noble and deeply-felt conclusion of his work,
a portion of which must be cited, although it is no fair
example of his ordinary style:

'So that by religion I mean, such a sense of divine truth as
enters into a man, and becomes a spring of a new nature within
him; reforming his thoughts and designs, purifying his heart,
and sanctifying him, and governing his whole deportment, his
words as well as his actions; convincing him that it is not enough,
not to be scandalously vicious, or to be innocent in his conversation, but that he must be entirely, uniformly, and constantly,
pure and virtuous, animating him with a zeal to be still better
and better, more eminently good and exemplary, using prayers
and all outward devotions, as solemn acts testifying what he is
inwardly and at heart, and as methods instituted by God, to be
still advancing in the use of them further and further into a more
refined and spiritual sense of divine matters. This is true
religion, which is the perfection of human nature, and the joy
and delight of every one that feels it active and strong within
him: it is true, this is not arrived at all at once; and it will have
an unhappy alloy, hanging long even about a good man; but, as
those ill mixtures are the perpetual grief of his soul, so it is his
chief care to watch over and to mortify them; he will be in a
continual progress, still gaining ground upon himself; and as he
attains to a good degree of purity, he will find a noble flame of
life and joy growing upon him. Of this I write with the more
concern and emotion, because I have felt this the true, and indeed
the only joy which runs through a man's heart and life: it is
that which has been for many years my greatest support; I
rejoice daily in it: I feel from it the earnest of that supreme joy
which I pant and long for; I am sure there is nothing else can
afford any true or complete happiness. I have, considering my
sphere, seen a great deal of all that is most shining and tempting
in this world: the pleasures of sense I did soon nauseate;
intrigues of state, and the conduct of affairs, have something in
them that is most specious; and I was for some years, deeply
immersed in these, but still with hopes of reforming the world,

and of making mankind wiser and better: but I have found that which is crooked cannot be made straight. I acquainted myself with knowledge and learning, and that in a great variety, and with more compass than depth: but though wisdom excelleth folly as much as light does darkness, yet as it is a sore travail, so it is so very defective, that what is wanting to complete it cannot be numbered. I have seen that two were better than one, and that a threefold cord is not easily loosed; and have therefore cultivated friendship with much zeal and a disinterested tenderness; but I have found this was also vanity and vexation of spirit, though it be of the best and noblest sort. So that, upon great and long experience, I could enlarge on the preacher's text, "Vanity of vanities, and all is vanity," but I must also conclude with him; Fear God, and keep his commandments, for this is the all of man, the whole, both of his duty and of his happiness. I do therefore end all in the words of David, of the truth of which, upon great experience and a long observation, I am so fully assured, that I leave these as my last words to posterity: " Come, ye children, hearken unto me: I will teach you the fear of the Lord. What man is he that desireth life, and loveth many days, that he may see good? Keep thy tongue from evil, and thy lips from speaking guile. Depart from evil, and do good; seek peace, and pursue it. The eyes of the Lord are upon the righteous, and his ears are open to their cry; but the face of the Lord is against them that do evil, to cut off the remembrance of them from the earth. The righteous cry, and the Lord heareth and delivereth them out of all their troubles. The Lord is nigh unto them that are of a broken heart, and saveth such as be of a contrite spirit." '

Burnet's reputation as an historian also rests in considerable measure upon another important work, his *History of the Reformation in England*, published in 1679. This great subject, frequently, variously, and never successfully handled, may some day make a first-class reputation for an historian as yet concealed in the future. That a satisfactory history of it should be written in Burnet's day was impossible, and it was equally impossible that his

work should either exhibit the liveliness, or possess the
unique value of his *History of his Own Times*. The theme
is one for a graver and more eloquent historian than he,
capable of rising to greater heights, and wielding far more
absolute command over the resources of language. Nor
can his laborious collections from state papers and former
historians rival the importance of his narrative of transactions in which he was a busy actor, full of particulars
only to be obtained from himself. With all these inevitable imperfections, his *History of the Reformation* is still
an excellent book, eminently readable, just and accurate in
its broad views, however needing correction on points of
detail; and, considering that it was the work of a Scotch
Protestant writing in the thick of the Popish Plot, surprisingly candid and impartial. It is of course the work
of a partisan, but he who does not feel sufficient interest
in the Reformation to be a partisan on one side or the
other is not likely to write its history at all, and had
better not. Probably no history of the English Reformation has since been written that does not exhibit more
party feeling than Burnet's, or that can reasonably claim
to supersede it.

Burnet's *History of his Times*, as we have seen, may be
regarded as a connecting link between history and *mémoires
pour servir*. The age of Charles II. was favourable to this
latter class of composition, which is, indeed, the form
which the narrators of public transactions in which they
themselves have borne a leading part, naturally fall. The
period was still more fertile in the diary, which may be
defined as the autobiographic memoir in a rudimentary
stage. One writer of the day, Samuel Pepys, has placed
himself for all time at the head of this class of composition, by an achievement little likely to be repeated.
Among memoir-writers proper the most important is

Edmund Ludlow, the Cato of the Commonwealth (1617-1692).

Ludlow, the son of a Wiltshire knight of extreme political views, enlisted at the commencement of the Civil War in the bodyguard of the Earl of Essex, and afterwards highly distinguished himself by his obstinate, though unsuccessful defence of Wardour Castle, in his native county. He was made prisoner, exchanged, and took part in several encounters in the West of England. Elected member for Wiltshire, he sided with the more extreme party, and was one of the king's judges. He became a member of the Council of State, and at the beginning of 1651 was sent to Ireland as second in authority to Ireton, whom he assisted in completing the subjugation of the country, and subsequently filled the same position under Fleetwood. Bitterly opposed to Cromwell's Protectorate, he resigned his civil appointment, but contrived to retain his military position until 1655, when, coming over to England, he was arrested and imprisoned in Beaumaris Castle. When at length he was admitted to an audience of Cromwell, 'What,' asked the Protector, 'can you desire more than you have?' 'That which we fought for,' replied Ludlow, 'that the nation might be governed by its own consent'—words which recall Augereau's repartee to Napoleon on the re-establishment of Roman Catholicism in France. Ludlow was kept under surveillance until the death of Cromwell, when he became exceedingly active, and upon the abdication of Richard Cromwell was sent again to Ireland in a position of authority. Returning, he sought in vain to mediate between the Parliament and the army, and distinguished himself in the Convention Parliament by a vain protest against the Restoration. He fled the country to avoid the vengeance of the new government, and took refuge in Switzerland, where he composed his memoirs, and abode in comfortable circumstances, although occasionally molested by plots against his life or liberty, until his death in 1692. The Revolution of 1688 had brought him back to England for an instant, but the public feeling against regicides was still too strong, and, returning to his refuge at Vevay, he carved over his door :

'Omne solum forti patria quia Patris.'

Ludlow was not one of the greatest or wisest characters of his time, but is one of the most estimable in virtue of his sturdy honesty. He was one of that hopelessly inconsistent class of persons, the believers in the divine right of a republic as the sole form of political institution consistent with reason, who in the same breath assert and take away the nation's right to choose its own form of government by forbidding its exercise unless the form has the allowance of a theory impersonated in themselves. On the principle of popular sovereignty, no form of government could be more legitimate than the Restoration monarchy, which, nevertheless, Ludlow was always seeking to overthrow. Cromwell's title was by no means so clear, and Ludlow's firm resistance to the Protector at the height of his power, if proving his inability to ' swallow formulas,' and look solely to the public good, is nevertheless most honourable to his courage and fortitude. If inaccessible to reason, he was even more so to self-interest. The historical value of his memoirs is very great, especially for the troubled interval between Cromwell's death and the Restoration. Carlyle, Guizot, and Firth unite in following him with implicit confidence when he speaks as an eyewitness, when he relies upon others he is frequently inaccurate and confused. The *Memoirs* virtually commence with the outbreak of the Civil War, and extend to 1672. The interest of the latter years is of course mainly personal. The style is clear and unadorned. The following passage is a good example of the writer's power of conveying antipathy by sarcasm:

'Different were the effects that the death of Cromwell produced in the nation: those men who had been sharers with him in the usurped authority were exceedingly troubled, whilst all other parties rejoiced at it: each of them hoping that this alteration would prove advantageous to their affairs. The Commonwealthsmen were so charitable to believe that the soldiery being delivered from their servitude to the General, to which they were willing to attribute their former compliance, would now open their eyes and join with them, as the only means left to preserve themselves and the people. Neither were the Cavaliers without great hopes that new divisions might arise, and give them an opportunity of advancing their minion, who had been long endeavouring to unite all the corrupt interests of the nation to his party. But neither the sense of their duty, nor the care of their own safety, nor the just apprehensions of being overcome by their irreconcilable enemy, could prevail with the army to return to their proper station. So that having tasted of sovereignty under the shadow of their late master, they resolved against the restitution of the Parliament. And in order to this it was agreed to proclaim Richard Cromwell, eldest son of Oliver, Protector of the Commonwealth, in hopes that he, who by following his pleasures had rendered himself unfit for public business, would not fail to place the administration of the government in the hands of those who were most powerful in the army. Accordingly the proclamation was published in Westminster, at Temple-Bar, and at the Old Exchange, with as few expressions of joy as had ever been observed on the like occasion. This being done, the Council issued out orders to the officers of civil justice to act by virtue of their old commissions till new ones could be sent to them: and that nothing might be omitted to fortify the new government, various means were used·to procure addresses from all parts, which were brought in great numbers from the several counties in England, Scotland, and Ireland, as also from divers regiments of the army. One of the first acts of the new government was, to

order the funeral of the late usurper; and the Council having
resolved that it should be very magnificent, the care of it was referred to a committee of them, who sending for Mr. Kinnersley,
master of the wardrobe, desired him to find out some precedent,
by which they might govern themselves in this important affair.
After examination of his books and papers, Mr. Kinnersley, who
was suspected to be inclined to popery, recommended to them the
solemnities used upon the like occasion for Philip the Second,
king of Spain, who had been represented to be in purgatory for
about two months.   In the like manner was the body of this great
reformer laid in Somerset House: the apartment was hung with
black, the daylight was excluded, and no other but that of wax
tapers to be seen.   This scene of purgatory continued till the
first of November, which being the day preceding that commonly
called All Souls, he was removed into the great hall of the said
house, and represented in effigy, standing on a bed of crimson
velvet covered with a gown of the like coloured velvet, a sceptre
in his hand, and a crown on his head.   That part of the hall
wherein the bed stood was railed in, and the rails and ground
within them covered with crimson velvet.   Four or five hundred
candles set in flat shining candlesticks were so placed round near
the roof of the hall, that the light they gave seemed like the rays
of the sun: by all which he was represented to be now in a state
of glory.   This folly and profusion so far provoked the people,
that they threw dirt in the night on his escutcheon that was placed
over the great gate of Somerset House.   I purposely omit the
rest of the pageantry, the great number of persons that attended
on the body, the procession to Westminster, the vast expense in
mourning, the state and magnificence of the monument erected
for him, with many other things that I care not to remember.'

William Lilly, the astrologer (1602-1682), to be discussed more fully among the writers of personal memoirs,
claims a few words here as the author of an account of
Charles I. whose justice and liveliness would have met
more general recognition, but for the author's character
as a fortune-teller, and if it had not been mingled
with the apparently serious exposition of idle prophecies

respecting the White King.   So long as he keeps clear of
the occult, Lilly is a shrewd and discriminating, as well as
a highly entertaining writer.   His enumeration of individual traits in Charles's character is correct and instructive, and free from any misleading bias.   He was in fact
a time-server, whose main purpose was to stand well with
the powers that were, and whose sketch of Charles would
have worn another aspect if he had written after the
Restoration; but this frame of mind, at all events,
exempts him from political passion, nor does his complacency carry him to the length of misrepresentation,
much less calumny.   He is destitute of the literary power
which would have enabled him to fuse single traits into
an harmonious character; but he has supplied others with
very valuable material towards such an undertaking.   One
merit the book certainly possesses in an eminent measure,
it is one of the most readable in the language.   The following passage indicates the author's real insight into
Charles's attractive, but infirm character; and, adversary
as he is, his remarkable agreement with Clarendon, of
whose work he had no knowledge :

'He had much of self-ends in all that he did, and a most difficult thing it was to hold him close to his own promise or word:
he was apt to recede, unless something therein appeared com-
pliable, either unto his own will, profit, or judgment; so that
some foreign princes bestowed on him the character of a most
false prince, and one that never kept his word, unless for his own
advantage.   Had his judgment been as sound, as his conception was quick and nimble, he had been a most accomplished
gentleman: and though in most dangerous results, and extraordinary serious consultations, and very material, either for state or
commonwealth, he would himself give the most solid advice, and
sound reasons, why such or such a thing should be so, or not so ;
yet was he most easily withdrawn from his own most wholesome
and sound advice or resolutions ; and with as much facility drawn

on, inclined, to embrace a far more unsafe, and nothing so wholesome a counsel.   He would argue logically, and frame his arguments artificially ; yet never almost had the happiness to conclude
or drive on a design in his own sense, but was ever baffled with
meaner capacities.   He feared nothing in this world, or disdained
any thing more than the convention of a Parliament ; the very
name was a bugbear unto him.   He was ever refractory against
the summoning of a Parliament, and as willingly would embrace
an opportunity to break it off.   This his averseness being well
known to some grave members, they contrived at last by wit, and
the necessity of the times, that his hands were fast tied up
in granting a triennial sitting, or a perpetuity as it were unto this
present Parliament, a thing he often blamed himself for subscrib-
ing unto, and as often those who importuned him thereunto.'

Bulstrode Whitelocke (1605-1676) has few pretensions
to rank as a man of letters ; but his *Memorials* are far too
valuable a source of historical information to be omitted
from a survey of the literature of the period.   The author,
a barrister and a Templar, was elected to the Long Parliament in 1641, and appointed chairman of the committee
for drawing up the charges against Strafford.   He held
various offices under the Parliament, and was employed in
negotiations with Charles, of whose execution he disap-
proved.   He was subsequently a member of the Council of
State, and one of the commissioners of the Great Seal.   In
1653 he was sent on an embassy to Sweden, which he has
described in a valuable work.   During the confused period
between the death of Cromwell and the Restoration he
was successively a commissioner of the Great Seal and a
member of the Council of State.   He had some difficulty
in obtaining pardon at the Restoration ; but ultimately
Charles II. admitted him to his presence, and received
him graciously, with a speech which Whitelocke's biographer thinks extraordinary, but which appears very sensible : ' Mr. Whitelocke, go into the country ; don't trouble

yourself any more about state affairs; and take care of your wife and your sixteen children.' Whitelocke profited by the royal admonition, and died at a good old age. His *Memorials* extend from 1625 to 1659, and are a valuable body of material, being for most of the time a diurnal record of all occurrences of importance. They are the student of history's indispensable companion for the period, but aim at no more exalted position in literature than that of a matter-of-fact register.

Another diarist of a similar description to Whitelocke, but not, like him, a busy actor in the scenes which he describes, is Narcissus Luttrell (1657-1732), a scion of the well-known family of Luttrell of Dunster, Somersetshire. Luttrell, who was a man of literary and antiquarian tastes, and the collector of the Luttrell Ballads, now in the British Museum, kept a diary from 1675 to 1714, which attracted little attention until Macaulay's frequent references to the MS. induced the University of Oxford to publish it in 1857.

Leaving diarists out of account, the most important writer of historical memoirs after Ludlow is Sir William Temple (1628-1699), whose memoirs treat of his own political career from 1672 to 1680. Temple, the son of an Irish judge, entered the diplomatic service after the Restoration under the auspices of Arlington, and soon found himself minister at Brussels. While occupying that post it was his good fortune to perform one of the most creditable diplomatic achievements on record, the negotiation of the triple alliance between England, Holland, and Sweden, which checked the conquests of Louis XIV., and, but for the venality and faithlessness of Charles II., would have long secured peace to Europe. When Temple's work was undone he retired into private life, but the failure of Charles's disgraceful policy brought him again into diplomacy, and his memoirs down to 1679 are occupied with foreign affairs. In 1677 he had rendered his country one of the greatest services that any man ever did, by bringing about, in conjunction with Danby, the marriage of William of Orange with the Princess Mary; and in 1679 he found himself, to his discomfort and dismay—for if wise as a serpent he was timid as a dove—charged with the mission of reconciling king and people, who, from the discovery of Charles's baseness in accepting a pension from France, seemed on the verge of entire estrangement. Temple attempted to attain this end by the creation of a council of thirty advisers, as a perpetual check upon the king's actions. The scheme might have succeeded if thirty disinterested politicians had been forthcoming; but the entire kingdom could barely have furnished the number requisite for the redemption of Sodom. Temple's memoirs give a lively picture of the mortifications he underwent as he gradually dwindled into a cipher; but the modern reader will prefer to study the story in Macaulay's famous essay, which, if exaggerated in his expression of scorn for Temple's irresolution, is not unfair as a statement of fact. At length he escaped to his books and gardens, and spent the rest of his life in the enjoyment of a character for consummate statesmanship, which he took care never to bring to the test. Wisdom and virtue he certainly did possess, but both with him were too much of the self-regarding order. His claims to rank as a restorer of English prose are better founded, though these, too, have been exaggerated. Johnson's assertion that Temple was the first writer who attended to cadence in English prose merely evinces how completely the power of appreciating the grand harmonies of the Elizabethan period had died out in the eighteenth century. He must, notwithstanding, be allowed an honourable place among those who have rendered English prose lucid, symmetrical, and adapted for business; and Macaulay has justly pointed out that the apparent length of his sentences is mainly a matter of punctuation. The elegance of the writer, and the egotistic caution of the man, are excellently represented by the concluding passage of his *Memoirs :*

'Upon the survey of all these circumstances, conjunctions, and dispositions, both at home and abroad, I concluded in cold blood, that I could be of no further use or service to the king my master, and my country, whose true interests I always thought were the same, and would be both in danger when they came to be divided, and for that reason had ever endeavoured the uniting them; and had compassed it, if the passions of some few men had not lain fatally in the way, so as to raise difficulties that I saw plainly were never to be surmounted. Therefore, upon the whole, I took that firm resolution, in the end of the year 1680, and the interval between the Westminster and Oxford parliaments, never to charge myself more with any public employments; but retiring wholly to a private life, in that posture take my fortune with my country, whatever it should prove: which as no man can judge, in the variety of accidents that attend human affairs, and the chances of every day, to which the greatest lives as well as actions are subject; so I shall not trouble myself so much as to conjecture: *fata viam invenient.*

'Besides all these public circumstances, I considered myself in my own humour, temper, and dispositions, which a man may disguise to others, though very hardly, but cannot to himself. I had learned by living long in courts and public affairs, that I was fit to live no longer in either. I found the arts of a court were contrary to the frankness and openness of my nature; and the constraints of public business too great for the liberty of my humour and my life. The common and proper ends of both are the advancement of men's fortunes; and that I never minded, having as much as I needed, and, which is more, as I desired. The talent of gaining riches I ever despised, as observing it to belong to the most despisable men in other kinds: and I had the occasions of it so often in my way, if I would have made use

of them, that I grew to disdain them, as a man does meat that
he has always before him.   Therefore, I never could go to
service for nothing but wages, nor endure to be fettered in
business when I thought it was to no purpose.   I knew very
well the arts of a court are, to talk the present language, to
serve the present turn, and to follow the present humour of the
prince, whatever it is : of all these I found myself so incapable,
that I could not talk a language I did not mean, nor serve a turn
I did not like, nor follow any man's humour wholly against my
own.   Besides, I have had, in twenty years experience, enough
of the uncertainty of princes, the caprices of fortune, the corruption of ministers, the violence of factions, the unsteadiness
of counsels, the infidelity of friends ; nor do I think the rest of
my life enough to make any new experiments.

'For the ease of my own life, if I know myself, it will be
infinitely more in the retired, than it has been in the busy scene :
for no good man can, with any satisfaction, take part in the
divisions of his country, that knows and considers, as I do, what
they have cost Athens, Rome, Constantinople, Florence, Germany, France and England : nor can the wisest man foresee how
ours will end, or what they are like to cost the rest of Christen-
dom as well as ourselves.   I never had but two aims in public
affairs ; one, to see the king great as he may be by the hearts of
his people, without which I know not how he can be great by
the constitutions of this kingdom : the other, in case our factions
must last, yet to see a revenue established for the constant
maintaining a fleet of fifty men of war, at sea or in harbour, and
the seamen in constant pay ; which would be at least our safety
from abroad, and make the crown still considered in any foreign
alliances, whether the king and his parliaments should agree or
not in undertaking any great or national war.   And such an
establishment I was in hopes the last parliament at Westminster
might have agreed in with the king, by adding so much of a new
fund to three hundred thousand pounds a year out of the present
customs.   But these have both failed, and I am content to have
failed with them.

'And so I take leave of all those airy visions which have so
long busied my head about mending the world ; and at the same
time, of all those shining toys or follies that employ the thoughts

of busy men : and shall turn mine wholly to mend myself; and, as far as consists with a private condition, still pursuing that old and excellent counsel of Pythagoras, that we are, with all the cares and endeavours of our lives, to avoid diseases in the body, perturbations in the mind, luxury in diet, factions in the house, and seditions in the state.'

CHAPTER XI.

Two private diarists, whose autobiographic records remained unknown to their contemporaries, have justly obtained classic rank by the publication of their records in the nineteenth century. One of these, Samuel Pepys, stands incontestably at the head of the world's literature in his own department. John Evelyn, possessing neither the humour, the *naïveté*, the shrewdness, or the uncompromising frankness of his rival and friend, occupies a much lower place as an autobiographer, though more highly endowed as a scholar and a man of letters. Born in 1620 of a prosperous county family, whose fortune had been made by the manufacture of gunpowder, he found himself an idle young Templar at the outbreak of the Civil War. Three days' service in the royal army sufficed him, and in 1643 he obtained the king's permission to travel. This does not seem very heroic conduct, but the family estate, lying at Wotton, near Dorking, was probably in the actual occupation of the Parliamentarians. He remained abroad until 1647, and his notes on art and antiquity are among the most valuable portions of his diary. Study and gardening were his chief occupations under the Commonwealth, varied with some cautious intriguing on behalf of the exiled king. Under the Restoration he was in great favour, and, although taking no part in politics,

filled several honourable public offices. A sincere Churchman, he was greatly alarmed by James II.'s illegalities,
and acquiesced in the Revolution as a necessary evil. In
1695 he was appointed treasurer to Greenwich Hospital.
He died in 1706. The general view of his character is
that expressed by Mr. Leslie Stephen, who describes him
as ' the typical instance of the accomplished and public-
spirited gentleman of the Restoration.' The chief dissen-
tient from this favourable estimate is a person of weight,
De Quincey, who, in a conversation with Woodhouse,
violently attacks Evelyn's *Diary*, three years after its publication, as ' a weak, good-for-nothing little book, much
praised by weak people,' and abuses the author as ' a
shallow, empty, cowardly, vain, assuming coxcomb,' ' a
mere literary fribble, a fop, and a smatterer affecting
natural history and polite learning.' There is just this
much of truth in this splenetic onslaught, that Evelyn
was an amateur in authorship, and that his high character
and influential friendships no doubt contributed much to
the esteem with which the works published in his lifetime
were regarded in his day. The *Diary* stands on a different
footing; it appealed to a remote and impartial public, and
the appeal has been justified by edition after edition.

Evelyn's claims to literary distinction rest principally
upon his *Diary* and his *Sylva*, which will be noticed in
another place. The chief literary merits of the *Diary* are
its unassuming simplicity and perfect perspicuity of style
and phrase. Infinitely less interesting than Pepys's, it
has the advantage of covering a much more extensive
period, and faithfully reflecting the feelings of a loyal,
pious, sensible Englishman at various important crises of
public affairs. Unlike Pepys, whose estimates of men and
things are very fluctuating, Evelyn is consistent, and we
may feel sure that any modification of sentiment that may

be observed in him faithfully represents the inevitable influence of circumstances upon a man of independent judgment. His personal loyalty to the house of Stuart is manifestly cooled, though not chilled, by the scandals of Charles II.'s reign ; but it is not until Church and King come into open conflict in the reign of James II. that Evelyn gives any countenance to a violent change of government, which it is clear he would most willingly have avoided. The extreme caution and moderation of his language lend weight to his disapprobation, and indicate more forcibly than any vigour of declamation how completely James had alienated his true friends. Evelyn's position was that of one who could neither lift a hand against the Government or stretch one out to defend it. His unaffected style almost rises into poetry as he succinctly enumerates the omens which heralded the downfall of James :

' *October* 14. The King's birthday. No guns from the Tower as usual. The sun eclipsed at its rising. This day signal for the victory of William the Conqueror against Harold, near Battel, in Sussex. The wind, which had been hitherto west, was east all this day. Wonderful expectation of the Dutch fleet. Public prayers ordered to be read in the churches against invasion.'

The interest of the early part of the *Diary* is of a different kind. It is occupied with the author's continental travels, and shows what was thought best worth seeing in that age, with many curious incidental traits of manners, and examples of the hardships and perils with which wayfarers were then beset. As always, we have to lament that the traveller was in that day so much of a mere sightseer, and took so little pains to acquaint himself with the moral, intellectual, or industrial life of the

nations he visited. This was the universal failing of the
age, and of all preceding ages; not until the eighteenth
century do we meet with a really philosophical traveller.
Evelyn, however, is not insensible to humanity when it is
thrust upon his attention; and his study of painting in
his youth, and the taste for arboriculture which produced
his *Sylva*, qualify him beyond most of his contemporaries
for the description of the aspects of nature. The feeling
for nature and the feeling for humanity are well combined
in the following passage :

'We went then to visit the galleys, being about twenty-five in
number; the Capitaine of the Galley Royal gave us most
courteous entertainment in his cabin, the slaves in the interim
playing both loud and soft music very rarely. Then he showed
how he commanded their motions with a nod, and his whistle
making them row out. The spectacle was to me new and
strange, to see so many hundreds of miserably naked persons,
their heads being shaven close and having only high red bonnets,
a pair of coarse canvass drawers, their whole backs and legs
naked, doubly chained about their middle and legs, in couples,
and made fast to their seats, and all commanded in a trice by an
imperious and cruel seaman. One Turk amongst the rest he
much favoured, who waited on him in his cabin, but with no
other dress than the rest, and a chain locked about his leg, but
not coupled. This galley was richly carved and gilded, and most
of the rest were very beautiful. After bestowing something on
the slaves, the capitaine sent a band of them to give us music at
dinner where we lodged. I was amazed to contemplate how
these miserable caitiffs lie in their galley crowded together; yet
there was hardly one but had some occupation, by which, as
leisure and calms permitted, they got some little money, insomuch as some of them have, after many years cruel servitude,
been able to purchase their liberty. The rising-forward and
falling-back at their oar, is a miserable spectacle, and the noise
of their chains, with the roaring of the beaten waters, has something of strange and fearful in it to one unaccustomed to it.
They are ruled and chastised by strokes on their backs and

soles of their feet, on the least disorder, and without the least
humanity, yet are they cheerful and full of knavery.'

Evelyn's *Diary*, however, with all its desert, sinks into
insignificance beside the *Diary* of Samuel Pepys, but the
same remark applies to almost every diary in the world.
Pepys's *Diary* has been frequently compared with Boswell's
Life of Johnson, and with justice in so far as the charm of
each arises from the inimitable *naïveté* of the author's self-
revelations. Boswell had a much greater character than
his own to draw, but Pepys had to be his own Johnson. It
is giving him no excessive praise to say that he makes
himself as interesting as Johnson and Boswell together.
There cannot be a stronger proof of the infinite interest and
importance of humanity that when we for once get a fellow-
creature to depict himself as he really is, the most trivial
details become matters of serious concern. We sympathize with Pepys as we sympathize with Ulysses, and are
for the time much more anxious about the liquidation of
his tailor's bill, or the adjustment of his misunderstandings
with his wife, than 'what the Swede intends or what the
French.' The only drawback is that the Pepys in whom
we are so deeply interested is, after all, not altogether the
true Pepys; not the distinguished civil servant or the
intelligent promoter of science ; not the man as he appeared
to his friends and contemporaries, but an incarnation of
whatever was petty, or ludicrous, or self-seeking in a man
of no inconsiderable official and intellectual distinction.
' A very worthy, industrious, and curious person,' says
Evelyn, ' universally beloved, hospitable, generous, learned
in many things, skilled in music, a very great cherisher of
learned men, of whom he had the conversation.' All these
traits are abundantly confirmed by passages in the *Diary*,
and yet, so infinitely more vivid is the delineation of the

writer's foibles, that one attempting to draw his character from the *Diary* would hardly have noticed them.

Pepys's life is chiefly remarkable for the extraordinary good fortune which raised him from an humble and precarious position to one in which he was enabled to render great service to his country. The son of a London tailor, whose family came from Brampton in Huntingdonshire, he had the good fortune to be distantly related to Sir Edward Montagu, afterwards Earl of Sandwich, one of the chief agents in the Restoration, to whose patronage he owed everything. A sizar and scholar at Cambridge, he married somewhat early and imprudently, accompanied his patron when he went as admiral to the Sound in 1658, and upon his return appears to have filled an inferior clerkship in the Exchequer. The Restoration brought him into the Admiralty, and for long after his history is one of rapid rise and increasing wealth, mainly acquired by means which would now be thought most reprehensible in a civil servant, but which the lax official morality of his day absolved or but faintly condemned. In 1669 the weakness of his eyes compelled him to discontinue his *Diary* and to solicit leave of absence from official duty on a tour in France and Holland. Shortly after his return he lost his wife, whose leaning to the Roman Catholic religion gave colour to a charge against himself of being a concealed Romanist, the object of which was to invalidate his election to Parliament for Aldborough. These proceedings failed, but in 1679 he was imprisoned for a short time on an accusation of being concerned in the Popish Plot, and, notwithstanding the absurdity of the charge, found it advisable to withdraw for a while from the Admiralty. He was reinstated in 1684, having in the interim made a voyage to Tangier on public business. Under James II., who understood naval affairs and knew the worth of Pepys, he attained to great

influence, and the navy to this day is deeply indebted
to him for the improvements he introduced into its administration. He lost his employments at the Revolution,
and retired to a life of scholarly leisure, dying in 1703.
In 1684 he had become President of the Royal Society, of
which he had been one of the earliest members, and long
after his retirement the members continued to meet at his
house.

Pepys bequeathed his library to Magdalen College, Cambridge, where it is preserved in exactly the same condition
as he left it. The immortal *Diary* was among the books,
but attracted no notice until about 1811. It was shortly
afterwards deciphered by the Rev. J. Smith, and published
in 1825 by Lord Braybrooke, who omitted much of the
most racy and characteristic part as below the dignity
of history. These omissions were principally supplied in
the edition of the Rev. Mynors Bright, 1875 ; and Mr.
Henry Wheatley is now publishing an edition absolutely
complete, with the exception of some few passages positively
unprintable.

No work of the kind in the world's literature can for a
moment be compared to Pepys's *Diary* ; but many circumstances must combine ere the existence of such a book is
possible. It is characteristic of Pepys to be at once a very
extraordinary and a very ordinary person. In one point of
view he is the most perfect representative imaginable of the
bourgeois type of humanity, worthy, sensible, indispensable,
and at the same time dull, prosaic, and narrow-minded.
Yet this solid citizen has a dash of the Gil Blas in him too ;
and his little rogueries and servilities appear the more
amusing by contrast with the really estimable and respectable background of his character. These qualities combined make a perfect hero of autobiography ; his ordinary
qualities awaken a fellow-feeling for so characteristic a

specimen of average humanity, and his deviations from the straight path communicate the piquancy of comedy, sometimes the exuberance of farce. Extraordinary he is too, for assuredly no one ever recorded his thoughts and actions with such absolute sincerity; or if anyone ever did, his thoughts and actions were not worthy of record. Those of Pepys, somehow, always seem worthy of being perpetuated. However trivial they may sometimes be, they are saved by the writer's admirable manner, and the contagious earnestness of his conviction that they are in truth of deep concern. The reader, moreover, is continually exercised by the problem whether his author is really aware of the display he is making of himself. If he is, he is a miracle of courage; if not, his obtuseness is equally extraordinary. The *Diary*, besides, is no less admirable as a delineation of the macrocosm than of the microcosm. It paints the official and private circles in which the author moved, the course of public affairs, the humours of social life, with no less truth and frankness than it reveals the author himself. It is by far the most valuable document extant for the understanding of the times; better than all the histories and all the comedies. It seems an unequalled piece of irony that the supreme piece of workmanship in its way and the most lucid mirror of its age should be the performance of an ordinary citizen who had not the least idea that he was doing anything remarkable; who expected celebrity, if he expected it at all, from his official tasks and scientific recreations; who shrouded his work in shorthand lest the world should profit by it; and who would have been dismayed beyond measure if he had foreseen that it would be published after his death. Many chances have conspired for its preservation; it is wonderful that the writer should not have destroyed it; beyond expectation that he should have bequeathed it to Magdalen College; fortunate, to say the least, that it should have been so well preserved there, and have attracted attention at last.   We shall never be able to determine whether we have more reason to be thankful that it was carried on so long, and so fortunately preserved, or to lament that it was not continued throughout the periods of the Popish Plot and the Rye House Plot, of Monmouth's rising, and of the Revolution.

The *Diary* extends from January 1st, 1660, to May 31st, 1669, when Pepys writes, 'And thus ends all that I doubt I shall ever be able to do with my own eyes in the keeping of my journal.' He recovered his sight, at least to a great extent, but the habit was broken, and never resumed. He had in the interim seen and described the Restoration, the Great Plague, the Great Fire, and the great disaster of 1667, when the Dutch burned the English fleet in the Medway.   During this time he had seen continually and been on terms more or less intimate with Charles II., the Duke of York, Monk, Clarendon, Sandwich, Shaftesbury, Sir William Coventry, and a multitude of persons of lower degree of almost every class of society except the Puritans, who are only represented by his worthy predecessor in office, Mr. Blackburne. He has displayed himself to us in almost every possible attitude, attending to accounts, drafting state papers, measuring the timber in the dockyards, giving and taking bribes, defending himself before the House of Commons, alternately a Mercury and a Mentor to his patron, dissipating at the theatre, flirting and something more with actresses and pretty servants, helping to set the Royal Society going, sitting for his portrait, practising music, buying and binding books, a perfect Proteus, yet always the same Pepys, a true type of his age in its peculiar idiosyncrasies, and of human nature in its essential sameness, heroic in no respect, yet admirable in many, and, with many

meannesses, by no means despicable, as good an example as
can be found of the truth of Goethe's dictum :

> ' Ein guter Mensch in seinem dunkeln Drange
> Ist sich des rechten Weges wohl bewusst.'

It is impossible to pass over so unique a work as the
Diary without extract, yet extracts can only convey the
impression of bricks from a building. The following have
been selected chiefly with reference to their incomparable
quaintness and raciness, the one grace which our literature
has forfeited without hope of recovery.

' *July* 18, 1660. Thence to my Lord about business, and being
in talk in comes one with half a buck from Hinchinbroke, and it
smelling a little strong my Lord did give it to me. I did carry
it to my mother.

' *July* 8, 1661. But, above all, our trouble is to find that his
estate appears nothing as we expected, and as all the world
believes; nor his papers so well sorted as I would have had
them, but all in confusion, that break my brains to understand
them. We missed also the surrenders of his copyhold land,
without which the land would not come to us, but to the heir-at-
law, so that what with this, and the badness of the drink, and the
ill opinion I have of the meat, and the biting of the gnats by
night, and my disappointment in getting home this week, and the
trouble of sorting all the papers, I am almost out of my wits with
trouble, only I appear the more contented, because I would not
have my father troubled.

' *Feb.* 19, 1665. In the evening comes Mr. Andrews, and we
sung together, and at supper hearing by accident of my maids
their letting in a roguing Scotch woman that haunts the office, to
help them to wash and scour in our house, and that very lately,
I fell mightily out, and made my wife, to the disturbance of the
house and neighbours, to beat our little girl, and then we shut
her down into the cellars, and there she lay all night.

' *July* 12, 1667. Thence after dinner home, and there find my
wife in a dogged humour for my not dining at home, and I did
give her a pull by the nose and some ill words, which she pro-

voked me to by something she spoke, that we fell extraordinarily
out, insomuch that, I going to the office to avoid further anger,
she followed me in a devilish manner thither, and with much ado
I got her into the garden out of hearing, to prevent shame, and so
home, and by degrees I find it necessary to calm her, and did,
and then to the office, where pretty late, and then to walk with
her in the garden, and pretty good friends, and so to bed with my
mind quiet.

'*Aug.* 18, 1667. I walked towards White Hall, but, being
weary, turned into St. Dunstan's Church, where I heard an able
sermon of the minister of the place; and stood by a pretty,
modest maid, whom I did labour to take by the hand; but she
would not, but got further and further from me; and at last I
could perceive her to take pins out of her pocket to prick me if I
should touch her again; which seeing I did forbear, and was glad
I did spy her design. And then I fell to gaze upon another
pretty maid in a pew close to me, and she on me; and I did go
about to take her by the hand, which she suffered a little and then
withdrew. So the sermon ended, and the church broke up, and
my amours also.

' *Oct.* 4, 1667. To see Sir W. Batten. He is asleep, and so I
could not see him; but in an hour after word is brought me that
he is so ill that it is believed he cannot live till to-morrow, which
troubles me and my wife mightily, partly out of kindness, he
being a good neighbour, and partly out of the money he owes
me, upon our bargain of the late prize.'

The *naïveté* of these passages, and of hundreds more
like them, remains unequalled in literature. Novelists,
as Le Sage in *Gil Blas* and Thackeray in *Barry Lyndon*,
have striven hard to make their personages paint themselves as they really are, but their art is far excelled by
Pepys's nature. If, as Carlyle deems, speech and hearing
were principally bestowed upon us that ' our brother might
impart to us truly how it stands with him in that inner
man of his,' no man has turned the former of these gifts to
better account than Pepys. The same sincerity renders
him a truthful mirror of public sentiment; and his very

limitations, intellectual and moral, enhance the value of his testimony. He has no bias to interfere with the veracity of his delineation ; he simply reports what people around him are saying and thinking; he can show us how the stream goes, because he is borne along with it himself. The lively description which we are about to quote of the consternation caused by the Dutch irruption into the Thames in 1667, is an admirable example of his power of reproducing the atmosphere around him :

'June 13th. No sooner up but hear the sad news confirmed of the Royal Charles being taken by them, and now in fitting by them, which Pett should have carried up higher by our several orders, and deserves, therefore, to be hanged for not doing it, and burning several others ; and that another fleet is come up into the Hope. Upon which news the King and Duke of York have been below since four o'clock in the morning, to command the sinking of ships at Barking-Creek, and other places, to stop their coming up higher: which put me into such a fear, that I presently resolved of my father's and wife's going into the country ; and, at two hours' warning, they did go by the coach this day, with about £1,300 in gold in their night-bag. Pray God give them good passage, and good care to hide it when they come home ! but my heart is full of fear. They gone, I continued in fright and fear what to do with the rest. W. Hewer hath been at the banker's, and hath got £500 out of Backewell's hands of his own money ; but they are so called upon that they will be all broke, hundreds coming to them for money : and they answer him, "It is payable at twenty days—when the days are out, we will pay you;" and those that are not so, they make tell over their money, and make their bags false, on purpose to give cause to retell it, and so spend time. I cannot have my 200 pieces of gold again for silver, all being bought up last night that were to be had, and sold for 24 and 25/ a-piece. So I must keep the silver by me, which sometimes I think to fling into the house of office, and then again know not how I shall come by it, if we be made to leave the office. Every minute some one or other calls for this or that order ; and so I forced to be at the office most of the day about the fire-ships which are to be suddenly fitted out; and it's a most strange thing that we hear nothing from any of my brethren at Chatham: so that we are wholly in the dark, various being the reports of what is done there; insomuch that I sent Mr. Clapham express thither to see how matters go. I did, about noon, resolve to send Mr. Gibson away after my wife with another 1,000 pieces, under colour of an express to Sir Jeremy Smith; who is, as I hear, with some ships at Newcastle; which I did really send to him, and may, possibly, prove of good use to the King; for it is possible, in the hurry of business, they may not think of it at Court, and the charge of an express is not considerable to the King. The King and Duke of York up and down all the day here and there; sometime on Tower Hill, where the City militia was; where the King did make a speech to them, that they should venture themselves no further than he would himself. I also sent, my mind being in pain, Saunders after my wife and father, to overtake them at their night's lodging, to see how matters go with them. In the evening, I sent for my cousin Sarah and her husband, who come; and I did deliver them my chest of writings about Brampton, and my brother Tom's papers, and my journals, which I value much; and did send my two silver flagons to Kate Joyce's: that so, being scattered what I have, something might be saved. I have also made a girdle, by which, with some trouble, I do carry about me £300 in gold about my body, that I may not be without something in case I should be surprised: for I think, in any nation but our's, people that appear, for we are not indeed so, so faulty as we, would have their throats cut.'

'July 14th (Lord's day). Up, and my wife, a little before four, and to make us ready; and by and by Mrs. Turner come to us, by agreement, and she and I staid talking below, while my wife dressed herself, which vexed me that she was so long about it, keeping us till past five o'clock before she was ready. She ready; and, taking some bottles of wine, and beer, and some cold fowl with us into the coach, we took coach and four horses, which I had provided last night, and so away. A very fine day, and so towards Epsom, talking all the way pleasantly, and particularly of the pride and ignorance of Mrs. Lowther, in having of her train carried up. The country very fine, only the way very dusty. To Epsom, by eight o'clock, to the well; where much company, and I drank the water: they did not, but I did drink four pints. And to the town, to the King's Head; and hear that my Lord Buckhurst and Nelly are lodged at the next house, and Sir Charles Sedley with them: and keep a merry house. Poor girl! I pity her; but more the loss of her at the King's house. W. Hewer rode with us, and I left him and the women, and myself walked to church, where few people to what I expected, and none I knew, but all the Houblons, brothers, and them after sermon I did salute, and walk with towards my inn. . . . Then I carried them to see my cousin Pepys's house, and 'light, and walked round about it, and they like it, as indeed it deserves, very well, and is a pretty place; and then I walked them to the wood hard by, and there got them in the thickets till they had lost themselves, and I could not find the way into any of the walks in the wood, which indeed are very pleasant, if I could have found them. At last got out of the wood again; and I, by leaping down the little bank, coming out of the wood, did sprain my right foot, which brought me great present pain, but presently, with walking, it went away for the present, and so the women and W. Hewer and I walked upon the Downs, where a flock of sheep was; and the most pleasant and innocent sight that ever I saw in my life. We found a shepherd and his little boy reading, far from any houses or sight of people, the Bible to him; so I made the boy read to me, which he did, with the forced tone that children do usually read, that was mighty pretty, and then I did give him something, and went to the father, and talked with him; and I find he had been a servant in my cousin Pepys's house, and told me what was become of their old servants. He did content himself mightily in my liking his boy's reading, and did bless God for him, the most like one of the old patriarchs that ever I saw in my life, and it brought those thoughts of the old age of the world in my mind for two or three days after. We took notice of his woollen knit stockings of two colours mixed, and of his shoes shod with iron, both at the toe and heels, and with great nails in the soles of his feet, which was mighty pretty: and, taking notice of them, why, says the poor man, the downs, you see, are full of stones, and we are fain to shoe ourselves thus;

and these, says he, will make the stones fly till they ring before me. I did give the poor man something, for which he was mighty thankful, and I tried to cast stones with his horn crook. He values his dog mightily, that would turn a sheep any way which he would have him, when he goes to fold them: told me there was about eighteen score sheep in his flock, and that he hath four shillings a week the year round for keeping of them: and Mrs. Turner, in the common fields here, did gather one of the prettiest nosegays that ever I saw in my life. So to our coach, and through Mr. Minnes's wood, and looked upon Mr. Evelyn's house; and so over the common, and through Epsom town to our inn, in the way stopping a poor woman with her milk-pail, and in one of my gilt tumblers did drink our belly-fuls of milk, better than any cream; and so to our inn, and there had a dish of cream, but it was sour, and so had no pleasure in it; and so paid our reckoning, and took coach, it being about seven at night, and passed and saw the people walking with their wives and children to take the air, and we set out for home, the sun by and by going down, and we in the cool of the evening all the way with much pleasure home, talking and pleasing ourselves with the pleasure of this day's work. Mrs. Turner mightily pleased with my resolution, which, I tell her, is never to keep a country-house, but to keep a coach, and with my wife on the Saturday to go sometimes for a day to this place, and then quit to another place; and there is more variety and as little charge, and no trouble, as there is in a country-house. Anon it grew dark, and we had the pleasure to see several glow-worms, which was mighty pretty, but my foot begins more and more to pain me, which Mrs. Turner, by keeping her warm hand upon it, did much ease; but so that when we come home, which was just at eleven at night, I was not able to walk from the lane's end to my house without being helped. So to bed, and there had a cere-cloth laid to my feet, but in great pain all night long.'

Pepys's correspondence forms a useful adjunct to his diary. Some of the letters addressed to him are very entertaining, especially that from Sir Samuel Morland on his matrimonial misadventures. His own letters are

P

usually couched in a formal full-dress style, contrasting strongly with the careless ease of the *Diary*. Numerous letters and other documents from Pepys's pen on Admiralty affairs are extant in various repositories, and should be collected and published. He is also the author of an anonymous work on the deposition of Alphonso VI. of Portugal, entitled *The Portugal History, or a Relation of the Troubles that happened in the Court of Portugal in the years* 1667 *and* 1668 (published in 1677), which deserves more notice than it has received. It is a curious history of a palace revolution, which must have been written to order by the help of official documents, and is the more remarkable from the close family connection of the Portuguese and English Courts, which latter must have approved, if it did not instigate the publication.

Much space has here been given to Pepys, and not unreasonably, for his will be to all ages the classical model of the diary, and a model to which not only no one ever will attain, but to which no one will endeavour to attain. Such transparent candour and artless *naïveté* will hardly in any future age of the world be found united to his parts and knowledge. He is as supreme in his own sphere as Milton in his; and another Milton is more likely to appear than another Pepys.

Another diarist, who, though far inferior to Pepys, deserves to be named along with him, is Sir John Reresby (1634-89), a Yorkshire baronet, of Thrybergh Hall, in the West Riding, a person of great influence by his standing and property in the county. His objects in writing, he informs us, were 'to instruct posterity how long it has pleased Providence to continue us Reresbys in the same name and place; to save the labour of turning over a great many obscure papers; and to preserve memorials of some things of use as well as of curiosity.'

This seems like the prelude to a family history; the really important part of the book, however, is not the introductory sketch of Reresby's ancestors, but a diary with very wide gaps devoted in the main to setting forth the writer's relations with the Court and his neighbours. To the latter he is the grand seigneur; towards the former his attitude is not unlike that of Pepys; he aims to provide as well for himself as possible without dipping too deeply into corruption or absolutely selling himself to promote the designs of arbitrary power. He attaches himself to Danby, whose leading maxim was to build upon the support of the country gentry; successively follows him and Halifax with some misgivings; and, though a devoted servant of James II., his enumeration of that monarch's tyrannical acts is so honest, that, if every document of the age had perished except his diary, enough might be deduced from this to justify the Revolution. At this time he was Governor of York, where he was surprised and imprisoned; and death overtook him shortly afterwards hesitating between the old king and the new. His memoirs, imperfectly published in 1734, were edited from the original MS. by Mr. Cartwright in 1875.

Rich as the age was in the diaries of private men and memoirs of public transactions, it did not produce many narratives of private lives in strictly autobiographic form. The most important was that of William Lilly the astrologer, whose character of Charles I. has been already noticed. If, as most think, an astrologer must be either a fool or a knave, there can be no doubt under which class to range this entertaining author. Born (1601) at Diseworth in Leicestershire, 'a town of great rudeness,' he was indebted for his grammar-school education to his father's decayed estate, which made the farm not worth following, and for his transfer to London to his total unfitness for all agricultural work. He walked up to London by the side of the carrier's waggon, got a place in London as general servant, where 'I saw and ate good white bread, contrary to our diet in Leicestershire;' but, on the other hand, 'sometimes helped to carry eighteen tubs of water from the Thames in one morning.' Within a few years he made his fortune by marrying his master's widow, and devoted himself for the rest of his life to mathematical and astrological pursuits. He died, in good circumstances, in 1681, and was honourably interred at the expense of Elias Ashmole, to whom his autobiography is addressed. His numerous astrological writings do not concern us here; his memoirs are no less valuable than entertaining for the glimpses they afford into bygone manners and contemporary feeling on public affairs, and particularly for the lively portrayal of the singular characters with whom Lilly was professionally brought into connection, prototypes of the spiritualistic mediums of a later day, and not unfairly represented by William Hodges, 'whose angels were Raphael, Gabriel, and Uriel; his life answered not in holiness and sanctity to what it should, having to deal with those holy angels.' The following description of a Welsh conjuror is a characteristic example of Lilly's graphic touch:

'It happened on one Sunday 1632, as myself and a Justice of Peace's clerk were, before service, discoursing of many things, he chanced to say, that such a person was a great scholar, nay, so learned, that he could make an almanack, which to me then was strange: One speech begot another, till, at last, he said, he could bring me acquainted with one Evans in Gun-Powder-Alley, who had formerly lived in Staffordshire, that was an excellent wise man, and studied the black art. The same week after we went to see Mr. Evans. When we come to his house, he having been drunk the night before, was upon his bed, if it be lawful to call that a bed whereon he then lay; he roused up himself, and, after some compliments, he was content to instruct me in astrology. I attended his best opportunities for seven or eight weeks, in which time I could set a figure perfectly : Books he had not any, except Haly de judiciis Astrorum, and Origanus's Ephemerides ; so that as often as I entered his house, I thought I was in the Wilderness. Now something of the man : He was by birth a Welshman, a Master of Arts, and in sacred orders ; he had formerly had a cure of souls in Staffordshire, but now was come to try his fortunes at London, being in a manner enforced to fly for some offences very scandalous committed by him in these parts where he had lately lived ; for he gave judgment upon things lost, the only shame of astrology : He was the most saturnine person my eyes ever beheld, either before I practised or since ; of a middle stature, broad forehead, beetle-browed, thick shoulders, flat-nosed, full lips, down-looked, black curling stiff hair, splay-footed ; to give him his right, he had the most piercing judgment naturally upon a figure of theft, and many other questions, that I ever met withal ; yet for money he would willingly give contrary judgments, was much addicted to debauchery, and then very abusive and quarrelsome, seldom without a black eye, or one mischief or other : This is the same Evans who made so many antimonial cups, upon the sale whereof he principally subsisted ; he understood Latin very well, the Greek tongue not at all : He had some arts above, and beyond astrology, for he was well versed in the nature of spirits, and had many times used the circular way of invocating, as in the time of our familiarity he told me.'

Considering the fertility of the age in personal memoirs, its barrenness in biography is remarkable. Apart from the lives by Mrs. Hutchinson and Izaak Walton, to be noticed presently, and a few brief accounts of celebrated men prefixed to their writings, almost the only example is the cluster of valuable and entertaining family histories for which we are indebted to Roger North (1653-1734), and one of these is an autobiography. Roger North, brother of Francis, Lord Guilford, Chief Justice of the Common Pleas and Jeffreys's predecessor in the Great Seal, was a

barrister, and a man of sound, though hardly shining
parts, who owed his extensive practice at the bar to the
influence of his relative. It fell off under the malevolent
discouragement of Jeffreys, and, at the Revolution, Roger,
unable to take the oaths to the new government, retired to
his country estate in Norfolk, where he spent a vigorous
old age in gardening, building, vindicating the memory of
his brothers, writing his own biography, and 'cheerfully
communicating to all, without fee or reward, his great
knowledge of the law'—virtuous behaviour, but unpro-
fessional. Two of the Norths were men of unusual ability,
the Lord Keeper and Sir Dudley, the eminent Turkey
merchant, who returned from a prosperous career at
Constantinople to pack juries, as his enemies alleged,
in the storms of the Exclusion Bill agitation, and to
signalize himself as an authority on questions of trade and
finance. The Norths, a jovial race, full of sap and substance, were staunch Cavaliers, and Roger's biographies of
his brothers grew out of a vindication of the Lord Keeper
against the attacks of Bishop White Kennett. His apolo-
getic *Examen*, not published until after his death, though
important for the history of the time, can hardly rank as
literature. The biographies and autobiography, on the
other hand, are very good literature, though Dr. Jessopp
is hardly warranted in styling them English classics.
They are neither planned with classic symmetry nor
executed with classic elegance; but are charming from
their artless loquacity and the atmosphere of fraternal
affection in which they are steeped, as well as most entertaining from their wealth of anecdote and their portraits,
partial, but not intentionally unfair, of remarkable men.
Two elements in these books are sharply contrasted, the
political and the anecdotic. The former affords a melancholy but useful representation of the factious unreason

of political parties in that age, especially Roger's, and of the prejudices which kept Englishmen apart until they learned toleration from Locke and Hoadly. It is to Roger's credit that, although he had done his best to put it into James II.'s power to overthrow the Church and trample on the laws, he recoiled when the crisis came. A page or two after expressing his opinion that good citizens never resist arbitrary power, he is found inconsistently, though very rightly, lauding his brother Dudley for refusing, under the strongest pressure from James, to mortgage his vote in Parliament; and the whole tenor of his memoirs shows that, although his principles would not allow him to acquiesce openly in the Revolution, he was at the bottom of his heart by no means sorry for it. His antipathy to Jeffreys, who had enacted towards his brother the part which Laud had formerly performed towards Abbot, may have had something to do with this attitude. His portraits of eminent lawyers, such as Hale, Saunders, and Maynard, though sometimes disfigured by party feeling, have signal value. The anecdotic part of the memoirs, on the other hand, is delightful reading, being full of good-natured fun, shrewd observation, and interesting glimpses of the manners of the times, sometimes well worth noting, as, for example, this testimony to the popularity of the Church of England in Wales in Charles II.'s time: 'I remember the doctor' (Roger's brother John, Master of Trinity College, Cambridge) 'told us that when he came to his parish, he found the humour of the people very different from what, on like occasions, was often found in England. For, instead of grumbling at and affronting a new tithe-monger came down amongst them, too often known in English villages, the parishioners came about him and hugged him, calling him their pastor, and telling him they were his sheep.' There are two especial

repositories of anecdotes in North's volumes, that of
stories of circuits and eminent lawyers in his memoir of
the Lord Keeper and his own autobiography, and the
Turkish and Levantine sketches in the life of his brother
Dudley. The latter gives a most curious picture of the
relations of Mussulmans and Christians in the days when
this was the fashion in which unbelievers were noticed by
sultans :

'The great officers about the Grand Signor, with whom he
[Dudley North] had transacted and familiarly conversed, told his
majesty that there was now in the city of Constantinople an
extraordinary *gower* [Giaour], as well for person as abilities to
transact the greatest affairs. The Grand Signor declared that
he would see this extraordinary *gower :* and accordingly the
merchant was told of it ; and at the time appointed an officer
conducted him into the seraglio, and carried him about till he
came to a little garden, and there two other men took him by
the two arms and led him to a place where he saw the Grand
Signor sitting against a large window open in a chamber not very
high from the ground ; the men that were his conductors, holding
each an arm, put their hands upon his neck and bowed him down
till his forehead touched the ground ; and this was done more
than once, and is the very same forced obeisance of ambassadors
at their audiences. After this he stood bolt upright as long as
the Grand Signor thought fit to look at him ; and then, upon a
sign given, he was taken away and set free again by himself to
reflect on this his romantic audience.'

This 'extraordinary *gower*' appears to have been the
perfect ideal of an orientalized John Bull. Having, as his
brother assures us, 'an uncommon disposition to truth,' it
is surprising to find him actively concerned in the subornation of perjury in Turkish law-courts, but this Roger considers a demonstration of the strength of his mind :

'One must have a strong power of thought to abstract the
prejudices of our domestic education and plant ourselves in a
way of negotiating in heathen remote countries.'

Another biography of the time unknown to the age
which produced it, but a standard work
Mrs. Hutchinson's Life of Col. Hutchinson. and general favourite since its republication early in the nineteenth century, is the life of Colonel Hutchinson, by his widow. Lucy Hutchinson, third daughter of Sir Allen Apsley, Governor of the Tower, was born in 1620, and in 1638 married Colonel John Hutchinson, of a good Nottinghamshire family, who, after having taken an active part on the parliamentary side during the Civil War, acted as one of the king's judges, and retired into private life rather than accept employment under Cromwell. He escaped prosecution at the Restoration, but afterwards, upon suspicion of engaging in plots, was imprisoned in Deal Castle, where he died from the unwholesomeness of his quarters. His widow wrote his life between 1664 and 1670, but it was not published until 1806. It is naturally an unqualified panegyric upon her husband, redeemed from insipidity by the conjugal affection and devotion which inspire it, and the elegant simplicity of the style. In panegyrizing her husband, Mrs. Hutchinson unwittingly extols herself; she has no doubt that he was among the wisest as well as the best men of his time, and her simple conviction is so touching, that the reader is almost persuaded to think so too. One of the most high-minded he certainly was, but his independence verged upon impracticability. The strictly historical value of the work is small, except as regards incidents of the Civil War in Nottinghamshire. Mrs. Hutchinson was a highly accomplished woman, and made a metrical translation of Lucretius, which is extant in MS. in the British Museum. The time of her death is not known.

The most important ecclesiastical biography by a contemporary writer is the life of Archbishop Williams, by

Bishop Hacket (1592-1670), the munificent restorer of Lich-
field Cathedral, which, although first published in 1693, was
completed in 1657, and will be more fitly noticed under the
pre-Restoration period. This, though more

Religious
Biography:
Izaak
Walton,
1593-1683.

intrinsically valuable, is much less known
than a series of little religious biographies
which owe their fame partly to the superior
attractiveness of the characters depicted, partly
to their more manageable compass, and partly
to the charm of a tender and pious spirit, rather than of
style. Singularly enough, the author owes a still larger
measure of fame to another book composed in a similar
spirit, but on a subject at first sight (were it not for the
profession of St. Peter) wide as the poles asunder from
ecclesiastical biography. Izaak Walton, biographer of
Donne, and author of *The Complete Angler*, was born at
Stafford in 1593, and died at Winchester in 1683. He
appears to have settled in London as a draper about 1616,
in a little shop over the Exchange, 'seven feet long and five
feet wide.' In 1624 he was established in Fleet Street, near
the south-west corner of Chancery Lane. In 1643, having
secured a competency by trade, and probably finding that
his churchmanship and royalism exposed him to annoyance
in London, he gave up business and withdrew into the
country, living, Wood says, 'mostly in the families of the
eminent clergymen of England,' unquiet habitations in
those times, one would imagine. He had, during his
residence in London, greatly ingratiated himself with the
dignified clergy, and distinguished himself as the biographer of one of the most eminent among them, though
this seems to have been a mere accident, Sir Henry Wotton
having requested him to collect materials for a life of
Donne, which he intended to have written himself. Wotton
dying without having performed his purpose, his mantle

fell upon Walton, whose memoir, prefixed to an edition of Donne's sermons, published in 1640, obtained so much success that he was requested to write the life of Wotton himself. This was completed in 1644, and appeared in 1651 along with the *Reliquiae Wottonianae*, a collection edited by Walton. The lives of Hooker and Herbert (the former a commission from Archbishop Sheldon) were written shortly after the Restoration, under the roof of Morley, Bishop of Winchester; the life of Bishop Sanderson was written as late as 1675. Meanwhile the *Complete Angler, or Contemplative Man's Recreation*, the book on which Walton's fame after all principally rests, had appeared in 1653, with copies of complimentary verse prefixed which seem to prove that it was ready for the press in 1650. One of these effusions, by Thomas Weaver, dated 1649, is a poem of unusual merit, much in the style of Marvell. Walton, who had married a sister of Bishop Ken, died in the house of his son-in-law, Prebendary Hawkins of Winchester, in 1683. His will, which he had himself drawn up a short time previously, shows the undiminished vigour of his faculties, and the endurance of his connection with his native county. His character may be read in every page of his writings, and is such as to prove that with him angling was indeed the recreation of a contemplative man.

The maxim *noscitur a sociis* is entirely in Walton's favour, for his ecclesiastical heroes are the flower of the Church of England of his day. His treatment is in general very satisfactory, entirely sympathetic, the first qualification of biography, and much less marred by prejudice and party spirit than was to have been expected from the agitated character of the times. The simple unaffected style almost verges upon garrulity. Though not a scholar, Walton seems to have possessed sufficient acquaintance with theology to avoid misrepresentation of eminent divines; while the chief value of his work consists in its portrayal of almost ideal charity, meekness, and learning; and in the curious anecdotes embedded in it, such as Pope Clement VIII.'s high appreciation of Hooker, James I.'s influence upon the composition of Sarpi's *History of the Council of Trent*, Charles I.'s translation of Sanderson (unfortunately lost), and his infatuated regret expressed to the same divine for having consented to the abolition of episcopacy in Scotland. Walton, into whose composition mirth entered, but not humour, records this with the same gravity with which he chronicles Charles's injunction to the Merry Monarch to be above all things diligent in the study of Richard Hooker. Some light may possibly be thrown upon the vexed question of the interpolation of the last three books of the *Ecclesiastical Polity*, by the statement of Hoole, a contemporary schoolmaster, when exhorting his scholars to good penmanship, that many of Hooker's sermons had been destroyed after his death from the impossibility of deciphering his handwriting.

CHAPTER XII.

DIVINITY.

PASSING from the biographers of divines to the divines themselves, we observe that, with the signal exception of *Pilgrim's Progress*, nearly all the writers in this department whose productions have established a claim to rank among English classics belong to 'the company of the preachers.' This is not in itself surprising; preaching stimulates eloquence, and the homilist enjoys a much greater freedom of range, and a fuller exemption from restraint, than the writer upon strictly technical or professional subjects. It does, however, at first sight seem remarkable, that an age so generally decried for immorality as the Restoration should, with the decade immediately preceding, have been the golden age of the English pulpit. In fact, as we have implied when treating of the drama, the apparent licence of the age did not really extend much beyond gay and fashionable circles, which could not greatly affect the pulpit except to its advantage, by furnishing it with impressive topics. Even in these circles immorality was far from necessarily implying irreligion; and the sober citizens who crowded churches and meeting-houses, and the universities, whose routine afforded so many opportunities for the delivery of discourses from the pulpit, were much as heretofore. In the rudimentary condition of the press

The Pulpit in the Restoration epoch.

as an organ of public information and education, and when the meeting was hardly an institution as yet, the spoken word possessed a power of which the newspaper has since gone far to deprive it. In times of public disquiet, such as the days of the Exclusion Bill or those which preceded the Revolution, churches and chapels were crowded with people seeking guidance, popular sermons went through edition after edition, and popular divines were almost tribunes of the people. Theological considerations moulded political opinion to a degree now hardly conceivable; the storm of pamphlets on both sides called forth by the resipiscence or tergiversation of a leading divine like Sherlock shows what importance attached to his conduct upon either view of it. The age, moreover, was in the stage of literary development most favourable for pulpit eloquence. As a huge glacier takes longer to melt than a small one, the quaint and involved periods of the Elizabethan pulpit stood out longer than ordinary prose against the disintegrating influence of seventeenth century taste, and while the new movement was triumphant in most branches of literature, it in general only affected the style of the sermon so far as to chasten and mellow it, leaving it still that sonorous dignity and that flavour of the antique with which stately and impressive eloquence can rarely dispense. The two greatest preachers, Barrow and South, stand just upon this culminating point of excellence, uniting the majesty of the old style to the ease and clearness of the new. Tillotson, going a step further, and bringing the pulpit down to the level of ordinary educated society, performed indeed a most useful work, but inevitably prepared the way for the sensible but unimpressive preaching of the next century.

Isaac Barrow, Master of Trinity College, was the son of a respectable tradesman, linendraper to Charles I.

His royalist and Arminian opinions kept him back under the Commonwealth, but after the Restoration he was acknowledged as the first mathematician of his country, except, as he was the first to allow, another Isaac whose surname was Newton. Newton, who had been Barrow's pupil, revised his lectures on optics (1669), an epoch-making work, but composed in Latin, as were his scarcely less celebrated lectures on geometry. His reputation as an English classic rests upon two great theological works, his *Treatise on the Pope's Supremacy* (edited, after his death, by Tillotson) and his *Exposition of the Creed*, and upon his sermons, which do not seem to have been extremely popular in his own day, though gaining the suffrage of such dissimilar men as Locke and Charles II., who called Barrow ' an unfair preacher, because he exhausted every topic, and left no room for anything to be said by anyone who came after him.' It may be reasonably conjectured that when Barrow preached before Charles he did not indulge in the inordinate expansiveness, it was not prolixity, that sometimes drove away his congregation. It is to the king's honour that his bestowal of the mastership of Trinity upon Barrow was entirely his own act.

Isaac Barrow (1630-1677).

Robert South, on the whole perhaps the greatest preacher of his age, was born in 1633, and educated at Westminster and Christ Church. He is accused by Antony Wood, the principal authority for his life, of having been a timeserver, who sided successively with the Independents, the Presbyterians, and the Church of England in the days of their power. Wood seems, however, to have had some private grievance against him ; and if South was really at the same time so pliant and so able, it seems strange that he should have attained no higher preferment than stalls at Christ Church

Robert South (1633-1716).

and Westminster. Quarrelsome he certainly was, and he entered into a most acrimonious controversy with Sherlock, which it required a royal proclamation to compose. He died in 1716.

Unlike South's, the character of John Tillotson is no

John Tillotson
(1630-1694).

matter for controversy. With the possible exception of Archbishop Herring,[1] he was the most amiable man that ever filled the see of Canterbury, and was pronounced by the discerning and experienced William III. the best friend he had ever had and the best man he had ever known. To the meekness of the pastor Tillotson added the qualities of the statesman, and happy was it for the Church of England that such a man could be found to fill the primacy at such a time. As a master of oratory he is greatly inferior in eloquence to both Barrow and South, but historically is more important than either, for Addison was influenced by him, and his discourses long gave the tone to the English pulpit, affording the almost universally accepted model throughout the greater part of the eighteenth century.

Of these three great preachers South is certainly the greatest as respects eloquence and energy of diction. Almost every sentence is striking, and at the same time in

---

[1] On the flyleaf of a copy of Birch's *Life of Tillotson* in the British Museum is a transcript of a letter from Archbishop Herring to the author, in which, acknowledging his dedication, he says: "I think myself extremely honoured in having my inconsiderable name connected with that of the best of my predecessors. I feel the disparity of the characters, and must submit to the censure which will arise from a comparison so infinitely to my disadvantage. But, as posterity, when the real object is out of sight, may imagine from your picture that there might be some distant shadow of a resemblance, I think I may, I think I ought to enjoy the contemplation." The resemblance was closer than the good archbishop's modesty would admit.

perfect good taste. By so much, however, as he surpasses his rivals in purely literary qualities, does he fall below them in others even more essential to the preacher. His judgment is often greatly at fault, he commits himself to plainly untenable propositions, and enforces them with the confidence of one displaying self-evident truths. After a few experiences of this kind the reader begins to look upon him as a rhetorician, and to prefer the more cautious, but still vivid and vigorous ratiocination of Barrow; or the ' sweet reasonableness' of Tillotson, inferior to Barrow, as he to South, in the gifts of the consummate orator, but more truly persuasive in the gentleness of his expostulation and his transparent candour.

Edward Stillingfleet, Bishop of Worcester (1635-1699), though a fine preacher, is less remembered in this capacity than for his unsuccessful controversy with Locke and his *Origines Sacrae*, a work of great learning in defence of the Church of England, which Coleridge in his *Notes on Books* emphatically prefers to the corresponding labours of Chillingworth. Coleridge was naturally prejudiced in favour of the antagonist of Locke, whose graces of mind and person, however, are attested by a dispassionate witness, Pepys.

Theology, apart from eloquence, is hardly entitled to a place in literary history; yet some of the theologians of the period were too illustrious to be passed over without mention. John Pearson, Bishop of Chester (1612-1686), ranks among the Fathers of the Church of England by his standard work on the Creed. ' Pearson's very dust,' says Bentley, ' is gold.' Barrow's great controversial treatise has been mentioned. George Bull, Bishop of St. David's (1634-1710), achieved even more, for he extorted the thanks of the clergy of France by his *Nicaenae Fidei Defensio* (1685), written in Latin, but afterwards translated

Q

into English.   The author's object was to prove the
orthodoxy of the Ante-Nicene Fathers, which had been disputed by several Protestant divines ; the cost of publication
was borne by the munificent Bishop Fell.   The French
prelates further paid Bull the equivocal compliment of
wondering why in the world so excellent a man did not
join the Church of Rome.   *Talis cum sis, utinam noster
esses.*   Bull expounded his difficulties in a treatise on the
corruptions of that church, the most popular of his works
at home, but which, being written in English, failed to
vindicate his position in the eyes of the Frenchmen.   Next
to these giants of learning may be named a very dissimilar
person, Richard Baxter (1615-1691), whom moderate men
had designated for a bishopric at the Restoration, but
whom the Bartholomew's Day of 1662 made a Nonconformist.   He wrote one hundred and sixty-eight books,
two of which have survived, *A Call to the Unconverted* and
The Saints' Everlasting Rest.   The latter Professor Minto
calls 'a volume of pious thoughts that have a peculiar
interest when we view them as the aspirations of an infirm
man turning wearily from the distractions of a time utterly
out of joint.'   The writings of George Fox, the founder of
Quakerism, mostly belong to a previous period; but the
No Cross, no Crown of William Penn (1644-1718) falls
within Restoration literature.   A far more important work
is the *Apology* of Robert Barclay (1648-1690).   This
remarkable book, which has been recommended by bishops
to theological students as the best available for many pur-
poses, is the standard exposition of Quakerism, and undoubtedly ranks among the classics of its period.   Mr.
Leslie Stephen describes it as 'one of the most impressive
theological writings of the century : grave, logical, and
often marked by the eloquence of lofty moral convictions.'
' The St. Paul of the Quakers,' says Coleridge of the

author. Barclay, the descendant of an old Scotch family, became a Quaker in 1667, following the example of his father. He underwent some persecution, but was in the main shielded by the favour of James II. His works were collected by Penn in 1692.

Two devotional writings of the age, besides Baxter's, obtained sufficient currency to merit a place in the history of literature. *The Whole Duty of Man*, first published in 1658, is an excellent representative of the sobriety and sound sense characteristic of the Church of England. At the same time it must be confessed that it has more reason than unction, and seeks rather to menace and upbraid than to allure men into the religious life. At the present day it would be pronounced grievously deficient in fervour, servile in its political teachings, and too exclusive in its appeals to prudential and self-interested motives; but its adaptation to a positive and prosaic age was sufficiently evinced by a circulation enormous for the period. The authorship is involved in mystery: it is usually attributed to Archbishop Sterne or Lady Pakington; but Sterne can hardly have had time to write the seven other treatises ascribed, apparently with good ground, to the same author; and it is clearly not the composition of a woman. Evelyn attributes it on the authority of Archbishop Tenison to a Dr. Chaplin, of University College, Oxford, who cannot be traced. Lately Mr. Dobie, in the *Academy*, has ascribed it and its companions on strong grounds to Richard Allestree, Provost of Eton, an intimate friend of Bishop Fell. The Bishop appears to have copied some of them in his own hand, and certainly was acquainted with the authorship. The most important of the other works ascribed to the writer of *The Whole Duty of Man* are *The Causes of the Decay of Christian Piety, The Gentleman and Ladies' Calling,* and *The Government of the Tongue.*

Another work of edification, which almost rivalled the popularity of *The Whole Duty of Man*, was the *Practical Discourse concerning Death* (1689), by William Sherlock (1641-1707), Master of the Temple and Dean of St. Paul's, the divine whose tergiversations respecting the oath of allegiance to William and Mary are so amusingly detailed by Macaulay. It is a model of clear and forcible writing, but on the lowest plane of unspiritual selfishness. 'How unreasonable is it for us to trouble ourselves about this world longer than we are like to continue in it!' exclaims Sherlock, with the air of one apologizing for enunciating a truism.

Natural theology had a representative of much higher moral calibre than professional theology found in Sherlock in John Ray (1628-1705). Ray, a Cambridge man, prevented by scruples from ministering in the Church of England after the fatal legislation of 1662, but substantially accepting her doctrines, was the first English naturalist of eminence, and wrote chiefly in Latin, but composed his treatise on *The Wisdom of God in the Creation* in his mother-tongue. The anthropomorphism of this earnest, lucid, and ingenious book, the prototype of Paley's, is a defect hardly to be avoided in an age when the Deity was almost universally conceived as an artificer; and yet Ray comes very near indeed to the conception of a power immanent in Nature. His style is limpid and persuasive; his reasoning cogent; his good sense is apparent in his discussion of spontaneous generation and the stories related in its support, although the caution and modesty of his temper sometimes incline him to defer too much to authority. He has no mercy, for example, on frogs rained from the sky, but will not, in the face of the testimony of eye-witnesses, carry scepticism to the point of disputing that they may have been occasionally found immured in the middle of stones.

Ray's teleology had allies in Derham (1657-1735), an observant naturalist and author of *Astro-Theology*, and in the Hon. Robert Boyle, the best of men in disposition, and an admirable natural philosopher, but feeble and diffuse as a natural theologian.

Thomas Burnet, Master of the Charter House, is the reverse of Boyle in most respects; a visionary as natural theologian and natural philosopher, but the only writer of his day, the great preachers excepted, who attained to sublimity in prose. A Cambridge man and a pupil of Tillotson, Burnet was elected Master of the Charter House in 1685, and signalized himself by his courage in resisting James II.'s attempted intrusion of Roman Catholics into the foundation. He became Clerk of the Closet to William III., which post he was obliged to resign from the freedom of his criticism of the Mosaic narrative, but retained his mastership unmolested to his death. He left behind him two theological works in Latin, privately printed, but soon afterwards published, *De Fide et officiis Christianorum* and *De Statu mortuorum et resurgentium*, in which he carried the liberty of speculation very far. The book on which his fame rests, *The Sacred Theory of the Earth*, was also originally composed in Latin, to which circumstance it is probably indebted for much of its exceptional dignity of style. It was intended by the author as sober natural philosophy, but to a scientific age appears a poetical vision of the former immersion and future conflagration of the earth, justly compared by Mr. Gosse to the gorgeous apocalyptic imaginings of Danby and Martin. According to Burnet the earth was originally an egg both in shape and smoothness, enclosing the waters in an 'antediluvian abyss.' At the universal deluge the earth sank into this internal cavity. Upon the subsidence of the waters the land partly emerged

Thomas Burnet (1635?-1715).

in the confused shapes into which it had been tumble
by the crash, partly remained beneath the sea. The argu
ment is very ingenious and entertaining, and instruc
tive also, for it exhibits to perfection two of the mos
ordinary causes of fallacy, the assuming imaginary dat
as unquestionable premises and the enthusiast's adoptio
of sublimity as the standard of truth. Burnet's min
was the mind of a poet; he had just enough science t
misguide him, and more than enough learning to glos
over the vagaries of his science. He is quite as much a
home in expounding the catastrophe of the future, th
final conflagration, as the watery catastrophe of which h
believes the traces to be visible everywhere around him
At the same time he has a strong affinity to the rationali
ing divines, even more visible in his strictly theologic
writings, and would not for the world propound anythin
of whose reasonableness he has not first convinced himsel
As a writer he stands high, combining the splendour an
melody of a former age with the ease and lucidity of hi
own. The following is a fair average specimen of hi
picturesque imagination and impassioned diction:

‘ Thus the Flood came to its height; and 'tis not easy to repre
sent to ourselves this strange scene of things, when the Delug
was in its fury and extremity; when the earth was broken an
swallowed up in the abyss, whose raging waters rose higher tha
the mountains, and filled the air with broken waves, with a
universal mist, and with thick darkness, so as nature seemed t
be in a second chaos; and upon this chaos rid the distrest Ark
that bore the small remains of mankind. No sea was ever s
tumultuous, as this, nor is there anything in present nature t
be compared with the disorder of these waters; all the poetr
and all the hyperboles that are used in the description of storm
and raging seas, were literally true in this, if not beneath i
The Ark was really carried to the tops of the highest mountain
and into the places of the clouds, and thrown down again int

the deepest gulfs; and to this very state of the Deluge and of
the Ark, which was a type of the Church in this world, David
seems to have alluded in the name of the Church, Psalm xlii. 7,
Abyss calls upon abyss at the noise of thy cataracts or water-
spouts; all thy waves and billows have gone over me. It was
no doubt an extraordinary and miraculous providence, that
could make a vessel, so ill manned, live upon such a sea; that
kept it from being dashed against the hills, or overwhelmed in
the deeps. That abyss which had devoured and swallowed up
whole forests of woods, cities, and provinces, nay the whole
earth, when it had conquered all, and triumphed over all, could
not destroy this single ship. I remember in the story of the
Argonautics, Dion. Argonaut. l. i., v. 47, when Jason set out to
fetch the Golden Fleece, the poet saith, all the gods that day
looked down from Heaven to view the ship, and the nymphs
stood upon the mountain-tops to see the noble youth of Thessaly
pulling at the oars; we may with more reason suppose the good
angels to have looked down upon this ship of Noah's; and that
not out of curiosity, as idle spectators, but with a passionate
concern for its safety and deliverance. A ship, whose cargo was
no less than a whole world; that carried the fortune and hopes
of all posterity, and if this had perished, the earth for any thing
we know had been nothing but a desert, a great ruin, a dead
heap of rubbish, from the Deluge to the conflagration. But
death and hell, the grave, and destruction have their bounds.
We may entertain ourselves with the consideration of the face of
the Deluge, and of the broken and drowned earth, in this scheme,
with the floating Ark, and the guardian angels.'

The most eminent natural theologian of the time after
Ray, and one who would have surpassed Ray in importance
if his labours in this department had been more than a
brief episode in a busy career, was Richard Bentley, whose
power of destructive criticism in other fields proved how
formidable a champion he could be on the negative side of
any question. Bentley's massive intelligence, however,
aptitude for broad commonsense views, and impatience of
niceties and subtleties, entirely qualified him to embrace

and expound the form in which natural theology commended itself to the vast majority of the thinkers of his day. He dealt solely with the materialism of Hobbes, 'there may be some Spinosists beyond seas,' he says, but to him *de non existentibus, et de non apparentibus, eadem est ratio.* The questions and the answers of a Goethe would have been equally unintelligible to him ; if Newman would certainly have thought him shallow, he would as certainly have thought Newman whimsical. He must be judged from the standpoint of his own day, and from this his argument, delivered as the Boyle lecture for 1691 and 1692, must be pronounced a splendid and cogent piece of reasoning. It is particularly remarkable for its absolute reliance on the doctrines of Newton's *Principia*, when Newton had hardly a disciple out of England.

CHAPTER XIII.

So great an endowment is genius, that neither the effect produced nor the fame achieved by all the eloquent and learned divines of Charles II.'s age can be for an instant compared to the achievement of a poor and almost illiterate mechanic, whom Macaulay classes with Milton as one of the only two men of that period—he might have excepted Thomas Burnet—to whom had been vouchsafed any considerable measure of imagination. John Bunyan, the one man who has attained to write a successful prose allegory on a large scale, and to infuse true emotion into an exercise of ingenuity, and who probably owed less to study and training than any other of the great authors of the modern world, was born at Elstow, a village in the neighbourhood of Bedford, in November, 1628. He is usually described as a 'tinker,' but, as he was not an itinerant, 'brazier' would be a more correct appellation. The trade was his father's, who was also a very small freeholder. Bunyan probably received some instruction at Bedford grammar school, and his narrative of his boyhood shows that he must have had considerable knowledge of the Bible, which impressed his imaginative temper more than he knew at the time. According to his own account he was wild and profane in his youth, but nothing very definite can be extracted from these self-accusations, and it

John Bunyan (1628-1688).

would rather appear that it was only for a short time that he could even be described as careless. In 1644, partly perhaps from grief at the death of his mother and dissatisfaction with his father's speedy re-marriage, he enlisted into the army, doubtless the Parliamentary force, though he strangely or prudently leaves the point uncertain. About the end of 1648 he married, and through the influence of his wife, whose name he does not tell us, and by the aid of two religious books which she brought him among her scanty possessions, he accomplished what he afterwards came to consider a merely outward reformation. The attempt to subjugate the inward man involved him for several years in the most distressing spiritual conflicts, described with extreme power in his *Grace Abounding*. They conducted him eventually to peace, and into the Baptist congregation of Mr. Gifford, who had been helpful to him. In 1655 he became a preacher, and in the following year produced his first book, *Some Gospel Truths Opened*, to which was prefixed a recommendatory letter by John Burton, who says, 'This man is not chosen out of an earthly, but out of the heavenly university.'

In 1660 the revival under the Restoration government of obsolete enactments against conventicles, with no endeavour to discriminate between seditious conspirators like the Fifth Monarchy men and harmless worshippers like the Baptists, compelled the reluctant Bedford magistrates to arrest and imprison Bunyan as an unlicensed preacher. He might have escaped, or have obtained release by a trifling submission, but with the spirit of a Christian martyr he disdained either course, and abode contentedly in prison for nearly twelve years. His captivity in the commodious county gaol was by no means oppressive; indeed, in the first part of it he enjoyed a large measure of liberty, afterwards withdrawn. He sup-

ported himself by making tagged laces, as well as by the
publication of some books, of which *Grace Abounding*
(1666) is the most important. The first part of *Pilgrim's
Progress* was also written in prison, but, as Bunyan's best
biographer, Dr. John Brown, almost proves, during a
second and comparatively brief confinement in 1676. In
1672 Bunyan published his *Defence of Justification by
Faith*, a coarse and violent attack on the *Design of Christianity*, by Dr., afterwards Bishop Fowler, one of the most
tolerant divines of the age, but who was provoked to
reply with almost equal acrimony. In the same year
Charles II.'s merciful but entirely illegal suspension of
all statutes against Papists and Nonconformists liberated
Bunyan, who even obtained a licence to preach, and became stated minister of the Baptist congregation at
Bedford, then meeting in a barn in an orchard. Notwithstanding some few molestations, of which the second
imprisonment in 1675-76 was the chief, the remainder of
his life was in general tranquil and prosperous. The first
part of *Pilgrim's Progress* appeared in 1678, and, though
not half-a-dozen copies of it are now known to exist,
immediately attained the highest popularity. Edition
followed edition, the first two or three with remarkable
additions and improvements. Bunyan frequently visited
London, where he became a popular preacher; his influence
was courted, though unsuccessfully, by the government
itself, and in 1688, the year of his death, he had become
in some sort chaplain to the Lord Mayor, ' an Anabaptist,
a very odd ignorant person,' says Evelyn. His principal
works in the interval had been: *The Life and Death of
Mr. Badman*, 1680; *The Holy War*, 1682; the second part
of the *Pilgrim's Progress*, 1684; *The Jerusalem Sinner
Saved*, 1688. His death, on August 31st, 1688, took place
in London, and was occasioned by cold contracted on a

journey which he had undertaken to reconcile a father with his son.

Of Bunyan's character there can be but one opinion, he was a truly Apostolic man. As no one's diction is more forcible, unadulterated Saxon, so no life has better expressed the sturdy, sterling virtues of the Englishman. A wider culture would have enriched both his mind and his writings, but with the probable result of turning a remarkable man into an ordinary one. His good sense and his humility are illustrated by a charming anecdote. 'Ah, Mr. Bunyan,' said a grateful hearer, 'that was a sweet sermon!' 'You need not tell me that,' replied Bunyan, 'the devil whispered it to me before I was well out of the pulpit.'

It is unnecessary to dwell at any great length upon the characteristics of so famous and universally known a book as *Pilgrim's Progress*. Though professedly a vision, and treating of spiritual things, it ranks with *Robinson Crusoe* and *Gulliver's Travels* as one of the great realistic books of the English language. All three are examples of the possibility of rendering scenes wholly imaginary, and in fact impossible, truer to the apprehension than experience itself by the narrator's own air of absolute conviction, and by unswerving fidelity to truth of detail. In Bunyan's case the triumph is the more remarkable, as his personages are not even imaginary men and women, but mere embodiments of moral or theological qualities. Yet Faithful and Hopeful are as real as Crusoe and Friday. Before he began to write he must have realized what he wished to describe with a vividness only conceivable by regarding it as an outward expression of his own spiritual experience. He had himself been Christian and Faithful and the captive in Doubting Castle; he had gazed on Vanity Fair, and passed through the Valley of the Shadow of Death. The fact that his allegory is in truth an auto-biography explains what Macaulay calls the characteristic peculiarity of *Pilgrim's Progress*: 'it is the only work of its kind which possesses a strong human interest. Other allegories only amuse the fancy. The allegory of Bunyan has been read by many thousands with tears.' Elsewhere he says, '*Pilgrim's Progress* is perhaps the only book about which, after the lapse of a hundred years, the educated minority has come over to the opinion of the common people.' It may be added that *Pilgrim's Progress*, unlike other celebrated works, is a *bona fide* and unmistakable allegory. *Don Quixote* may have a much deeper purpose than that of satirizing chivalric romances, but not one reader in a hundred cares to fathom it. Spenser undoubtedly intended to shadow forth Elizabeth in Gloriana; but the perception of the poet's purpose contributes nothing to the enjoyment of his poem. In Bunyan, however, the allegory is the book, too plain to be overlooked by the most careless reader; and all the minor allegories that combine to enrich the main action are equally apparent for what they are, and yet the obvious invention has all the force of reality. 'Bunyan,' says Macaulay, 'is almost the only writer who ever gave to the abstract the interest of the concrete. In the works of many celebrated authors men are mere personifications. The mind of Bunyan, on the other hand, was so imaginative that personifications, when he dealt with them, became men. A dialogue between two qualities, in his dream, has more dramatic effect than a dialogue between two human beings in most plays.' Macaulay proceeds to compare Bunyan in this particular with Shelley, and the comparison is just; but it is surprising that neither he nor Mr. Froude should have dwelt on Bunyan's deeper affinity to a great predecessor of whom he assuredly never read a line—Dante.

Dante's personifications, indeed, are feeble compared to Bunyan's; it is doubtful whether some of them are even intended as such. The might of his imagination, however, like Bunyan's, is shown in his power of reconciling us to its wildest flights by the intensity of his realism; and the chief distinction is that while Bunyan's materials are necessarily drawn from the only worlds he knew, the narrow and prosaic world of Bedford and the sublime world of the Bible, Dante disposed of all his age could give in philosophy, political life, human learning, the influence of art and the scrutiny of nature. Bunyan is hence a very contracted and terrestrial Dante, but so far as he goes he is a true Dante; he cannot soar with his great predecessor, but if Dante had succeeded him he would not have disdained to have built upon his massive groundwork. Both suffer from the inevitable progress of mankind beyond the conceptions which in their day were accepted as matters of course. Dante's *Inferno* now seems rather grotesque than terrible. Christian's forsaking his kindred in the City of Destruction, which to Bunyan appeared a duty, now seems selfishness. That the fame of both should have survived such profound modifications of belief is one of the most striking evidences of their greatness. One great advantage Bunyan possessed: the Bible had prepared the way for him. There is probably no other such instance of the assimilation of one literature by another as the domestication of the Bible in England. The Greek and Hebrew authors of the Scriptures were better known to the public that Bunyan principally addressed than the majority of their own writers, and he had no need, like other men of original genius, to painfully create the taste by which he was ultimately to be judged. From the first *Pilgrim's Progress* took rank as a classic; well might Dr. Arnold call it ' a complete reflection of Scripture.' Its chief blemish, the somewhat prosaic and self-seeking character of its piety, harmonized entirely with the current teaching of the pulpit, and offered no stumbling-block to a generation which had not so much as heard of 'other-worldliness.' Its popularity soon received the usual attestation of piracies, spurious continuations, and imitations in all languages. The question whether Bunyan was indebted for his allegory to any predecessor is hardly worth discussing. Some general resemblance must necessarily exist between books treating of pilgrimages, and here the resemblance is no more than general. The second part was published in 1684. Its inferiority to the first part is universally admitted, but is less than is usually entailed by the endeavour to append an artificial supplement to an inspired book. Many passages are fully worthy of the first part, and as a whole it abounds with life and variety.

Three only of Bunyan's numerous publications, besides *Pilgrim's Progress*, claim a place in literature : *The Holy War* (1682) ; *The Life and Death of Mr. Badman* (1680) ; *Grace Abounding* (1665). Of these *The Holy War* is the most important, and affords a highly instructive contrast with *Pilgrim's Progress*. It is the peculiar virtue of the latter, while full of wisdom and profitableness, to be in no way professedly didactic. Bunyan himself tells us that he did not sit down to compose it; the thoughts came spontaneously into his mind; he wrote it because he could not help himself. There was thus no need for laboriously instilling lessons which inhered in the original conception, and came forward of themselves as the story flowed along. The elaborate construction of *The Holy War* precludes belief in a like inspiration. There can, in fact, be little doubt that the idea is consciously derived from *Paradise Lost*. In both the banished fiends cast about for some means of retaliating upon their omnipotent foe ; in Milton their attack is levelled against the Garden of Eden, in Bunyan against the soul of man. All human attributes, virtuous or vicious, are allegorized with graphic liveliness, but at length one wearies of the crowd of abstractions; and where strength was most necessary, Bunyan is weak. Emanuel is not godlike, and Diabolus is not terrible. The book is perhaps chiefly interesting as an index to the great progress effected since Bunyan's time in spirituality as regards men's religious conceptions, and in freedom and enlightenment as concerns the things of earth. No one would now depict the offended majesty of Heaven as so like the offended majesty of the Stuarts; or deem that the revolters' offence could be mitigated by the abjectness of their submission; or try criminals with such unfairness; or lecture them upon conviction with such lack of judicial decorum. Bunyan's own spirit seems narrower than of old; among the traitors upon whom Emanuel's ministers execute justice he includes not only Notruth and Pitiless, but also Election-doubter and Vocation-doubter, who represent the majority of the members of the Church of England. The whole tone, in truth, is such as might be expected from one nurtured upon the Old rather than the New Testament, and who had never conceived any doubts of the justice of the Israelites' dealings with the Canaanites. The literary power, nevertheless, is unabated; much ingenuity is shown in keeping up the interest of the story; and there is the old gift of vitalizing abstractions by uncompromising realism of treatment. The following passage is a remarkable instance of the dependence of Bunyan's style upon his inward mind. Seldom have joy and elation of spirit elevated homely diction into so near an approach to magnificence:

'Well, I told you before, how the prisoners were entertained by the noble Prince Emmanuel, and how they behaved themselves before him, and how he sent them away to their home with pipe and tabor going before them. And now you must think, that those of the town that had all this while waited to hear of their death, could not but be exercised with sadness of mind, and with thoughts that pricked like thorns. Nor could their thoughts be kept to one point; the wind blew with them all this while at great uncertainties, yea, their hearts were like a balance that had been disquieted with shaking hand. But at last as they, with many a long look, looked over the wall of Mansoul, they thought that they saw some returning to the town; and thought again, who should they be? At last they discerned that they were the prisoners. But can you imagine, how their hearts were surprised with wonder! Especially when they perceived also in what equipage, and with what honour they were sent home. They went down to the camp in black, but they came back to the town in white; they went down to the camp in ropes, they came back in chains of gold; they went down to the camp with their feet in tatters, but they came back with their steps enlarged under them; they went also to the camp looking for death, but they came back from thence with assurance of life; they went down to the camp with heavy hearts, but came back again with pipe and tabor playing before them. So, so soon as they were come to Eye-gate, the poor and tottering town of Mansoul adventured to give a shout; and they gave such a shout, as made the captains in the Prince's army leap at the sound thereof. Alas! for them, poor hearts, who could blame them, since their dead friends were come to life again! For it was to them as life from the dead, to see the ancients of the town of Mansoul to shine in such splendour. They looked for nothing but the axe and the block; but behold! joy and gladness, comfort and consolation, and such melodious notes attending of them, that was sufficient to make a sick man well. So when they came up, they saluted each other with Welcome, welcome, and blessed be he that spared you. They added also, we see it is well with you, but how must it go with the town of Mansoul, and will it go well with the town of Mansoul, said they? Then answered them the Recorder, and my lord Mayor, Oh! tidings! glad tidings! good tidings of good; and of great joy to poor Mansoul! Then they gave another shout, that made the earth to ring again. After this, they enquired yet more particularly, how things went in the camp, and what message they had from Emmanuel to the town. So they told them all passages that had happened to them at the camp, and every thing that the Prince did to them. This made Mansoul wonder at the wisdom and grace of the Prince Emmanuel; then they told them what they had received at his hands, for the whole town of Mansoul; and the Recorder delivered it in these words, Pardon, Pardon, Pardon for Mansoul; and this shall Mansoul know to-morrow. Then he commanded, and they went and summoned Mansoul to meet together in the market-place to-morrow, there to hear their general pardon read.

'But who can think what a turn, what a change, what an alteration this hint of things did make in the countenance of the town of Mansoul; no man of Mansoul could sleep that night for joy; in every house there was joy and music, singing and making merry, telling and hearing of Mansoul's happiness was then all that Mansoul had to do; and this was the burden of all their song, "Oh! more of this at the rising of the sun! more of this to-morrow! Who thought yesterday, would one say, that this day would have been such a day to us? And who thought, that saw our prisoners go down in irons, that they would have returned in chains of gold! Yea, they that judged themselves as they went to be judged of their judge, were, by his mouth, acquitted, not for that they were innocent, but of the Prince's mercy, and sent home with pipe and tabor."'

The Life and Death of Mr. Badman is a piece of prose indeed, and its realism is, perhaps, the more effective from being wholly devoid of the least particle of imagination. The genesis and purpose of the book are thus stated by the author: 'As I was considering with myself what I had written concerning the progress of the Pilgrim from this world to glory, and how it had been acceptable to many in this nation, it came again into my mind to write, as then of him that was going to heaven, so now of the life and death of the ungodly, and of their travel from this world to

hell.' Had this conception been strictly carried out, the narrative must have been a failure from the want of admixture of
light and shade. The Christian of the *Pilgrim's Progress* is
a mixed character, and though we are scarcely in doubt as
to the ultimate success of his adventure, this is sufficiently
chequered with peril and hardship to keep our interest
alert. This evidently cannot be the case with Mr. Badman,
whose career is not only a monotony, but a monotony of
sordid evil; and who only excites a flickering sort of
interest in virtue of the sympathy naturally felt for the
victim of the animosity of his creator. Bunyan, however,
has not been faithful to his original plan, and has in a
measure redeemed one fault in art by committing another.
As a rule, nothing is more reprehensible in a fiction than
inordinate digression; but here it is the greatest relief to
be turned away from the repulsive career of Mr. Badman
to the running commentary in which Bunyan opens his
mind on a variety of subjects, spiritual and secular, ranging
from earnest rebukes of the maxim to be anon formulated
as 'buy in the cheapest market and sell in the dearest,' to
foolish stories of the deaths of persecutors, quite in the
vein of the Methodist anecdotes satirized by Sydney Smith.
This garrulity is greatly promoted by the inartistic
character of the machinery employed, a dialogue between
Mr. Wiseman and Mr. Attentive, which allows the writer
to say whatever he pleases. It is evident that he has real
persons and actual transactions continually in his mind,
and it would not be surprising to learn that his book
made no inconsiderable commotion in the town of
Bedford.

Grace Abounding resembles thousands of similar narratives in essentials, differing principally in the vigour with
which a terrifying religious experience is portrayed. It
does not, as some seem to have taken for granted, termi-

nate with what would be technically considered as Bunyan's conversion; on the contrary, a large portion is employed in recording his agonies of apprehension long after he had become a recognized religious instructor, even so late as the beginning of his imprisonment, when he was so little acquainted with the law as to suppose himself in jeopardy of the gallows. Much might be said in censure or compassion of his lamentably distorted views of divine things; but one thing cannot be said: there is not from first to last the slightest symptom of cant. The book is more sincere than Rousseau's *Confessions*, but could not, like that book, have helped a Carlyle or a George Eliot to learn that there was something in them. As *Pilgrim's Progress* may be termed a prosaic Divine Comedy, so might the Bunyan of *Grace Abounding* rank as a prosaic Augustine, but an Augustine without a Monica. With the rarest exceptions, self is its beginning, middle, and end; it is only when the author for a space becomes, unlike Cardinal Newman, conscious of the existence of something besides God and his own soul, that we catch the real moral of his tale, which he himself was far from intending or perceiving. In his own incomparably forcible words: ' I went myself in chains to preach to them in chains; and carried that fire in my own conscience that I persuaded them to beware of. I can truly say, and that without dissembling, that when I have been to preach I have gone full of guilt and terror even to the pulpit-door, and there it hath been taken off; and I have been at liberty in my mind until I have done my work, and then immediately, even before I could get down the pulpit-stairs, I have been as bad as I was before.' What is this but to own that self-seeking is unprofitable even when cloaked with piety and contrition; that there is no true peace save in disinterested service?

Violent indeed is the transition from John Bunyan to Aphra Behn, but in fact the living fiction of the age is almost summed up in these two names. But for the demonstration of the contrary afforded by the state of French literature since 1830, one would almost have been inclined to formulate it as a maxim that the drama and the novel cannot flourish together. The almost utter barrenness of the Restoration age in the latter class of literature is certainly very remarkable. All needful conditions seemed present in a teeming national life, clever writers, and a public that craved to be amused. It seems difficult to offer any explanation except that it had as yet occurred to none to depart from French models, and that the French exemplars of the day, like Samuel Weller, disdained all under the degree of 'a female markis.' Hence the healthy realism without which the English novel cannot prosper was impossible, and it was left to the Fieldings and Smolletts of the next age to effect a momentous revolution in art by the simple discovery that for the novelist's purpose, 'Jack was as good as his master.' One variety of fiction, apparently still popular at the Restoration, gradually died out—the interminable romance of the Clelia class, by which French polite society under Louis XIII. had replaced the exploded romance of chivalry. Of the few examples of this which English literature still produced, it will suffice to name Lord Orrery's *Parthenissa*, whose heroine, as an example of chastity, lived long enough to be dethroned by Pamela. Mrs. Behn's tales, it need not be said, are constructed upon principles in every respect antipodal to *Parthenissa* ; they are, however, much less objectionable than her comedies. They are on the French pattern, brief and bright, but inevitably conventional. At the present day, however,

(side note) Aphra Behn (1640-1689).

when the disuse of an equally conventional fashion is
restoring action to the rank from which it had been almost
displaced by dialogue, Mrs. Behn's tales might be not un-
profitably read as examples of movement and condensation ;
and occasionally of strong situation, of which she rarely
makes the most.   The most celebrated is *Oroonoko*, the
groundwork of Southern's play, and itself founded on facts
within the authoress's knowledge.   Among other remarkable passages is one descriptive of the effects of the electric
eel.   Mrs. Behn's stories are types of a large number of
miniature romances, apparently little noticed in their own
day, and utterly unknown in ours, which they have not
always reached in other fashion than Protus's

> ' Little tract on worming dogs,
> Whereof the name, in sundry catalogues,
> Is extant yet.'

' This class of literature,' says Mr. Gosse, ' was treated
with marked disdain, and having been read to pieces
by the women, was thrown into the fire.'   One specimen,
Incognita, deserves a word of mention as the first work of the
youthful Congreve.   Some variety was introduced into
pure fiction by the importation from France by Mrs.
Manley, already mentioned as a dramatist, of the political
novel, in which the actions of living monarchs and states-
men were represented under transparent disguises.   The
presses of Amsterdam and Cologne had long teemed with
such productions, and Mrs. Manley's *Atalanta* and *Zarah*
are conspicuous English examples.   Another romance, *A
New and further Discovery of the Isle of Pines*, in a letter
professing to emanate from Cornelius van Sloetton, a
Dutchman (1668), deserves some attention from its possible influence on Defoe.   It has been represented to be
connected with Australian discovery, with which it has in

fact nothing to do, the imaginary island being placed in the very centre of the Indian Ocean. It afforded the theme for Voltaire's joke about the Englishman *qui travaillait si bien* that the island on which he was wrecked was shortly afterwards found to be peopled by twelve thousand English Protestants.

CHAPTER XIV.

THE most important part of the posthumous papers of Samuel Butler, the discovery of which in the eighteenth century has been mentioned, was his *Characters*, composed upon the model of Theophrastus, and fairly entitling him to the appellation of the English Theophrastus, which is not the highest encomium imaginable. As the only work of the kind which has come down to us from antiquity, the *Characters* of Theophrastus, which are in reality much later than the time of that successor of Aristotle, have passed as models, a reputation in excess of their desert. They offer an acute and entertaining enumeration of various peculiarities of character, but do not succeed in presenting the personage as a whole, and have much the air of being compiled from traits delineated with a real truth of representation by the comic poets. Butler's *Characters* are of just the same kind, and his work is rather a museum of particulars than a gallery of portraits. The age of Charles II. by no means lives in him as the age of Anne lives in Addison. La Bruyère, Butler's more celebrated French successor, who certainly never read and probably never heard of him, fell into precisely the same error from too timid an adherence to Theophrastus; and the improvement upon him effected by Addison may be compared to the service rendered to sculpture by Dædalus,

the first, it is said, to show the human form in motion. '
Isolated remarks in Butler's essays are frequently very
shrewd and pregnant; as when he says of the newsmonger,
' He would willingly bear his share in any public calamity
to have the pleasure of hearing and telling it;' or of the
hunter, ' Let the hare take which way she will, she seldom
fails to lead him at long-running to the alehouse;' or the
description of a prince's unworthy favourite as ' a fog
raised by the sun to obscure his own brightness.' Many
of Butler's miscellaneous thoughts, appended to the *Characters*, are highly acute, and exhibit a happy talent for
illustrating abstract ideas by comparison with sensible
objects, as for instance: ' Oaths and obligations in the
affairs of the world are like ribands and knots in dressing,
that seem to tie something, but do not.' In politics Butler
is, of course, a loyalist; and one whose loyalty is intensified
by his æsthetic dislike to Puritanism, in which he was
constitutionally incapable of seeing anything but cant.
At the same time, the contempt which as a man of understanding he could not help entertaining for the conduct of
affairs under the Restoration, and disappointment at the
neglect with which he was himself treated, seem to have
almost reduced him to a condition of political scepticism
' The worst governments are the best when they light in
good hands; and the best the worst, when they fall into
bad ones '—a remark condensed into a famous couplet by
Pope, who appears to have become acquainted with Butler's
MS. through Atterbury. It is worth observing that Butler
not only prefers Ben Jonson to Shakespeare, but seems to
take his superiority for granted: ' Virgil, who wanted
much of that natural easiness of wit that Ovid had, did
nevertheless with hard labour and long study arrive at a
higher perfection than the other with all his dexterity of
wit, but less industry, could attain to. The same we may

observe of Jonson and Shakespeare; for he that is able to think long and judge well will be sure to find out better things than another man can hit upon suddenly, though of more quick and ready parts, which is commonly but chance, and the other art and judgment.' One special distinction of Butler's is to have been perhaps the first English satirist of mark who made parody a political weapon, or at least showed its capabilities for this purpose, as it does not appear that any of his political parodies were printed in his lifetime. Jack Cade's speeches in Shakespeare are, indeed, a sufficient model, but Butler worked out the hint elaborately in his fictitious speeches in the Rump Parliament; his mock eulogium of this body or segment of a body in the oration supposed to be delivered at Harrington's Rota; and the parody of Prynne's style in the imaginary correspondence between him and John Audland, the Quaker.

Butler's remains were only partially printed in 1759, but the MSS. from which Thyer's publication was drawn were acquired in 1885 by the British Museum. His selection seems to have been in general exceedingly judicious, but the opportunity may be taken of giving some examples of Butler's unpublished thoughts:

'There is no better argument to prove that the Scriptures were written by divine inspiration than that excellent saying of our Saviour, If any man will go to law with thee for thy cloak, give him thy coat also.

'Birds are taken with pipes that imitate their own voices, and men with those sayings that are most agreeable to their own opinions.

'If the French nobility should follow our fashions, and send their children over to learn our language, and receive their education from us, we should have as glorious an opinion of ourselves, and as mean a value of them, as they have of us; and

therefore we have no reason to blame them, but our own folly '
for it.'

It is interesting to learn Butler's opinion of Dryden as
a critic:

'Dryden weighs poets in his virtuoso's scales that will weigh
to the hundredth part of a grain, as curiously as Juvenal's lady
pedantess—

> "Committit vates, et comparat inde Maronem,
> Atque alia parte in trutina suspendit Homerum."

He complained of Ben Jonson for stealing scenes out of Plautus.
Set a thief to find out a thief.'

George Savile, Marquis of Halifax, who ranks with
Shaftesbury and Temple among the few politicians of that
age entitled to the appellation of statesman, enriched English
literature with a small volume of essays, the most important
of which are his vindication of his own political course and
principles in *The Character of a Trimmer* and *The Anatomy
of an Equivalent.* Of these Macaulay justly says: 'What
particularly strikes us is the writer's passion for generaliza-
tion. He was treating of the most exciting subjects in the
most agitated times; he was himself placed in the very
thick of the civil conflict; yet there is no acrimony, nothing
inflammatory, nothing personal. He treats every question
as an abstract question, begins with the widest propositions, argues these propositions on general grounds, and
often, when he has brought out his theorem, leaves the
reader to make the application, without adding an allusion
to particular men or to passing events.' The effect of this
remarkable breadth of view was not with Halifax, as so
frequently the case, to paralyze energy, and render the
comprehensive mind unfit for practical action. He was

not retained in equilibrium by the difficulty of deciding
between two courses, but was an enthusiast for the *via
media*, as great a zealot for compromise as zealots commonly are for strong measures; and, though sometimes
too yielding or too speculative for the unquiet times in
which his lot was cast, would have made an almost ideal
prime minister for the nineteenth century. His praise of
trimming, which to more fiery spirits must have seemed
an ignoble policy, rings with the eloquence and passion of
the most genuine conviction:

'Our Trimmer adores the Goddess Truth, though in all ages
she has been scurvily used, as well as those that worshipped her.
'Tis of late become such a ruining virtue that mankind seems to
be agreed to commend and avoid it; yet the want of practice,
which repeals the other laws, has no influence upon the law of
truth, because it has root in heaven, and an intrinsic value in
itself that can never be impaired. She shows her greatness in
this, that her enemies, even when they are successful, are ashamed
to own it. Nothing but power full of truth has the prerogative
of triumphing, not only after victories, but in spite of them, and
to put conquest herself out of countenance. She may be kept
under and suppressed, but her dignity still remains with her,
even when she is in chains. Falsehood with all her impudence
has not enough to speak ill of her before her face. Such majesty
she carries about her that her most prosperous enemies are fain
to whisper their treason, all the power upon the earth can never
extinguish her. She has lived in all ages, and let the mistaken
zeal of prevailing authority christen any opposition to her with
what name they please, she makes it not only an ugly and an
unmannerly, but a dangerous thing to persist. She has lived
very retired indeed, nay, sometimes so buried that only some few
of the discerning part of mankind could have a glimpse of her;
with all that, she has eternity in her, she knows not how to die,
and from the darkest clouds that shade and cover her she breaks
from time to time with triumph for her friends, and terror to her
enemies.

'Our Trimmer, therefore, inspired by this divine virtue,

thinks fit to conclude with these assertions, That our climate is a trimmer between that part of the world where men are roasted and that part where they are frozen : That our Church is a trimmer between the phrenzy of phanatic [1] visions and the lethargic ignorance of Popish dreams : That our laws are trimmers between the excess of unbounded power and the extravagance of liberty not enough restrained : That true virtue has ever been thought a trimmer, and to have its dwelling in the middle between the two extremes : That even God Almighty himself is divided between his two great attributes, his mercy and his justice.

'In such company our Trimmer is not ashamed of his name, and willingly leaves to the bold champions of either extreme the honour of contending with no less adversaries than nature, religion, liberty, prudence, humanity, and common sense.'

Burnet might well be puzzled by a man who 'seemed to have his head full of Commonwealth notions,' and yet concurred in the worst measures of Charles II.

The most important of Halifax's other essays are his advice to his daughter, excellent for sense and curious as an illustration of the manners of the age, and his character of Charles II., nicely balanced between half-sincere censure and half-sarcastic apology.   There is nothing in Charles's history to refute Halifax's view of him as a man whose master passion was the selfish love of ease ; but much to prove that his abilities and discernment were far greater than Halifax chooses to allow.   Halifax's aphorisms, as usual, are too numerous to attain a uniformly high standard, but some are exceedingly good.

'A fool hath no dialogue within himself.

'Malice may be sometimes out of breath, Envy never.   A man may make peace with hatred, but never with envy.

[1] All the editions have *Platonic*, but this must be a misprint.

'An old man concludeth from his knowing mankind that they know him too, and that maketh him very wary.

'He that leaveth nothing to chance will do few things ill, but he will do very few things.'

An allusion in these aphorisms to the Bank of England proves that Halifax went on writing till nearly the hour of his death in 1695. Of his other writings, the most remarkable is the *Advice to a Dissenter* (1687), a masterly dissuasive against abetting the illegalities of James.

Possibly, when Halifax penned the last-quoted aphorism, he was thinking of Sir William Temple, well known to him at the council-board, of whom Macaulay says, 'It was his constitution to dread failure more than he desired success.' This elegant writer, whom we have already met as an historian and as a speculator upon government, for once did a rash thing when he entered into the controversy respecting the comparative merits of the ancient and modern writers, knowing little of either. Macaulay has done full justice to the ignorance and carelessness of this well-worded composition; but Macaulay has said nothing of its extraordinary want of insight. Temple need not be blamed for having been unable to make up his mind whether the blood circulated, and whether the earth went round the sun (the Grand Duke Cosmo found Cambridge disputing against the latter proposition in 1669); what is really astonishing is that he should have been utterly blind to the stupendous consequences which Giordano Bruno had pointed out a century before. 'If they are true,' he says, 'yet these two great discoveries have made no change in the conclusions of astronomy, nor in the practice of physic, and so have been of little use to the world, though perhaps of much honour to the authors.' After this, Temple's essays are not likely to be referred to in quest of intellectual wisdom, and their chief value, apart from the purity and elegance of their style, consists in their illustrations of contemporary opinions and practices. This is especially the case with the essay on *Health and Long Life*. Temple enumerates with suppressed amusement the various sanatory fads he has known, among which he seems to reckon tea and coffee. Unconsciously confirming an anecdote of Charles II. and his physicians, related by Evelyn, he tells us that Peruvian bark was at first received with prejudice and suspicion, but was becoming rehabilitated in his day, and fairly confounds us by his faith in ' that little insect called millepedes; the powder whereof, made up into little balls with fresh butter, I never knew fail of curing any sore throat.'

The letter-writers of the age who have any claim to a place in literature as such are but few, and none of their epistles were intended for publication. Dryden, as elsewhere, takes the lead, and his letters, though scanty and occasional, occupy a pleasant chamber in the edifice of his prose writings. The first, dated 1655, and addressed to a female cousin in language of complimentary gallantry, is of especial interest as showing how early his prose style was formed. Notwithstanding the strain of high-flown sentiment enforced by the occasion, it is far less fanciful and involved than similar compositions of the early Caroline period, and is in all essential respects an example of the sound, clear prose of the Restoration. The letters to the two Rochesters, the man of letters and the man of office, are models of ingenious flattery in different styles; those to his publisher, Jacob Tonson, apart from their personal interest, are important for the light they throw upon the relations between publishers and authors at a period when publishers were as yet mere tradesmen, and the most popular author could hardly subsist by authorship. The latest of all, addressed to his Northamptonshire kindred, are mellow as with the light of a setting sun, and afford pleasant glimpses of the occasional ruralizings of the most urban of poets.

Sir William Temple is so thoroughly identified with the Restoration period, that although the charming letters of his betrothed, Dorothy Osborne, were written in 1652-54, and not published until 1888, they may be regarded as belonging to it. The young lady was well known from Macaulay's account of her in his essay upon her husband, and many of her letters had been published in Courtenay's life of her husband, ere the whole, so far as preserved, recently became accessible in the edition of Mr. Edward Abbott Parry. Intended for no other eyes than her lover's, these letters have given Lady Temple high rank among English epistolographers. Though they are exceedingly well written, their charm is personal rather than literary. No biographer or novelist has painted a truer picture of the English maiden, high-minded and high-spirited, heroically constant and at the same time full of engaging frailties and arch teasing ways, than is depicted in these artless self-revelations. Temple seems to have behaved perfectly well throughout their protracted engagement; and his fulfilment of it after Dorothy's beauty had been destroyed by the smallpox may be reasonably believed to have been the effect of inclination, no less than of honour and duty. The very slight glimpse we obtain of their married life reveals Lady Temple's interest in his political career; had this been guided by her his life would probably have been less comfortable, and his memory more glorious.

The letters of Humphrey Prideaux, Dean of Norwich, to John Ellis, Secretary of the Treasury, edited for the Camden Society by Sir Edward Maunde Thompson,

Lady Temple's letters (1652-1654).

though ordinary familiar correspondence, are too curious
a repertory of gossip to be passed over
without notice. They are mostly written
from Oxford, and retail the scandal of the
university in a lively fashion, although
the writer, a middling classical and oriental scholar, known
by his edition of the *Arundel Marbles* and his *Life of
Mahomet*, seems rather a matter-of-fact personage. His
relish for scandal, however, occasionally makes him
humorous, as when he describes the deportment of his
predecessor in the Norwich deanery: 'His whole life is
the pot and the pipe, and, go to him when you will, you
will find him walking about his room with a pipe in his
mouth and a bottle of claret and a bottle of old strong
beer (which in this country they call nog) upon the table,
and every other turn he takes a glass of one or the other
of them.' The book is rich in such vignettes; its more
serious interest consists in its illustration of the practical
refutation of the theory of divine right previously held by
the majority of the clergy by James II.'s misgovernment.
The beginning and the end of the correspondence are in
violent political contrast; and the metamorphosis is entirely effected during the last two years of James's reign.

Dean Prideaux's letters (1674-1710).

Literary history is necessarily among the latest developments of literature. The nearest approach to it in the
England of the seventeenth century was the younger
Gerard Langbaine's (1656-92) *Account of the English
Dramatic Poets*, Oxford, 1691. Langbaine laid himself
out particularly to discover the sources from which dramatists had borrowed their plots, and is styled by Dr.
Johnson 'the great detector of plagiarism.' He has been
accused of having read poetry for no other purpose, but is
vindicated by Mr. Sidney Lee. The value of his work is
much increased by the manuscript notes and additions of

S

Oldys and others, copies of which are in the British Museum and Bodleian. The literary compilations of Edward Phillips are so poor that they would have deserved no notice if he had not been Milton's nephew, and the first English author to mention *Paradise Lost*.

CHAPTER XV.

THE pursuit of antiquarianism has always flourished in England since her inhabitants have enjoyed sufficient culture to be aware that they possessed a past. Even the poetry of Layamon is in a certain measure antiquarian, and Chaucer, Spenser, Milton appear progressively more and more leavened with antiquarian sentiment, which, as a factor of literary inspiration, attains perhaps its highest conceivable development in the works of Robert Burton and Sir Thomas Browne. The Restoration period produced no such examples of antiquarian men of genius; but several excellent antiquarian writers, whose works are of sufficient compass and intrinsic importance, and are distinguished by sufficient attention to diction, to bring them within the domain of literature. It may be said of all the principal of these laborious men, that they have erected imperishable monuments to themselves, and have left little room for successors, except in the capacity of editors and annotators. Of Anthony à Wood, the historian and biographer of Oxford, it is almost enough praise to say that two centuries have elapsed without producing anyone capable either of continuing his Oxonian labours on the same scale, or, since the late Mr. C. H. Cooper's work has remained incomplete, of performing the like for the sister university. A terrible

Anthony à Wood (1632-1695).

toiler, a loyalist and high churchman, as beseemed the
Oxonian of his day, but apparently with few serious interests in life except the fame of his beloved Alma Mater,
he sat down at thirty in his college (Merton), and delved
resolutely until he had produced his *History and Antiquities* (1674) and his *Athenae Oxonienses* (1691). The former
was originally published in a Latin version made by one
Peers, and seriously garbled at the instigation of Dr. Fell.
The original English text, however, was published in the
eighteenth century. The labours of Wood's nineteenth
century editor, Dr. Bliss, upon the *Athenae*, are universally
known. Wood is not a pure or elegant writer, but his
works will last as long as Oxford.

Thomas Rymer has already been mentioned with due
disrespect among critics, and his more useful
Rymer's and honourable labours as an antiquary do not,
Foedera. strictly speaking, entitle him to be named
among men of letters, being mainly those of an editor.
It is impossible, however, to pass over in silence a collection of such unspeakable value as his *Foedera*, ten folio
volumes of most precious documents relating to English
history from 1102 to 1654. Rymer the Dryasdust, however, cannot quite forget Rymer the Longinus; his work
is graced with a Latin address to Queen Anne, more like
a dithyrambic than a dedication.

Next to Wood, the most important antiquary of the age
was Sir William Dugdale, of little account as
Sir William a mere author, but whom his industry and the
Dugdale assistance he was successful in enlisting from
(1605-1686). various quarters, enabled to achieve several
works, any one of which would have sufficed to gain him
immortal renown as an antiquarian. These were his
monumental *Monasticon Anglicanum* (1655-1673), a gigantic
work, but founded in great part upon the collections of

Roger Dodsworth; his *Antiquities of Warwickshire* (1656),
an immense improvement upon everything that had previously been effected in the department of county history,
and the model of all that has been accomplished since; his
History of St. Paul's Cathedral (1658), and his *Baronage of
England* (1675-1676). He was also the author of several
other works. So eminent a genealogist was naturally a
Cavalier, and, when he lost his appointment as Chester
herald during the Civil Wars, is said to have made his
living by the deaths of persons of quality, whose funerals
he conducted *secundum artem.* Private patrons and em-
ployers helped him on until the Restoration, when, as successively Norroy and Garter King-at-Arms, he attained
great prosperity, making numerous visitations, and approv-
ing himself a terror to heraldic pretenders. He died at
eighty, of a fever contracted 'by attendance too much on
his worldly concerns.' His son-in-law, Elias Ashmole,

Elias Ashmole
(1617-1692).

was an eminent antiquary of a different
order, although his principal work, *Institution, Laws, and Ceremonies of the Order of
the Garter*, might well have proceeded from Dugdale's pen.
His turn, however, was rather for the collection of curiosities, 'the greatest virtuoso and curioso that ever was known
or read of in England before his time.' In this capacity
he collected the Ashmolean Museum, which has preserved
his name more effectually than anything he wrote or was
capable of writing. He was also an astrologer, the friend
of Lilly and Booker, and in his younger days an alchemist.
This latter pursuit was so far serviceable, that it led him to
preserve by printing twenty-nine rare old alchemical books.
After his history of the order of the Garter, his principal
work is his diary, which briefly but amusingly records the
vicissitudes of his generally prosperous life; his gain of
estate and loss of quiet by his second marriage; his

acquaintance with old Mr. Backhouse, the Rosicrucian,
'who told me, in syllables, the true matter of the philosopher's stone;' his prosperity under Charles II. as Wind-
sor herald and holder of several other offices; his third
marriage, with the daughter of his friend Dugdale; above
all, his acquisition of the Tradescant antiquities, which
formed the nucleus of the Ashmolean Museum.   This
and his collection of manuscripts were bequeathed to the
University of Oxford; the catalogue of the latter forms a
goodly volume.

Of far less importance than Dugdale or Ashmole as an
antiquary, John Aubrey is better remembered
as an author. His strictly literary qualifications are few; setting aside his collections for
local history, his writings consist of little else than detached memoranda.   Their merit lies partly in the interest
of their themes, but still more in their artless simplicity
and the transparent revelation of the amiable if not dignified character of one who might have sat to Addison for
Will Wimble.   Aubrey remarks concerning himself that
he might have succeeded in life if he had been a painter.
Of his artistic powers we cannot judge, but the simple,
cheerful, social temper that befits the itinerant landscape
painter was his beyond question.   For all more serious
careers he was totally unfit. He had lost money and estate
before middle life, and spent the remainder of his days
with much more satisfaction to himself in visiting, or,
when pressed by pecuniary difficulties, 'delitescing' at the
mansions of country friends, a welcome and innocent para-
site.   The guiding spirit of his literary work is charmingly
expressed by himself: 'Methinks it shows a kind of grati-
tude and good nature to revive the memories and memorials of the pious and charitable benefactors long since
dead and gone.'   In the same spirit, after relating how he

John Aubrey
(1626-1697).

had seen Venetia Digby's bust 'standing at a stall at the Golden Crosse, a brasier's shop,' he exclaims, 'How these curiosities would be quite forgot, did not such idle fellows as I am put them down!' He has hence retrieved from oblivion a number of highly curious and interesting particulars about men of letters from Shakespeare downwards, and a most entertaining collection of stories of apparitions, warnings, prophecies, and similar matters. Much of the charm consists in the credulity and simplicity of the narrator, who is nevertheless by no means incapable of just and penetrating reflections on occasion, as when he says of Shakespeare: 'His comedies will remain wit as long as the English tongue is understood, for that he handles *mores hominum;* now our present writers reflect so much upon particular persons and coxcombeities, that twenty years hence they will not be understood.' Though exceedingly industrious as a collector, 'my head,' he says, 'was always working, never idle, and even travelling did glean some observations, some whereof to be valued,' he lacked the patience or the ability to reduce these observations into form, and they have been mostly incorporated with the works of succeeding antiquaries. He was born at Easton Pierse, in Wiltshire, in 1626, and died at Oxford in 1697. He is entitled to much credit for having brought to light the Druidical remains at Avebury in his native county, unnoticed before his time.

Along with the works of the antiquarians may be mentioned a book of great interest, and in its way of great merit, the *History of the Royal Society* by the convivial and facetious Dean of Westminster and Bishop of Rochester, Thomas Sprat (1636-1713), whom we have already met as a bad poet on his own account, but as the efficient

Sprat's *History of the Royal Society.*

coadjutor of Buckingham in the *Rehearsal*. Cautious, pliant, and self-indulgent, he almost incurred infamy and deprivation by his unworthy compliances under James II.; but he retracted just in time, rallied to the new order of things, and recovered credit through the sympathy excited for him as the object of a most diabolical plot in the manner of Oates and Bedloe.[1] Of his *History of the Royal Society* Johnson says: 'The *History of the Royal Society* is now read, not with the wish to know what they were then doing, but how their transactions are exhibited by Sprat.' If this was true at the time, it is true no more. Sprat's name is no longer a magnet; and, in truth, although his enthusiasm for scientific research is highly honourable to him, his style exceedingly lively, and many of his observations replete with good sense, his work as a whole is discursive and ill-digested, and so little of a history that it hardly ever gives a date. The writer himself confesses that it is only the second of his three books has any proper claim to the title of history. But it is important on grounds of its own, which render it of more real value than the more exact and pragmatical narratives which have superseded it. The glow of youth is upon it. It paints vividly the great scientific awakening which coincided with the accession of Charles II. The mere list of the experiments which the Royal Society had performed, or proposed to perform, attests the devouring scientific curiosity of the age, and shows at once the reaction of men's minds in the direction of the tangibly useful after a long series of fruitless theological and political controver-

---

[1] It is strange that Macaulay, who had told this story so graphically in his *History*, should have forgotten it when he came to write the *Life of Atterbury*. No English bishop, he says, had been taken into custody between the Seven Bishops and Atterbury, overlooking Sprat.

sies, and how deep in the long run had been the influence
of the great man who had lost his life in performing an
experiment.   At the same time there is a humorous side to
the picture: much of the curiosity of the time was idle, much
was founded on credulity. Many of the queries which Sprat
catalogues with such complacency would now be thought too
trivial to engage the attention of a learned society, and some
are not a little absurd. In the main, however, they are most
significant of the new spirit that had come into the world.
A counter spirit was necessarily called into being also.
Sprat combats the objections of churchmen by proving that
enthusiasts cannot be natural philosophers, and propitiates
wits like Butler by promising them new ideas for their
writings.   His demonstration that the design of the society
was in no respect prejudicial to the Church of England
may raise a smile now, but was probably by no means
superfluous at the time.   His remarks upon the utility of
experiments display the most vigorous common sense ; he
would evidently have subscribed heartily to a modern
definition of a fool as ' a man who never made an experiment in his life.'   ' If,' he says of the opponents of experi-
mental philosophy, ' they will persist in contemning all
experiments except those which bring with them immediate
gain and a present harvest, they may as well cavil at the
providence of God that he has not made all the seasons of
the year to be times of mowing, reaping, and vintage.'
He enumerates eleven classes of experiments actually instituted by the Royal Society, comprising a very large
number of separate essays, one of which, it is to be
feared, may not have perfectly succeeded, ' Of making a
deaf and dumb man to speak.'   His observations upon the
prospects of human improvement, the advantages of trans-
plantation and immigration, the national gain from encouraging inventors and projectors, are conceived in the

same bold and liberal spirit, contrasting forcibly with his timid and time-serving politics. In his advocacy of the claims of London to rank as the metropolis of science, and his exhortations to the English gentry to turn the leisure and opportunity afforded by a country life to account for the study of nature, he becomes what he never is when writing verse—something bordering upon a poet.

.. As has been remarked, the latter half of the seventeenth century was in England pre-eminently a scientific age. The ideas of Bacon were generally acted upon, and it was universally recognized that the only safe path to physical knowledge was through experiment. Newton and Hooke, in natural philosophy; Mayow, in chemistry; Sydenham, in medicine; Grew, in vegetable anatomy; Ray, in the classification of plants and animals, carried the fame of their country to greater heights than even Bacon's 'eagle-spirit' could have soared to imagine. But these illustrious men did little or nothing for literature, for such was not their design. The art of blending scientific research with elegant disquisition remained to be invented. Many of their works were composed in Latin; none were intended for a miscellaneous public. Science, in consequence, was far from exerting that influence upon creed and conduct which she exercises in our day, and an age of scientific discovery till then unexampled passed away without enriching literature by a single classic. Two books alone, neither of which can strictly be termed scientific, but both of which touch outlying provinces of natural history, added —one very considerably—to the literary wealth of the age. They are Evelyn's *Sylva* and Walton's *Complete Angler*— both by authors of whom we have previously had occasion to speak. If any reader of Evelyn's *Diary* should feel prejudiced by the carping criticisms of De Quincey, he may be safely referred to his *Sylva* (originally published in 1664, much augmented in later editions).

Evelyn's *Sylva*, 1664.

The writer here displays himself in a character most alien of all others to that of a time-server or a prig, that of an English country gentleman. His work is further inspired by a genuine love of nature, whose formality is justified by the stateliness of the theme, and tempered by the almost personal affection of the author for the trees he has known from a boy, or himself called into being. The scholar is everywhere apparent. 'I did not,' he says, 'altogether compile this work for the sake of our ordinary rustics, mere foresters and woodmen, but for the benefit and diversion of gentlemen and persons of quality, who often refresh themselves in the agreeable toils of planting and gardening.' It may be that Evelyn thought too much of the requisites of this class of readers, but, had he limited himself to a mere technical manual, he would not now be read. We do not know how his precepts are rated by the foresters and landscape gardeners of the present age; but even if he has not always shown the way, he has powerfully stimulated the wish to become a miniature creator by embellishing the countenance of Nature. His prose, more elaborate here than in his *Diary*, entitles him to rank among the refiners of the language.

The literature of England has this among other points in common with ancient literature, that it reckons books on fishing among its classics. Oppian, who sang of the sea and its inhabitants to Caracalla, is far from the worst among the Greek poets, and has in particular expressed the successful angler's exultation with a truth and terseness which no successor will surpass :

πολλὴ γὰρ βλεφάροισι καὶ ἐν φρεσὶ τέρψις ἰδέσθαι
παλλομενον καὶ ἐλισσομενον πεπεδημενον ἰχθυν.

Half a century later Nemesian gained equal fame among the Latins by a poem on the same theme, which has not come down to us. The piscatorial eclogues of Sanazzaro are an ornament of Italian literature, and were imitated by Milton in his *Lycidas;* [1] but the first and best modern poem on the technicalities of angling (*The Secrets of Angling,* by John Dennys, 1630) is English, and is one of the most pleasing didactic poems in the language. The subject was next to have been taken up by a better known writer, Sir Henry Wotton, but his intended work was never completed, and it remained for Izaak Walton, whom we have already met as an ecclesiastical biographer, to render it equally interesting to the professional fisherman and charming to the lover of idyllic pastoral.

The first edition (1653) is wellnigh the most prized of all rare old English books. It had four more editions in the author's lifetime, all with additions and amendments, and it is needless to observe that it has retained its popularity to our day as completely as *Paradise Lost* or *Pilgrim's Progress.* The technical details are no doubt sound, except for the author's defective acquaintance with fly-fishing; but the preservative against time has not been the didactic skill which others might rival or surpass, but the accompaniment of natural description and song and pictures of country life, conveyed in a style whose quaint simplicity, at once transparent and formal, is a survival from the old Elizabethan days, to which, with their pastorals and poetry, he himself looks back with so much affection :

'Look, under the broad beech-tree, I sat down, when I was last this way a-fishing, and the birds in the adjoining grove seemed

[1] A correspondent of the *Athenaeum* has pointed out, but the discovery seems to have been hardly noticed, that Shakespeare took the name of Ophelia from Sanazzaro's *Arcadia*—another argument for his acquaintance with Italian.

to have a friendly contention with an echo, whose dead voice seemed to live in a hollow tree, near to the brow of that primrose-hill; there I sat viewing the silver streams glide silently towards their centre, the tempestuous sea; yet sometimes opposed by rugged roots and pebble-stones, which broke their waves, and turned them into foam: and sometimes I beguiled time by viewing the harmless lambs, some leaping securely in the cool shade, whilst others sported themselves in the cheerful sun; and saw others craving comfort from the swollen udders of their bleating dams. As I sat there, these and other sights had so fully possessed my soul with content, that I thought, as the poet has happily exprest it,

> "I was for that time lifted above earth;
> And possessed joys not promis'd in my birth."

As I left this place and entered into the next field, a second pleasure entertained me; 'twas a handsome milk-maid, that had not yet attained so much age and wisdom as to load her mind with any fears of many things that will never be, as too many men too often do: but she cast away all care, and sung like a nightingale; her voice was good, and the ditty fitted for it: 'twas that smooth song, which was made by Kit Marlow, now at least fifty years ago: and the milk-maid's mother sung an answer to it, which was made by Sir Walter Raleigh in his younger days.

' They were old-fashioned poetry, but choicely good, I think much better than the strong lines that are now in fashion in this critical age.'

Passages like these create for the middle-aged man the joy and charm of Walton's *Angler*, which the boy devours as a manual of the piscatorial art. To the more advanced reader the chief use of the fish is as a vehicle for the pastoral; nevertheless, the great success of Walton's treatise is a proof that he was by no means inefficient from a more utilitarian point of view. Londoners have usually made good anglers, except, from want of opportunity, as fly-fishermen. Here it has been necessary to supplement Walton very largely; and indeed he himself confesses to having relied for such information as he does afford upon another angler. Elsewhere he approves himself master of his profession, and no doubt had trained many a pupil, perhaps made many a convert like the Venator who puts himself so readily under his tuition. Everyone knows the proem of his book, instinct with the freshness of the bright May morning, the otter hunt, a holy war in the eyes of the injured fisherman (O blissful days, when otters were yet to be found in the Lea!), and the earnest rhetoric of Auceps, Venator, and Piscator, contending for the pre-eminence of their favourite sports. It is characteristic of Walton's simplicity and candour that he should have placed the most beautiful passage of his book in the mouth of one of his opponents.

'These I will pass by, but not those little nimble musicians of the air, that warble forth their curious ditties, with which nature hath furnished them to the shame of art.

'As first the lark, when she means to rejoice; to cheer herself and those that hear her, she then quits the earth, and sings as she ascends higher into the air, and having ended her heavenly employment, grows then mute and sad to think she must descend to the dull earth, which she would not touch but for necessity.

'How do the blackbird and thrassel with their melodious voices bid welcome to the cheerful spring, and in their fixed months warble forth such ditties as no art or instrument can reach to?

'Nay, the smaller birds also do the like in their particular seasons, as namely the leverock, the tit-lark, the little linnet, and the honest robin, that loves mankind both alive and dead.

'But the nightingale, another of my airy creatures, breathes such sweet loud music out of her little instrumental throat, that it might make mankind to think miracles are not ceased. He that at midnight, when the very labourer sleeps securely, should hear, as I have very often, the clear airs, the sweet descants, the natural rising and falling, the doubling and redoubling of her voice, might well be lifted above earth, and say Lord, what music hast thou provided for the saints in heaven, when thou affordest bad men such music on earth!'

It has been remarked that it was necessary to supplement Walton's imperfect knowledge of fly-fishing. This task, a delicate one in his lifetime, was piously and successfully performed by a scholar, Charles Cotton, of Beresford, Derbyshire (1630-1687), whose appendix of dialogues appeared in the fifth edition of Walton's own treatise (1676) with some graceful introductory lines from Izaak himself, then in his eighty-third year. 'I have been so obedient to your desires,' he says, 'as to endure all the praises you have ventured to fix upon me.' Cotton, a country gentleman of good family, whose fishing cottage on the Dove stands to this day, obtained some reputation as a man of letters by a translation of Scarron's burlesque poem, and other versions from the French. He was also an authority upon cards, which possibly accounts for the pecuniary embarrassments which clouded the latter part of his life. His piscatorial teaching is no doubt quite sound; but his book, although a lively dialogue, is no idyll like his master's, and would be forgotten but for its association with the latter. The best passages are those depicting the horror of the London visitor at the steepness of the Derbyshire hills and the narrowness of the Derbyshire bridges. 'I would not ride over it for a thousand pounds, nor fall off it for two; and yet I think I dare venture on foot, though if you were not by to laugh at me, I should do it on all four.'

TRAVEL was well represented in the literature of the period, as could hardly be otherwise in an age distinguished by the awakening of a spirit of curiosity and intelligent inquiry. The time for systematic scientific exploration had not arrived; no Englishman devoted himself to travel as a profession with the steadiness of the Italian Della Valle, or described a foreign land with such thoroughness as in the Indian monograph of the French jeweller, Tavernier. But if no such monumental work was produced, there was no lack of standard ones. The two which have come nearest to attaining the rank of literary classics, however, were not the production of men of high attainments, but the work, or reputed work, of writers of imperfect education, whose chief claim to attention was the surpassing interest of their narratives.

Robert Knox belongs to the especially interesting class of travellers whose experience of foreign countries has been gained in captivity. Driven by a storm on to the coast of Ceylon in 1659, he was made prisoner and carried into the interior, then almost unknown to Europeans. Here he supported himself for nearly twenty years by knitting caps and hawking goods, resisting all inducements to enter the service of the native sovereign, whose caprice and cruelty he dreaded

Robert Knox
(1640?-1720).

with good reason. At length he escaped to a Dutch settlement, and returned safely to England, where he entered the service of the East India Company. After several more voyages to the East he retired, and died in good circumstances in 1720. His letters to his cousin, Strype, preserved in the University Library, Cambridge, show him, it is said, 'to have been a man of morose temper, rough manners, and a woman-hater.' The 'manuscripts of my own life,' bequeathed by him to his nephew, Knox Ward, have unfortunately gone astray. His account of his captivity was published in 1681, with a preface by the illustrious natural philosopher, Robert Hooke, who no doubt gave Knox much literary assistance, but happily abstained from tampering with the simplicity of his narrative. As a classic of travel this ranks with the similar works of Drury and Mariner, which also received literary form from intelligent collaborators, and it may have served in some measure as an example to Defoe.

William Dampier fills a more important place than
William Dampier (1652-1715). Knox in the history of travel, his experiences having been much more diversified, and his works being of much greater compass. Having gone in 1679 to the West Indies on a commercial adventure, he was persuaded to join a buccaneering expedition, many of the piratical incidents of which, judiciously passed over in his own narrative, are recorded in the manuscripts of his companions. It involved him in a series of adventures which took him all round the world, and from which he returned in 1691 with no other property than an 'amiable savage, curiously tattooed.' His voyage was published in 1697-99, and obtained such success that the government, overlooking or ill-informed of his piracies, employed him on a voyage of discovery to Australia. He was subsequently engaged in

two privateering expeditions, in the first as commander, in the second only as pilot. Alexander Selkirk was put on shore on Juan Fernandez in the first of these, and taken off in the second. Dampier's temper seems to have disqualified him for supreme authority, and he lost much of the reputation which he had formerly acquired. He died in 1715 in good circumstances, with a large amount of prize-money still owing to him. As a traveller he takes high rank from the interest of the occurrences he narrates, the clearness and simplicity of his style, his powers of description, and his practical knowledge. 'His *Discourse of the Winds*,' says Professor Laughton, 'may even now be regarded, so far as it goes, as a text-book of that branch of physical geography.' His literary merit, however, partly belongs to some unnamed coadjutor. 'I have,' says Charles Hatton, in the Hatton correspondence edited by Sir Edward Thompson, 'discoursed with Dampier. He is a blunt fellow, but of better understanding than would be expected from one of his education. He is a very good navigator, kept his journal exactly, and set down every day what he thought of, but, you must imagine, had assistance in dressing up his history, in which are many mistakes in naming of places.'

The times were not ripe for archæological exploration, or for profound investigation of the manners and institutions of foreign nations; and the most gifted travellers of the age wrote with one eye upon things abroad and the other upon affairs at home. Among such itinerant politicians the first place must be given to Burnet, rather, however, for his celebrity in other fields than for the special merit of his travels. He recorded, nevertheless, a number of intelligent observations upon Switzerland, Italy, and Germany. Burnet is always lively and sagacious, and much more impartial

Burnet and Molesworth.

than could have been expected in one so deeply concerned in political and theological controversies. His account of Venice is especially interesting. The book, written during his exile, was published in Holland, and was for some time prohibited in England. The somewhat similar work of Lord Molesworth (1656-1725) owes its existence to accident. Molesworth, a theoretical republican of Algernon Sidney's school, was English envoy at Copenhagen from 1690 to 1692, and was obliged to quit the country in consequence, as was asserted, of an insult offered by him to the king; considering, however, the favourable character he gives of the monarch, this appears hardly probable. Whatever the reason, he threw up his embassy, and avenged himself by a severe indictment of the system of absolute government established in Denmark by the memorable revolution of 1660, which he declared to have entirely impoverished the country. Himself a patrician, he finds the principal cause of this in the abasement of his own class; and he probably wrote rather from regard to the affairs of England than those of Denmark. He is a forcible, but, at the same time, a candid writer, admitting frankly that 'In Denmark there are no seditions, mutinies, or libels against the government; but all the people either are, or appear to be lovers of their king, notwithstanding their ill treatment, and the hardships they groan under. There are no clippers or coiners, no robbers upon the highway, nor housebreakers; which conveniency of arbitrary government, among the multitude of mischiefs attending it, I have likewise observed in France.' He is greatly impressed with the merits of the Danish laws, apart from their administration. 'For justice, brevity, and perspicuity, they exceed all that I know in the world. They are grounded upon equity, and are all contained in one quarto volume, written in the language of the country.' Such passages are conclusive as to his impartiality, and the violent attacks which his book provoked were probably mainly due to its exceedingly plain speaking about individuals. Of the Danes in general he says: 'I never knew any country where the minds of the people were more of one calibre and pitch than here; you shall meet with none of extraordinary parts or qualifications, or excellent in particular studies and trades; you see no enthusiasts, madmen, natural fools, or fanciful folks; but a certain equality of understanding reigns among them. Every one keeps the ordinary beaten road of sense, which in this country is neither the fairest nor the foulest, without deviating to the right or left.' Molesworth was a man of parts and independent character, who afterwards rendered his country considerable services in Ireland, where Swift dedicated one of the Drapier's letters to him as a patriot.

Paul Rycaut, secretary to the English ambassador at Constantinople, and author of an exceedingly

Paul Rycaut. valuable account of *The Present State of the Ottoman Empire* (1668), should perhaps hardly be reckoned among travellers, as he gives no account of his residence, and merely condenses the results of his observation of Ottoman manners and polity. The book must have been highly important at a time when the Ottoman still menaced Europe, and may be read with pleasure even now for its good sense and varied information, which includes a lively description of a palace revolution, and an account of the chief religious sects among the Turks.

Doctor Edward Browne, son of Sir Thomas Browne, was a highly accomplished man, whose travels in

Edward Browne. Eastern Europe (1673) contain a remarkable amount of accurate observation within a surprisingly narrow compass. It seems strange to find him foretelling a great territorial expansion of the Turkish empire at the expense of Christian Europe, but the prophecy came near being fulfilled by the peril of Vienna not long after Browne wrote.

This review of English travellers would not be complete without a brief notice of two foreign visitors to the country, whose narratives, translated into English, have probably been more read here than at home, and from whom much valuable information may be derived. Sorbière, a philosopher of Gassendi's school, a Protestant by birth, but who had become a nominal Catholic, visited England in 1663. Being, as he admits, entirely ignorant of the language, his attention was principally given to the intellectual aspects of the country, which were not unfamiliar to him, from his acquaintance with the works of Englishmen who had written in Latin. His accounts of Oxford and the Royal Society are neither unamusing nor uninstructive; he has a true veneration for English men of science, especially Bacon, whom he pronounces 'the greatest man for the interest of natural philosophy that ever was.' Of English letters he can only say that 'he understands that all English eloquence consists in mere pedantry.' Writing in the character of a courtier, Sorbière expresses himself antagonistically to the English constitution, but it is difficult to believe that his remarks are not sometimes ironical. He can hardly have thought it a very extravagant idea on the part of the commons 'that their king ought to apply himself entirely to maintain the public peace, to promote the happiness of his people, and to advance the honour and reputation of his country abroad, as much as possibly he can.' We are nevertheless informed that this and similar views arise from 'a particular inclination they have by nature to supply themselves with such disrespectful arguments.'

Foreign Travellers in England.

The travels in England of Duke Cosmo de' Medici, heir-apparent to the Grand Duchy of Tuscany, were performed in 1669, and described by Signor Magalotti, a member of his suite, whose manuscript account was translated into English, and published in 1821. They are more interesting than most foreign narratives of English travel, in so far as Cosmo, having landed at Plymouth and travelled up to London, and having afterwards made excursions to Oxford, Cambridge, and other places, saw more of English country life than usual, and inasmuch as they are accompanied by excellent sketches taken by artists in his suite. It is most delightful to be thus enabled to see towns and villages and country-houses exactly as they appeared in the days of Charles II., and it is only to be regretted that the artists did not exercise their pencils upon the streets of London. Magalotti is an intelligent and inquisitive traveller; but, voyaging in the train of a prince, and unacquainted with the language, he can tell us little respecting the people. His account of what fell within his sphere is sensible and impartial, with a few errors, such as the strange assertion that Clarendon had been secretly a Presbyterian! He is too much of a courtier to inform us respecting the court of Charles II., except in the enumeration of titled persons and officials, in which he is very exact. He gives a fair account of the Royal Society, and of the theatre; but seems unconscious of the existence of English literature outside the walls of the playhouse.

We have now accompanied the literature of the Restoration period from its apparently sudden manifestation contemporaneously with the return of the exiled monarch to its transition into what is so appropriately in one point of view, so unaptly in another, termed England's Augustan age. We have seen that this apparent abruptness was deceptive, arising from the interruption of English literary development by the Civil War and its consequences ; and that the Restoration literature represented tendencies which must inevitably have prevailed without the infusion of any French element. The old Elizabethan mode had become inadequate to the vastly extended needs of the time, and we are now able to recognize the literature of the Restoration in its proper connection as a transition to the thoroughly practical and business-like style of the eighteenth century, which, having worked itself out in its turn, and arrived at an impracticable position through the total negation of imagination by its most characteristic representatives,[1] brought about the revival of the Elizabethan spirit in the imaginative, spiritual, and at the same time intensely human literature of the nineteenth century. This in turn seems threatened with decay from the exaggeration of its characteristic qualities; and the antidote might be sought in less hopeful quarters than in the sound sense, manly vigour, and solid execution of the robust if prosaic writers of the Age of Dryden.

[1] Fox thought that Shakespeare's reputation would have stood higher if he had never written *Hamlet!*

CHRONOLOGICAL TABLE.

1660. Dryden's *Astraea Redux.*
      Pepys begins his *Diary.*

1662. Bentley born.
      Atterbury born.
      Royal Society incorporated.

1663. First part of *Hudibras* published.
      Dryden begins to write for the stage.
      London Gazette established.
      L'Estrange licenser of the press.

1664. Second part of *Hudibras.*
      Evelyn's *Sylva.*
      Vanbrugh born.

1665. Bunyan's *Grace Abounding.*

1667. *Paradise Lost.*
      Dryden's *Annus Mirabilis.*
      Dryden's *Essay of Dramatic Poesy.*
      Cowley died.
      Swift born.

1669. Pepys discontinues his *Diary.*

1670. Dryden made Poet Laureate.
      Walton's *Lives* collected.
      Congreve born.

1671. *Paradise Regained* and *Samson Agonistes.*
      The Rehearsal.

1672. Wycherley begins to write for the stage.
      Addison born.
      Steele born.

1674. Milton died.

1676. Barclay's *Apology*.
       Hoadly born.
1677. Barrow died.
1678. *Pilgrim's Progress*, first part.
       Cudworth's *Intellectual System*.
       Hudibras, third part.
       Dryden's *All for Love*.
       Farquhar born.
       Marvell died.
1679. Burnet's *History of the Reformation in England*.
1680. Bunyan's *Life and Death of Mr. Badman*.
       Otway's *Orphan*.
       Butler died.
1681. *Absalom and Achitophel*, first part.
       Thomas Burnet's *Sacred Theory of the Earth*.
1682. *The Medal*.
       Absalom and Achitophel, second part.
       Religio Laici.
       Otway's *Venice Preserved*.
       Bunyan's *Holy War*.
1683. Izaak Walton died.
       Oldham died.
1684. *Pilgrim's Progress*, second part.
       Berkeley born.
1685. Otway died.
1687. Newton's *Principia*.
       The Hind and the Panther.
       Waller died.
1688. Pope born.
       Bunyan died.
       Cudworth died.
1689. Locke's *Letter on Toleration*.
       Dryden deprived of the Laureateship.
       Richardson born.
1690. Locke's *Essay on the Human Understanding*.
       Dryden's *Don Sebastian*.
       Wood's *Athenae Oxonienses*.
1691. Ray's *Wisdom of God manifested in Creation*.

1691. Nathaniel Lee died.
1692. Bishop Butler born.
1693. Locke's *Treatise on Education*.
      Congreve's *Old Bachelor*.
      Congreve's *Double Dealer*.
1694. Tillotson died.
1695. Locke's *Reasonableness of Christianity*.
      Congreve's *Love for Love*.
1697. Dryden's translation of the *Aeneid*.
      Congreve's *Mourning Bride*.
      Dampier's *Voyages*.
      Vanbrugh begins to write for the stage.
1698. Collier's *Short View of the Immorality of the Stage*.
      Warburton born.
      Bentley's *Dissertation on Phalaris*.
1699. Farquhar begins to write for the stage.
      Stillingfleet died.
      Sir William Temple died.
1700. Dryden's *Fables*.
      Dryden died.
      Thomson born.

INDEX.

CHISWICK PRESS:—CHARLES WHITTINGHAM AND CO.
TOOKS COURT, CHANCERY LANE, LONDON.